VENTURE TO
OREGON

VENTURE TO
OREGON

GORDON HULL

The Patrice Press
Tucson, Arizona

The Patrice Press
1810 W. Grant Rd., Suite 108
Tucson, AZ 85745
1-800-367-9242

Printed in the United States of America

AUTHOR'S NOTE

Traveling the Oregon Trail in the mid-nineteenth century was very difficult. The diaries kept on the two-thousand-mile journey are filled with the suffering and the hardships the pioneers endured. Even the well-prepared and carefully organized wagon trains often experienced disease and death. Accidents claimed the lives of many on the westward trek. Ill-prepared travelers usually suffered the most tragedy, but it could happen to anyone on the trail.

This is not a story about a typical wagon train, but what was a typical wagon train? There was so much variation in the size of the trains, the kind of animals pulling the wagons, the extra animals and the capabilities of the leaders. This writer spent considerable research time before traveling several weeks following the Oregon Trail.

A big thank-you to Gregory Franzwa for his detailed *Maps of the Oregon Trail* and excellent guidebook, *The Oregon Trail Revisited.* His determination for accuracy was as great as a well-planned Oregon-bound expedition. The editing expertise of Betty Burnett and Gregory is greatly appreciated.

It was a thrill to walk in the ruts that are still visible on the old trail. To view the washed-out ruts at Windlass Hill near the beautiful Ash Hollow was awesome. It was enlightening to imagine the thousands of wagon wheels it took to wear the deep ruts in the sandstone ridges near Guernsey, Wyoming. It is almost necessary to walk on a hot afternoon in the dusty, barren desert to visualize the misery, the despair, and the choking dust the weary travelers experienced.

When I stood on the bank of the wide Snake River at the Three Island Crossing (two islands during Oregon Trail days), it made me respect the Oregon-bound traveler's courage. The sight of the water brought back memories of my youth along the James River and Timber Creek in South Dakota. I remember swimming the river and creek on horseback during high water.

One day my brother Vernon and I forded the usual, placid James with a team and wagon. We hit a large rock in midstream. We were plain stupid. With a horse and buggy, we forded a rain-swollen creek that we knew was dangerous. The current swept the buggy downstream and we survived only because of our powerful bald-faced mare.

Later, watching the Snake River, I could imagine the fear in the people's eyes as the oxen struggled in the strong current to reach the north bank. To travel the Cascades was to feel for the exhausted animals and humans as they fought and struggled their way to the top of the last steep grade.

This is a story of what might have happened if the hard-earned lessons of former travelers were put into practice. Following those lessons often made the difference of success or disaster.

Gordon Hull

1

J ed awakened when the first light of the April morning came through the open window of his room. The distant crow of a rooster reminded him that another day was dawning. When he remembered that he was in a second-story room of the Independence House and there was no need for him to get up early, he turned his back to the window and resumed his sleep.

When he awakened the second time bright sunlight filled the room. He closed his eyes again and listened to the sounds of the frontier town coming from the streets below—the braying of a mule, the ring of a blacksmith's hammer on his anvil, a young calf's bawling and a cow's deep-throated answer. He heard the faint whinny of a horse and the barking of several nearby dogs. The jingle of work harness chain tugs meant that a team was trotting by hitched to a light rig. The chuckle of the wheels of a heavily loaded wagon made Jed wonder if it was pulled by horses, mules, or oxen. The sharp crack of a blacksnake whip and the holler of "gee," told him the wagon was pulled by oxen and was turning the corner.

A conversation was taking place between two men directly below his open window, but one man spoke so softly that Jed could hear little of what he was saying. The other man's booming voice was so loud Jed heard every word.

"Yep, I know it's early but it looks like a lot fewer wagons are going to Oregon this year." A few seconds of near silence and the loud voice thundered again. "Last year at this time, they was hundreds of wagons around here and people filled the streets, buyin' supplies. Blacksmith shops were busy all night. Just a few wagon trains are going to Oregon this year, I'll bet on that. 1848 ain't gonna be our year."

When the voices faded away and the sound of their footsteps grew faint, Jed opened his eyes and frowned at the ceiling. He was disturbed by what he'd heard. He wondered if he'd be able to get work this year as a trail guide.

Then he noticed a change in the room and thought to himself, this hotel is getting better. They had finally replaced that little broken mirror with a large new one. Jed rolled onto his back, stretched to the full length of his five-foot, eleven-inch frame and thought how good this bed felt after spending so much of the last eleven years sleeping on the ground. He threw back the blanket and swung his legs over the side of the bed. When he sat up, he could see his head and shoulders clearly in the new mirror.

He couldn't resist smiling at himself and thought how rarely he'd seen himself in a mirror since he began living west of the Missouri River. Seeing how tousled his dark hair was, he reached for the piece of a comb that lay on the small dresser. His hair had last been cut in February and now it was hanging below his ears. Before he stood up, he ran the comb through his abundant dark beard as well, then smiled again in satisfaction.

He was wearing only his drawers, which he left on for sleeping when he shucked the rest of his clothes. The bright sunlight and the new mirror showed off the jagged scars on his body. He turned a little to get a better look at the one on his upper left arm and recalled the gash the Crow arrow had made nearly ten years ago. It had healed quite well. Jed turned to face the mirror squarely and looked at the scar on his rib cage. He felt the ridge on the rib that had been split by an arrow and winced at the memory of the pain.

Once more he noticed gratefully that he didn't have the furry body of his Welsh father. He grinned at his weathered face in the mirror and thanked his Cherokee grandmother for the smoothness of his skin. He was not ashamed of his one-quarter Indian blood, but it was a secret that must be kept until he was through with the job he was doing. Many white settlers were convinced that Indians were evil and that was not about to change.

Jed dressed, closed the window and went downstairs to the dining room.

"What's it gonna be for you, Jed?" the proprietor asked.

"Three fried eggs, Ely, and a half a loaf of corn bread."

"Comin' right up, Jed. Sure you don't want some jerky with it?"

Jed laughed, knowing Ely was ribbing him. When Jed had a chance to get fried eggs, he considered them a treat. Most of the year he ate bacon without eggs, hardtack, and jerky, and some days, nothing at all.

It was late enough this morning that most of the hotel's guests had already gone. He ate alone in silence at the big dining table, savoring his second cup of coffee in an almost empty room.

When he had finished breakfast, he put on his jacket and sauntered out the door, picking his way down the rutted street until he came to Tom's blacksmith shop. He walked in the open door just as Tom was finishing a door hinge. Jed sat on a sawhorse until the smith put the hinge away and said, "Long time, Jed."

The two men grinned at each other. "You aren't shoeing oxen today, Tom?" asked Jed. "No wagons to work on?"

Tom shook his head. "Last year at this time I was almost sold out of ox shoes. Now look at them bins on the wall. They's all full. I had to work late ever night last spring to make shoes. This winter, I made a lot so I wouldn't run out and now I've got most of them left. I hear lots more wagons are starting from St. Joe this year. I know two young smiths left here to try their luck there."

"Yeah, maybe," Jed replied thoughtfully, "but I think it's just that fewer people are going West this year. A party's camped around here. Noah left me a note at the Independence House that I should meet him here this morning. Said an emigrant train is looking for a guide."

"They was in here yesterday talking to Noah," answered Tom. "The liveryman sent them over to give you a recommend. Lucky for you, I had my sister's letter that Noah brought back in February. Well, I showed those three that part where she sang your praises, and they sure did take a keen interest in it. Man alive! If you and Noah weren't the shaggiest, dirtiest, most raggedy pair when you got here! But I guess there ain't many men crazy enough to come back from Oregon in the winter."

Jed nodded ruefully. "How has Noah done as an apprentice blacksmith?"

"Real good. Learns fast. He made a pile of shoes, helped me shoe oxen, mules, and horses, and he learned to forge-weld iron, too! He can cut a piece out of a wagon tire and weld it back together in nothin' flat."

"Yep, he's quick," agreed Jed. "And he's a darn good hunter. Noah could guide a wagon train to Oregon by himself, if he wanted to—but he doesn't want the problems." Jed laughed. "Guess that shows how smart he really is!"

A tall young man with a red beard ducked in the door and exclaimed, "Well, Jed, you made it back from the east side of the Mississip! How's your kin back there?"

"Just fine, Noah," replied Jed. "I have a lot more nieces and nephews than I had the last time I was home. Even my kid brother has four kids now."

"And you, Jed, you old wanderer," put in Noah, "you don't have a wife or even a hope of one."

A shadow flickered across Jed's face, then he laughed. "What woman would put up with me? I'm more comfortable with a mountain lion than with a female."

Noah's handsome face parted in a smile as he pushed his

hat back enough to expose thick locks of sandy colored hair.

"Jed, we'd better get over to Will's Livery. We don't want those folks going to Oregon without us."

"Let's go," answered Jed. "I'm as ready as I can get."

Noah's grin widened. "The quicker we get started, the sooner we'll get to Oregon."

Tom stood up. "In a hurry, are you?" He turned to Jed. "Do you suppose Noah's sweetheart's gonna wait a whole year for him?" he asked with a wink.

"Probably not," joked Jed and added, "she might marry someone else before we get back." When Jed's eyes met Noah's, he wished he hadn't said that.

Noah turned for the door. Jed threw an arm around his young friend as they walked into the street. "We were only joking," said Jed. "I know Beth pretty well, Noah. I know her folks said last fall that she was too young to marry you. You've got nothing to worry about."

"There's a dozen men for every single girl in Oregon!" exclaimed Noah. Then he relaxed a little. "But I guess I shouldn't worry. She knows I'm coming back."

Jed slowed his pace to match Noah's. When they entered the open door of the barn, Jed could see a knot of men at the other end. They walked in that direction. Will came forward and introduced the two guides to the three Oregon-bound men.

"This is Jedidiah Jones and Noah Taylor," said the liveryman. Jed studied the men as they introduced themselves. The first to step forward was a powerfully built man about five feet eight inches tall.

"My name is Elwood Yeager," he growled through his large mustache, "but they call me Sarge. I spent a few years in the army and now I'm a farmer."

The second man to shake Jed's hand was clean shaven, smallish, but with a powerful handshake. "Chester Hill from Illinois," he stated matter-of-factly. His blue eyes met Jed's steady gaze. "Call me Chet."

The third man towered above Chet by nearly a foot, and his

bushy beard made him look top heavy. When his long arm swung out to greet Jed, his face parted into a broad smile that showed he was missing several teeth.

"Gil Maddox from Kentucky, but I hope to be an Oregonian before the snow gits too deep in the Blue Mountains," he said, and he laughed at his own remark.

Jed cleared his throat and said, "You're thinking ahead—that's a good attitude to have."

Sarge's face grew serious again and Jed could see that he wanted to get down to business. His dark eyes and bushy eyebrows gave him an air of authority. I bet he was a hell-to-pay sergeant, Jed thought admiringly.

"We're trying to get a wagon train together west of here aways," said Sarge, "but we've got a long ways to go. We have about an equal number of people from three states so far—Illinois, Kentucky, and my home state of Missouri. We've heard we should have about forty to fifty wagons and the three of us think we need an experienced guide. Some of our people, especially the Missourians, don't think we need a guide. They think we can do it ourselves." He made a sound of disgust. "That's like having an army without a commander."

Chet broke in. "We thought we'd find out who's available. If you were our guide, what could you do for us?"

Jed liked Chet's direct approach. No time-wasting lollygagging here, he thought.

For nearly an hour as they sat on bales of hay in the stable, Jed talked about the trail—the drenching storms that were sure to come up, where they could find water and forage and where they couldn't. The Indians. The buffalo. The river crossings and the mountain passes. He'd taken trains to Oregon four times by now and knew the route as well as anyone.

When the questions finally died, Sarge turned to the others and said, "I think Jed and Noah ought to come out to our camp tomorrow afternoon. A few more families are going to join us by then."

The men nodded and Sarge continued, "Some of the

Missourians think I could lead us to Oregon because I was in the army. They know I've been over the Santa Fe Trail and to Texas. I'll tell you, along the way, I learned some hard lessons. I purt near died from thirst on one campaign in the jornada. A lot of men and some of the horses did die because of a stupid greenhorn officer from the East who wouldn't hire a guide to get us out of there. We wandered around for days without water." He shook his head and spat. "No cause for it."

The others nodded soberly. Sarge pounded the railing in front of him for emphasis. "We need a guide."

Not much was said after that. Noah and Jed agreed to be at their gathering at two o'clock the next day.

When the three men left, Jed and Noah looked at each other and grinned. Noah said, "I think we got us a job, partner."

They walked over to the yard next to the livery barn to check on the horses that they had brought from Fort John to Independence in February. Leaning on the top rail of the fence, they searched out their four horses. Noah spotted them eating hay at a manger.

Jed remarked with satisfaction, "They have sure gained well in the last two months."

"They should have," said Noah. "They've had two good feedings of oats and corn every day and darned good hay, too. They must've each lost a hundred and fifty pounds getting us here."

Jed said sadly, "It's hell on horses coming back east in the winter. Not much grass—it's either covered with snow or grazed down. We must've walked that whole last week. They were too scrawny to carry us—remember?"

"How could I forget?" exclaimed Noah. "And I won't forget walking through South Pass to keep our feet from freezing!"

"It *was* a mite cold in the high country," added Jed with a chuckle.

"*A mite* cold!" Noah shouted. "You old mountain men spend so much of your lives half froze you just take cold for granted."

"I can tell you got spoiled this spring with easy living,"

retorted Jed. "Your aunt's good cooking, sleeping in a bed, and working inside."

"If that's what you call spoiled," Noah said. "That's the way I want it to be. When we get to Oregon and I get married, I'm going to build me a blacksmith shop with a good roof and a warm house. When me and Beth lay in bed listening to the rain on the roof, I'll think of you wading through the snow of the Blue Mountains or huddled under a buffler robe at night in the South Pass with the wind blowing in your face."

Jed grinned at his young friend and said, "I might just surprise you and settle down in Oregon this fall. Sometimes I can feel my age and that winter trip gets a little harder each year."

Jed rubbed his eyes and said, "Come on, Noah, it's time to eat. I'll buy your dinner if you don't eat too much."

When they found a place, they concentrated on the important job of eating. After he had devoured his first pork chop, Jed wiped his greasy mouth with the back of his hand and grinned at his young friend.

"I'm itching to go out on the trail again, Noah," he said happily. "I can't take too much of this city life. I feel these buildings closing in on me and I start longing for the prairies and the mountains."

Noah poked a big chunk of cornbread in his mouth. "How're you ever gonna settle down, Jed? It'll take some special gal to make you quit traveling."

Jed squinted at the wall, pushing away memories. "I reckon." Later they found a bench on the south side of a building where the afternoon sun felt warm, and they planned what they'd say to the emigrants the next day.

"Won't be hard," concluded Jed. "Just stick to the truth."

Noah asked Jed what he thought of Sarge.

"Well, I'd say he's used to taking orders—and giving them. He seems to have good sense. I think he'll be a good man on the trail. What do you make of the little fellow, Chet Hill?"

"He asked some good questions—even wrote down the answers. Maybe he could be the orderly sergeant for the outfit. And Gil?"

"Oh, he'll keep things lively, I reckon," said Jed. "But I think he has a lot of sense, too, 'cept with his wife. He's got ten kids—did you hear that? Calls 'em his clan."

Noah whistled, then stood up. "Time to get back to the smithy. Say, how about coming over for dinner tomorrow night? My aunt's a larupin' good cook."

"You bet," agreed Jed. "I got used to home cooking at my mother's. Didn't realize how much I missed it."

Noah nodded. "See you tomorrow. Think I'll work on my diary tonight." He had kept a record of their trek last year and someday Beth and their kids would read it.

Jed thought about looking up some old friends in Independence. Perhaps he could find some freighters who might not have left for Santa Fe yet.

Noah headed for his uncle's shop, and Jed walked to the nearest saloon. Entering the dark room, he was met with the smell of spilled whiskey and beer and many unwashed bodies in the crowded room. Pipe and cigar smoke hung heavily in the air.

Jed nodded to a few bullwhackers he remembered slightly. He looked around at the riverboat men and a few customers, he guessed, were Oregon-bound farmers.

The saloon was so crowded Jed stepped outside, enjoyed a good breath of clean air, and continued down the street. Before he reached the next saloon, which was only four storefronts away, he noticed a man walking toward him on the dusty boardwalk. Something about his walk seemed familiar. When they got closer, Jed could see blond hair sticking out from under his cap and knew who it was.

They each reached the door of the saloon at the same time.

"Jed Jones, you old coot!"

"I'll be—if it ain't Wilbur Parker!" shouted Jed as the two men pumped each other's arms.

"So you got back from Oregon in one piece," said Wilbur with a wide grin. "Gonna try it again?"

"Sure will if I can get a job. Just got back from the East last night."

"What d'y'know—I'm just back from St. Louis myself!"

"Let's have a drink, you old buzzard. I'll even buy. We need to catch up!"

Inside, the pair squeezed up to the bar. WIlbur ordered a shot of whiskey and Jed ordered coffee. Only one table in the room was empty, but it held a half-full bottle.

"Let's take it," said Wilbur above the din. "If someone else claims it, we can move—or slit their throats! Har!"

They jostled their way to the chairs and sat down. Before he could down his coffee, Jed heard his name called. He turned to see a bullwhacker he'd met on the Santa Fe Trail during the driest summer he'd ever lived through.

"Hey, Cuz!" he shouted. "Come on over and join us."

Just then Jed noticed a terrible stench. He looked up at Wilbur, whose face was puckering into a frown. Cuz turned around and hurried back to his table.

"Oh, my God, it's Jake," they said in unison. Together they looked at the man standing behind Jed. Jed's eyes met Jake's bleary gaze that showed a slight recognition.

"Howdy, Jake," said Jed, inadvertently raising his hand to his nose. "How be you?"

"Howdy, yourself." Jake grabbed the bottle and took a few swallows before stumbling against the table. Jed's eyes met Wilbur's and they walked out the door.

They gasped at the fresh air for a moment and then Jed spoke. "Whew! I always knew Jake was dirty, but I've never seen—or smelled—him this bad."

"You know Jake pretty well?" asked Wilbur.

"Yep. We worked a freight train once. He was a good mule man—one of the best I've seen—and good with oxen, too. Today no self-respecting mule could stand to be near him!"

"He's a good worker, all right," agreed Wilbur. "He worked for me last year and you can't ask for a better man on the trail. He's got a real way with animals, but he's in bad shape now."

"Oh?" asked Jed.

Wilbur frowned. "I don't think he's drawn a sober breath for weeks. If he was sober, how could he stand them bugs crawlin' on him?"

Jed shuddered, remembering his last run-in with bedbugs—the curse of city living.

Wilbur gestured toward a bench and they sat down. "It was about this time last year, maybe a little later. We were ready to start breaking in some new oxen. Some of the boys hatched a plan—they couldn't stand to work with Jake, him stinking so bad. We all chipped in, including Bart, who owns the saloon." Wilbur chuckled.

"Yeah?" asked Jed. "So what happened?"

"We bought new duds, boots, and blankets and made a deal with Fritz, the barber, to get his hair cut. Well, Fritz said, 'Not in my place!' So we got a tin tub out back of his shop and rounded up some real strong lye soap—to kill the lice, you know.

"Well, one afternoon when Jake was drunk enough to pass out, the boys carried him off to the tub and scrubbed him clean. Even his whiskers and hair! They burned his old clothes, dressed him up in his new ones and brought him in to Fritz. Fritz cut off about a pound of hair. Jake looked almost human for a week or so. Course the clean wore off and here he is again, just as filthy as before." Wilbur shook his head and continued, "On the trail he gets rank, like we all do, but he gets washed off once in a while when we ford streams."

"Yeah, it's not easy keeping clean on the trail. Let's find us a piece of pie," Jed said abruptly. "I'm getting hungry."

Wilbur nodded in agreement and they moved down the street to a hotel. The crowd had thinned out by now and the friends found a table and enough quiet to talk.

"How's the freight business?" Jed asked, once they were settled with a slab of berry pie each.

Wilbur scratched his chin thoughtfully. "Well, pretty good, I reckon. Or at least it was last year. This year—"

Jed nodded. "Yeah, everybody says the number going to Oregon is a lot less this year."

Wilbur continued, "We'll check at St. Joe and Westport before we load up."

He explained that the supplier of Fort John and Fort Bridger sent freight according to the number of Oregon-bound wagon trains. Last year had been very busy for Oregon Trail freighters, but this year looked sparse. Wilbur had left some wagons at Fort John after they'd been unloaded and then had gone on to Fort Bridger, where he picked up furs and buffalo hides.

"We never bring extra wagons and oxen home," Wilbur said. "The forts sell them to the Oregon-bound people. You know, I've often wondered—how do the women and children stand all that hard walking they do?"

"Don't ever underestimate the strength of women, Wilbur. There are always a few that have trouble, but most of them walk all the way, cook the meals, tend the younguns, and wash clothes on days they don't travel. They might even bake a pie to boot!"

"Hey, why don't you find one of those women?" asked Wilbur.

Jed winced. "Aw, the good ones are already married," he said lightly. "You know that."

After a moment, Jed said he was ready to call it a day and bid his old friend goodnight, heading for his room at the Independence House.

2

T he next afternoon Jed met Noah near the emigrant camp. Noah complimented Jed on his buckskin shirt and slicked-down hair.

"Some people get the idea mountain men are illiterate savages who can only hunt critters and fight Indians," he said. But you look like a preacher! Maybe you oughta run for senator after you settle down."

They both laughed and headed for the meeting.

Sarge came to meet the two frontiersmen as they strode toward the meeting site. He was with a young blacksmith named Henry, who wanted to talk to Noah.

"I hope you vellows get das chob," Henry said in a thick German accent. "I don't vant to be der only smit on der train."

Noah nodded. "Lots of animals to shoe and lots of wagon tires to watch out for," he said.

There was a scattering of wagons and livestock at the camp. Several tents had been set up. Jed knew that many of these farmers had sold everything they had back home and planned to buy new wagons, oxen, and supplies in Independence. Some had brought their wagons and animals with them, along with their cooking utensils, food, tools, and household goods. It had been like this every year.

13

Sarge led the buckskin-clad men to the waiting crowd, which formed a crude half-circle around them. Some people sat on stools and others sat on the ground or on buffalo robes that had been thrown down over the dust. Sarge held up his hand. The murmuring in the crowd stopped. Jed could feel an air of tension.

Sarge's introduction was short. "Meet Noah Taylor," he said first, touching Noah on the shoulder. "He's a master buffler hunter and can shoot anything else that's edible, so I hear. He's also been an apprentice blacksmith for a few months now. He's Tom's nephew."

A few people in the crowd acknowledged this information with murmurs of approval.

"Tom's a good man," said one. "Once he helped me straighten a wheel rim and didn't charge a cent.

Turning to Jed, Sarge said, "This here is Jedidiah Jones, a genu-wine mountain man and explorer. He's been places most of us have never even dreamed of. And he's taken four wagon trains safely to Oregon. You can ask him the questions you've been badgering me with all week!"

"'Bout time we got some answers, Sarge!" someone cried.

"Hope you don't want to put us in no regiments, like Sarge does," called another.

All eyes were on Jed as Sarge and Noah moved off to the side. Jed had been through this before but he was always a little uneasy at first. He nervously lifted the front of his hat. He looked out over the crowd for a few seconds before starting. Families, lots of women and children. Good, he thought. Everyone sat expectantly, waiting for him to begin. The sounds of small children playing and mules braying seemed very far away.

Jed suddenly realized that he liked speechifying, liked the chance to tell these folks what he knew. Maybe he *would* run for Congress! Then he couldn't help but laugh at himself for thinking such a thought.

His voice was strong and loud as he began. "Howdy-do to you all. Most of you folks have been planning this trip for a long time and you've probably heard lots of different stories. Some of you may even know everything I'm going to say."

"If I did, I'd be standing up where you are," a man with red suspenders shouted. The others tittered and Jed felt the tension break. His voice relaxed and he started to speak normally.

"Okay. It looks like you want to go to Oregon, and I don't blame you. It's a great place. You'll be glad you made this decision. Right now every man can file a claim for 640 acres of free land, his wife for 320 and each child for 160."

Several people nodded enthusiastically. They could never hope to get that much land back east.

"The Willamette Valley is about forty miles wide," Jed continued, "and two hundred miles long. This valley is one of the most fertile in the world. You'll be able to get tremendous yields of grain, garden crops of all kinds, and your livestock can graze on green grass all year 'round. You can raise fruit of all descriptions—the sweetest berries you've ever tasted, apples, pears, and crops that haven't even been invented yet."

The crowd laughed with pleasure. This is what they wanted to hear.

"The summers," said Jed, "the summers are so mild you won't even raise a sweat and when the calendar says January, you won't believe it because it'll feel like April." He could feel their attentiveness. "It rains a lot in the winter, but it snows very little, and then it melts in a day or two. I spent one winter in the valley and I never saw ice. Never."

A few women clapped in glee.

"There are tremendous forests there—tall, straight trees with wood that produce lumber without any knots!"

Again a smattering of applause and a few cheers. "The Willamette River flows into the Columbia—that's like the Mississippi to you folks from back East—and this river can take you right to the Pacific Ocean and all the way to China. The fishing—I can guarantee you've seen nothing like it, no matter where you've been fishing before. Salmon so big it'll take two of you just to pull 'em out."

"You hear that, Mother?" a man called to his wife. "And how 'bout the hunting, Jed?"

Jed chuckled. "Ask Noah, there."

Noah chimed in, "The hunting's so good you could live on venison—or bear meat, elk, squirrel, rabbit, quail. Some of those animals are long gone from the East."

"Yeah, too many people back East," snorted a listener. "They've chased all the good hunting away."

"Any buffler?" someone wanted to know.

"I've never seen any in Oregon," said Jed. "You, Noah?"

"Nope, not there. But if they were any, you can bet they'd be juicy and more flavorful than any you've tasted."

"Plus," added Jed, "it's purely beautiful countryside—the mountains and the rivers—"

"Don't care 'bout that," a man said, "just give me them year 'round crops."

A dozen heads nodded in agreement.

"So how do we get to this land of milk and honey?" called Sarge. "Tell us about the trail!"

"There is one problem about going to Oregon, and that is you have to go through hell to get there. It's a good two thousand miles of hard traveling. It's not all like the rolling hills you see in the distance from here. Mountains—how many of you have seen mountains?"

A few people raised their hands. "The Ozarks," someone said. "Blue Ridge," someone else called out.

Jed nodded. "Hills," he said. "I'm talking about *mountains*, mountains you think you can never get up—and then don't want to get down 'cause it looks like it's a straight drop to nowhere. We'll have to cross rivers and ford a lot of streams, so many you'll give up tryin' to keep your feet dry. Sometimes we'll find bad water and sometimes no water at all.

"We'll cross deserts without grass. The heat'll knock you out and your skin will pucker from the dryness. Flies and mosquitos—big fellers like you never saw in Missouri—are goin' to want you for supper. And just when you're getting used to the heat, it'll turn cold and your teeth will chatter out of your head. If we don't get to the Blues in time, we'll be wading through snow past your knees.

"When a prairie thunderstorm rumbles up, you won't be able to hide in the barn 'cause there won't be any barns. There'll only be you and your wagon—and believe me, that's not much protection.

"This isn't a trip to Aunt Minnie's on a Sunday morning or a three-day stay at a camp meeting in Kaintuck. This is the roughest bit of travelin' you'll ever hope to see and you damn well better be prepared for it—for sloshing through mud, for picking your way around boulders, trying to get through deep sand, or slapping across hard-pan.

"There no place for mistakes and there's no place for slackers. Everybody's got to work together to make this trip successful. And if you do, I guarantee this will be the adventure of your lifetime."

Jed stopped speaking for a moment and the silence hung heavily over the camp. They all seemed to be holding their breath, watching him closely.

"Why do I think I can help you? You don't need anyone to show you the trail. It's well marked. Hundreds of wagons have gone over the trail in the last few years. You won't need help finding the trail.

"But you *will* need help managing the trip—deciding where and when to stop, how to cross the rivers and things like that—and you *will* need help with Indians."

There was a collective gasp.

"I spent a lot of time as a trapper and a freighter and I've met a lot of Indians. I can talk with most any tribe using sign language and I know a few words in Sioux and Cayuse. I've watched Indians for a long time and I understand the way they think.

"Now this is probably a good place to stop talking and let you ask some questions. Anybody got any questions?"

"Sure do," spoke up a middle-aged man with long side

whiskers. "I want to take my horses. My neighbors say I'd be crazy to. What do you think?"

"You horsemen might not like this, but oxen are the power you need to pull your wagons."

A groan went up from the crowd.

"Now listen," continued Jed. "Oxen can get along without grain better than horses or mules, and we won't have grain. Plus there'll be lots of coarse grass along the way that horses can't digest. Horses don't have the strength that oxen have and will give out halfway there if they have to pull these heavy loads. And most important—Indians love horses. You can't convince an Indian brave that it's a crime to steal horses. It's a badge of pride, like a medal. They're experts at horse-stealing and, short of keeping your horse under you each night, there's no way to keep him. Indians don't care about oxen—they're slow and they aren't as good eating as buffalo.

"Indians do like to eat dogs, though. I don't see any here— that's good. Dogs bark at the wrong time and get in the way. No dogs, no horses."

Seeing the unhappy faces, Jed continued, "All right, you can bring a riding horse or two—we could manage that. But no draft animals."

"How about wagons?" someone else called out.

"The big Conestoga wagons are no good for the Oregon Trail. From here it looks like that the size of your wagons is good. As your guide, I'd inspect every wagon in the train and all the animals that pull them. I won't let any wagon go that isn't good enough because that would hold us all up. The total weight that you haul in the wagons can't be much over two thousand pounds. You can have a little more than that to start with, but not more than a ton after traveling five hundred miles. That means almost no furniture. The mountains are full of castaway furniture that couldn't be pulled up the steep grades. You can send your furniture down to New Orleans on a steamboat and then on a ship to Oregon."

Chet stepped forward. "Must we travel on the Sabbath?"

he asked.

"That's up to the whole group to decide, and it should be decided before you leave. I've led trains that rested and those that kept going. Either way works. Those that observed a day of rest got there just about as soon because the animals can only go about so many miles in a week anyway. A day of rest seems to be good for both man and beast. Usually Sundays are not all rest because you have to use the time for shoeing horses or oxen and repairing and greasing the wagons or washing clothes or baking. Some trains like to have a worship time too. That is up to your group to decide.

"You've got to be practical though. If it's Sunday and there's poor grass or no water we have to press on. We must make as many miles as possible when the going is good."

"How many miles you think we can make in a day?" Sarge asked.

"Well, Sarge, if the grass is good enough to leave here by April 22, say, we should get to Oregon City by October 5. That gives us 165 days to travel nearly two thousand miles. That figures out to over twelve miles a day if we travel every day. If we don't travel on Sundays and lose some time ferrying over rivers and letting livestock graze where the grass is good, we might travel only 135 days. We'd need to average about fifteen miles a day, which means we need to travel twenty miles a day when the going is good. We can do that if we have a good oxen and wagons that aren't overloaded.

"If you go too fast on the first half of the trip and wear your animals down, they won't have the strength to make it up the mountains. You need extra oxen so you don't have to pay the high price for fresh ones at Fort Bridger or Fort Hall. You can sell two horses and buy nearly five oxen right here in Independence.

"I've found out the hard way that it's very important for you to have a good organization to decide these questions democratically. You should have a constitution, a set of rules to deal with problems along the way—and there are always problems. You should elect three men to be your leaders. One is the wagonmaster or captain, another is the secretary-treasurer, and the third oversees the night guard. These three men will have to make a lot of decisions along the way."

"What's this guard do?" asked a man toward the back.

"The night guard is very important. If it's real dark or the weather is threatening, the livestock must be in the circle of wagons, but all other times they should be out where there's the best grass. Every pound of flesh you keep on the oxen along the trail will be needed to climb the mountains.

"From the time we leave here until we get to Oregon we'll never all be sleeping at the same time. Three or four men will always be awake to guard the livestock and the wagon circle. You can bet your britches there'll be an Indian around who wants to look like a hero to his sweetheart.

"Every able-bodied man eighteen years of age and older must share in the guard duty. Depending on how large a wagon train we have, this usually means a three-hour shift every four or five nights. If someone gets careless and we lose some of our scouting, hunting, and night guard horses, we're in big trouble. We can't let that happen."

"What about the women?" Chet's wife Della asked. "Do you have any instructions for us?"

"Women are going to be very busy all the way to Oregon," he said and everyone listened intently. "Cooking in the open for six months is a real chore. Women and most of the children will walk right along side the men all the way to Oregon. Small children, babies, and sick people are the only ones who will ride in the wagons. Any other questions?"

"Just one." It was Gil. "How much you charge?"

"We ask eleven dollars per wagon. Noah and I'll furnish four good horses, two saddles, and rifles. I'll spend all my time guiding the train. Noah'll spend a lot of his time hunting and also be available to do blacksmith work for hire. Noah and I'll take our turns at night guard like all the rest of the men."

Jed looked around the group. He felt good about what he

saw. Sarge turned to the crowd and asked, "Do you think we should wait 'til tomorrow to give these men an answer or can we talk it over and give them a yes or no now?"

One of the oldest men in the crowd spoke up. "I think that if they want to take a little walk, we can give them an answer real soon. My mind's already made up." The others nodded.

Jed and Noah walked to the west, past some of the wagons. They approvingly noticed a few big oxen that probably had come from Illinois.

Jed said, "That price was a little low, but we both want to go to Oregon now and there might not be many jobs available."

Noah nodded. "I rather have a job and be underpaid than head back to Oregon on my own," he said.

"I figured you'd feel that way," said Jed.

Before they returned to the group, Sarge, Gil, and Chet came walking to meet them. They could tell by Gil's broad smile that they had a job.

"It looks like you fellers are goin' to have to put up with my jabbering this summer," Gil said. "Your speech sure did convince 'em to hire you and they elected us three fellers to bother them all along the trail. They let us decide who's gonna do what. So Sarge is the cap'n, Chet's our secretare-treasure, and I aim to keep the guard boys on the job. I might bore people with my chatter, but I usually don't rile 'em very much."

Even Sarge had a smile on his face when he said, "It went better than I thought. By gosh, Jed, you sure got a way with words. Right now the folks want you to give 'em some directions, so they can get started with their preparations."

Jed tried to keep his elation in check. He could hardly wait to get his new outfit in line and headed out to the West he loved. He turned back toward the camp with a spring in his step.

3

As soon as Jed and Noah got back to camp, the questions began in earnest.

"Come look at my wagon," one man called out. "Is it good enough?"

"And supplies—have I got the right ones?" another man chimed in.

All right," said Jed, "let's talk about wagons first." He walked over to the closest one. It looked almost new and had a new canvas top.

After he'd examined it, he turned to the crowd and said, "This is a good wagon for the Oregon Trail. It's not too heavy and it seems strong enough. Lots of good ash in the body. Wheels look like osage orange. See the tires? Mighty near three inches wide, to keep from going deep in the sand. And a good three-quarters of an inch thick. They'll make it to Oregon and back.

"These high wheels are very important—they roll over ruts better and they pull easier. You need the box high off the ground for fording rivers."

"Aw, it don't look like mine at all," said an obviously disappointed man. "Now what do I do?"

"I'll look at yours in a minute, but you can buy wagons like this one right here in Independence," said Jed. "Several supply outfits sell them. It looks like there'll be a small crowd going to Oregon this year, so shop around before you buy. You'll get a better deal that way.

"As to supplies—Noah's got a list of what you should have. He's also got a list of groceries you'll need. Someone can copy it off and pass it around. You're lucky you've got a good hunter going with you—otherwise you'd need more bacon. You'll be sick of bacon before you get to Oregon anyway!"

Noah's list included:

Food and other supplies per adult:

Bacon 100 lbs.	Sugar 20 lbs.	Salt 10 lbs.
Coffee 10 lbs.	Dried fruit 25-30 lbs.	Beans 5 lbs.
Baking powder	Spices	Soap and towels
Blankets	Clothes and extra shoes	

Some canned food
Flour 200 lbs. (some can be corn meal)

Supplies for each wagon:

Hammer	Hand saw	Hatchet
Good axe	Spade and pick	One wash tub
Water jugs	Cooking utensils	Tent
Trunk for valuables	A few boards (2x4s)	
Extra wagon axle	Spare reach	
Some light poles	Extra piece of canvas	

Neck ropes for all your animals
One hundred feet of 1/2" rope
One hundred feet of 1/4" rope
Enough chain to reach from the lead yoke of oxen
     to the hitch pin on the wagon
Twenty feet extra chain
One 30-gal. water barrel
One 15-gal. water barrel
Some assorted nails and bolts
Two sets of shoes for all the animals
Needle and cord to sew canvas
One grease bucket for greasing the wheels
One tar bucket for caulking up wagon beds
One wagon in every six should have 100 feet of 1" rope

Jed continued, "Now for those of you who are going to use oxen, you can pull these wagons easy with four good ones, but you should have at least one extra yoke of oxen for each wagon. You can change off some and if something happens to one yoke, you'll still have a spare one left. Some folks start out with eight oxen for each wagon. They're a lot cheaper here than at the forts along the way.

"And some of these here in town have been crossed with Texas Longhorns. They're real sturdy on the trail. Most of those for sale aren't trained, so you have a job to do in the next days. Get used to cooperating with each other right now. Those of you who have well-trained oxen can help get the wild ones tamed. Most of you are farmers and know all about working animals, so you'll do all right.

"One thing I've already mentioned—you can't use oxen for scouting or hunting. Noah and I each have two good horses, but our train needs a total of twenty—to ride and to pack with buffalo meat. Chet'll have to buy about twenty head of horses or mules for the company. The guard horses and the hunting and scouting horses can't be ridden every day. He also ought to buy a supply wagon and about eight oxen."

"This is getting more expensive by the minute," someone muttered.

"You wanta get there, don't you?" answered a voice. "Quitcher complaining."

Jed continued. "One of the liveries in town is getting a herd of horses in today. Their horses are usually good—about four years old, so they're mature enough for the hard trail use. They'll be green broke, but if you decide to buy, Noah and I'll finish training them as best we can."

"I know we'll think of more questions as soon as you go," said Sarge, "but I don't have any more for you now. When will you be back?"

"We'll be here first thing in the morning," replied Jed. "The next ten days are going to be busy for all of us." Jed's friendly eyes moved over the crowd as he spoke. His strong, warm voice carried easily to his listeners. His new hat and buckskins set off his well-trimmed dark beard, making an impressive sight. More than one woman watched him as closely as did the men.

Just before they left, Jed and Noah were hailed by a tall man who wanted to show them his horses. The four looked outstanding and Jed sensed his pride.

The man stuck out his hand and said, "Name's Matthew. Question is, if I could buy two more good horses to change off with these, could I make it to Oregon with them?"

"Possibly," said Jed, "but you wouldn't want to watch what would happen to them. They probably weigh about fourteen hundred pounds now and when we get to the Blue Mountains they'd be less than eleven hundred pounds. I can tell you care about your animals. When they're just skin and bones going up the grades in the mountains, will you have the guts to use a lash on them?"

Matthew frowned. He spoke softly. "No, I reckon not. I always feed my horses oats and I don't use a whip."

"That's just it," said Jed. "There won't be any oats except what you can take for the first week. If you sell your horses and buy oxen, you won't have to see fine animals suffer. There are a lot of horses in Oregon you can buy when you get there."

Jed and Noah left the troubled man and started back to the main part of town. Jed hadn't forgotten that he was to have supper with Noah's aunt. He remarked as he walked along, "I want to stop off at the Independence House and change clothes. These darn buckskins are too hot to wear indoors."

Noah nodded and said, "I'll change as soon as I get to the house."

Jed turned at the next corner and walked past Will's Livery. He was pleased to see that the horses Will said were coming in had already arrived. They were all in the yard by the livery. Jed couldn't resist going up to the fence to take a look.

He was studying them when Will approached, asking, "Whatcha think?"

"Oh," replied Jed without expression, "some of 'em might

do." He tried to cover a smile with his sleeve.

"Jed, you old liar! You know these are some of the best horses I've ever had. They've come about twenty-five miles today and look at 'em! Hardly look like they've gone a mile. You come back in the morning and look 'em over when they're fresh and see 'em prance. Hey—you get that job?

"Yep, thanks to you, we did, so we'll be busy from now on. Don't know yet how many horses we'll need. A lot less wagons going to Oregon this year. A lot less oxen and horses to be bought," remarked Jed.

"I suppose," said Will, "that in a few days you'll ask me to just give you all the horses you need, so I won't have to feed 'em all year."

Jed laughed and answered, "No, Will, we won't do that. Hey, I really feel obliged to you for this job. We'll give you some business. See you later!" Jed turned and hurried on to the Independence House.

During dinner, Jed kept his guard up, just like he had at his mother's house. When he was visiting her this spring, he tried not to eat too fast or to slurp, like he did the first time he came back after being in the mountains. That time his mother gave him a lecture as though he had no manners at all.

When the pie was finished and the coffee cups refilled, Jed noticed Noah's uncle's eyes were growing heavy and his head was starting to nod. Jed thanked his hosts for a pleasant evening and a tasty meal and headed out into the dark rutted streets, reminding Noah to meet him outside the Independence House early.

When Jed and Noah arrived at the camp the next morning, it was alive with activity. They found Sarge, Chet, and Gil huddled over a tablet. Chet was listing the families in the train. It looked like there would be thirty-six to thirty-eight wagons. Some large families hadn't decided if one wagon would be enough or if they needed two. The short-statured Chet looked up at his tall Kentucky friend.

"Whatcha think?" he asked.

Gil replied thoughtfully, "I know darned well we need another wagon. We got one good one and two yoke of well-broke oxen, but I got ten kids. Reckon I'll buy six more yoke of oxen so half of them'll get some rest. My three oldest boys are about growed, so I kin turn 'em loose at breaking the new oxen. We best be gettin' to buyin' right away."

Chet asked Noah and Jed if they'd help him buy oxen and a wagon for the company. The guides found out in a hurry what a shrewd yankee trader Chet was. They visited every dealer that sold wagons and oxen, and Chet drove a hard bargain. He told them, "If I pay more than the rest of them did, they'll be hard on me, that's for sure."

After they purchased a wagon and two oxen, they returned to camp. The rest of the buying would have to wait until afternoon. Chet said that his wife, Della, was expecting them for the noon meal and she wanted them to be on time.

Della was an attractive woman, an inch taller than Chet. She met them with a smile and friendly greeting. "Chester speaks so highly of you boys," she said. "I'm right glad you could join us."

Jed and Noah warmed to her at once and Jed wondered how the sober, business-like Chet had ever attracted her.

The wind wasn't blowing for a change, so cooking outside had gone well. After Chet offered thanks, they enjoyed a hearty meal of beef stew, fresh biscuits and honey, and warm apple pie. As they were drinking their coffee, Chet asked Jed what he usually did on the trail for food.

Jed replied, "I buy my own groceries. Always managed to find a family I can eat with on the road. I pay the cook, naturally. One year I shared meals with a couple of single men who had a wagon."

Jed shifted his position to watch Noah's reaction to his next statement. "We were all supposed to share in the cooking, but one fellow was such a good cook he couldn't put up with our messes, so he did most of it. My cooking's not the best."

Noah's coffee cup shielded his face for an instant, but when it came away his expression gave his opinion of Jed's cooking.

Chet took another sip of coffee and said, "Della and me talked about that last night and we'd like it if you and Noah could be close to Sarge and us. The Lord didn't bless us with children, so we could haul your food in our wagon and you could eat with us."

Della said, "If I'm gonna cook for one man, I may just as well cook for two more! We'd truly admire to have you in our camp."

Jed looked at Noah's smiling face and answered for both of them. "After eating your cooking, it'd be pretty foolish of us to turn down an offer like that."

Jed was saying his good-byes before finding the next wagon he had promised to check over when he felt a tug on his pants. He looked down to see a small boy with enormous eyes who had a large yellow dog on a rope. For a moment he thought it was someone else, and he gasped. Then his eyes focused again on the small boy in front of him.

"Please, mister," the boy said. "Can I keep my dog?"

Jed saw the tears starting to form and hunkered down so he could look the boy in the eyes.

"What's your name, son?"

"Jimmy. Can I keep my dog? He's my best friend."

"I'm sure he is, Jimmy," said Jed. "I've had dogs like that myself. I know that special tie you have with a dog. But, Jimmy, we're going to be traveling through Indian country. You know about Indians, don't you?"

Jimmy nodded. "Yeah. They scalp you and stuff."

"Yeah, and they steal from you. And one thing they like to steal is dogs. Know why they steal 'em?"

Jimmy shook his head.

"They eat 'em. Leave him here, with a family in Indepence. You can find somebody to take care of him."

"I don't think you understand how much this dog means to my son," said a woman's voice.

Jed looked up to see a light-haired woman looking intently

at him. He suddenly felt a strange pain in his chest and answered more gruffly than he intended, "Ma'am, the dog stays here. We're not taking him."

He got up abruptly and walked away.

"Say," said Noah, following him. "That's no way to get folks on your side. What got into you?"

Jed shook his head and kept on walking.

The next few days went by quickly. After much haggling, Chet bought seventeen horses from Will's Livery and three mules from another dealer. All the travelers wanted to get Jed's opinion of their wagons. He took the sizes and ages of the children in each family and then showed them on paper how much their supplies would weigh. If it was too much for one wagon, he told them where to get another and what to look for. Boys eighteen years and older could drive a wagon.

"Three wagons can haul your supplies with a little room to spare," Jed told a large family. They readily accepted his suggestion.

The camp was a scene of turmoil as the wagon trains prepared to depart. Oxen bawled and fought as unbroken ones were hitched with the steady ones. Many of the young animals refused to cooperate, but the veteran farmers kept after them and soon progress was evident. Noah and Jed rode several of the green-broke horses every day. A few took to training right away, but most of them needed more time than they had. They'd have to be trained on the way.

One morning Jed arrived at the camp to find a young man he didn't recognize. Jed held the reins of his green-broke horse tightly, not wanting the skittish horse to bolt. The young man introduced himself as Walter Samuelson and said his in-laws had been on the train Jed guided last year. Their name was Lee.

"I remember them well," said Jed. "A fine family, stable, hard workers and their young people didn't cause any trouble."

"We couldn't go with them last year," said Walter, "because

we didn't have enough money. We still might not have enough, but the wife wants to go to her folks so bad I told her I'd talk to you about it. She gets to bawlin', you know how women do, missin' her ma and all." Walter looked away, embarrassed.

"You brought a letter back from her folks last winter and left it with the liveryman. Her folks wrote just how much it cost on the road for ferry tolls and the Barlow Road toll. We've got enough money to buy four oxen, a wagon, and all the supplies, but nothing for an extra yoke of oxen or the toll money."

Jed was almost ready to see if he could find a loan for him, when he asked, "How big's your family?"

"We got a girl four years old, a son two, and my wife is expecting another one in a month or so."

Jed swallowed before he answered. He looked hard at the young man and shook his head. "Walter, I'll tell you straight. Babies are born on the trail every year. Some survive and some don't. One year we buried the baby and the mother both. Four young children were left without a mother. It's always hard, even if the mother and baby do survive.

"If you wait one more year, when the new 'un is nearly a year old and you have enough money saved, that'll go much easier for you. You tell your wife I said so. She doesn't want to lose that baby on the road. Now, if you want to send a letter to her folks, I'd be glad to deliver it to them."

The young man seemed more relieved than disappointed. Thanking Jed profusely, he hurried off.

Steamboats from St. Louis had been dropping off more westering families every day. Jed thought there were enough wagons to start the inspection, so Noah and he started down one of the lines of wagons. Many were new, with new white canvas covers. They found only a couple of wagons that would have to go to a blacksmith shop for repairs. One was the wagon belonging to Jimmy and his parents. Jed told them about the problem and Jimmy's dad readily agreed. Jimmy's mother would not look at Jed and Jed noticed that the dog was gone.

As they moved down the second row, Jed heard a high dry

cough and looked around to see a young man with flushed cheeks. Consumption, Jed thought. That's bad.

The young man held out his hand. "Name's Aaron," he said. "And this here's my wife, Annie."

"Pleased to meet you, ma'am," said Jed. "Say, Aaron, that cough sounds bad."

"I know," he said earnestly, "but you won't see me slacking. I can carry my own weight. Just ask Gil. We was neighbors for years."

"We think he'll get better once we get to the mountains," Annie said. "We sure hope so."

Jed nodded, but he made a note to discuss the situation with Sarge. He didn't like to sign up sick people—the trip was hard enough on those who were well.

The next day Jed and Noah arrived each carrying a large board across their saddles. When they got to Chet's wagon, Jed called out, "Hey, Chet! Got something for you!"

Chet and Della stopped packing and looked up. "Whatcha got?" she called. "An ironing board?"

"Help me out—grab an end."

A crowd started to gather as Chet reached up to take hold of one end of the board. Together they lowered it to the ground.

"But what's it for?" asked someone.

"Why, I'll be—looks like a table top!" said Della.

"Yep, it is." Jed said with pride. "Figured we could use it."

Jed untied the four 2x2s from the saddle, handed the reins to Noah, and jumped down. "Look," he said. One end of each of the 2x2s had been whittled round, and Jed pushed them into the four holes that had been bored into the top. When he turned the board over, he had a ten-foot long table.

Someone whistled in appreciation. "Look at that, Margaret!"

"You can make the legs any length you want and when it's time to load up and get on the road, you just pull the legs off and slide the board in the wagon along one side. It doesn't take much room and it sure is useful."

Della's sensitive fingers felt the smooth planed top of the table and her pleasant face turned and smiled at Jed. "My, yes, that looks like a very usable table. Thanks, Jedidiah."

"You're welcome," answered Jed. "I've learned over the years that these things work out real well."

Noah tied the horses and carried the other table down the row of wagons. He demonstrated how it worked to the folks gathered along the way. When he returned he said, "Think a lot of these tables are going to be made tonight."

Jed and Noah inspected the wagons they hadn't yet seen. There were more than forty now. Then they turned to the few stubborn oxen that were resisting training. Some oxen were being shod in the chutes at the blacksmith shop. Jed told the owners that most of the oxen could travel at least two weeks without shoes. Some could go even longer, saving them money.

That night it rained lightly, and it was still drizzling the next morning when Jed and Noah got to the camp. Sarge asked if the rain would cause problems crossing the creeks and rivers.

"I don't think so," answered Jed, "unless they had a hard rain farther upstream. This kind of rain is just what the grass needs. We can't leave until we're sure there'll be enough grass to keep the oxen going. We don't want them to start losing weight already."

The next day Jed and Noah bought new canvas for their bedrolls. They also bought new blankets because the old ones looked like rags. They decided to move to the campsite so they could help with last-minute preparations.

"Sure hate to give up my bed for sleeping on the ground, but it's got to happen sometime," Jed told Noah.

Noah nodded. "But every day gets us closer to leaving and I'm happy to give up my bed if we can get started. When do you think we can go?"

"We should be ready to roll in a few days. I think we should check out the grass up the trail before we head out. That blazed-faced gelding needs a good workout, Noah. Why don't you take him down the trail for about twenty-five miles."

"Sure," said Noah. "If he gets really tired, maybe we could work with him and see if he gets a little better about being touched around the ears."

"Right," said Jed. "Nothing more bothersome than a head-shy horse. Can't hardly bridle him."

When Jed helped Noah saddle Blaze in the morning, there was a cool mist in the air, but they were sure it would lift when the sun got higher. Jed watched the tall horse and rider until they disappeared into the mist about two hundred yards away.

It was about dark when Noah rode Blaze back into camp. The horse was sweat-stained and ganted up, but he was still stepping out in a long stride.

Jed took the horse and sent Noah to Chet and Della's wagon for supper. When Jed arrived later, Della poured a cup of coffee for him and Noah gave his report.

"That horse has a lot of bottom," he said. "I must of gone over twenty miles before I turned around. There's fair grass growing up there, and if we feed the animals a little grain the first few days, I think we can go."

Chet asked Jed, "Should we get Gil and Sarge and do some talking?"

"A good idea," said Jed. "I'll look up Gil if you find Sarge."

When they gathered around the fire, Jed asked, "Can you finish the loading and be ready to roll in three days?"

They looked at one another for a few seconds, then Sarge spoke. "I reckon so. What do you say, Gil?"

Gil turned to spit a long stream of brown juice before he returned his gaze to Sarge. "It's mostly just loadin' the food and things like that. Our wagons can be ready in one day. What d'you think, Chet?"

"Don't think I can make it in one. I'll have my wagon ready tomorrow, and we can finish loading the supply wagon the next day."

Jed remarked, "If we see by tomorrow night we can't make it, we can wait another day, but I think two days is plenty of time. Let's spread the word to everyone early tomorrow morning—they've got forty-eight hours."

Gil was grinning wide enough to show the gap in his teeth. "There's nothing like being well prepared," he said. "Like one of my neighbors back in Kaintuck. This young feller came home from the field and found his bride upset.

"'I feel terrible,' she told him. 'I was pressing your suit and I burned a big hole in the seat of your pants.'

"'Don't worry about it, hon," said her husband. "Remember I got an extra pair of pants with my wedding suit.'

"'Yep," his bride answered. 'It's right lucky you did. I used them to patch the hole.'"

Gil laughed as hard as the others. They shook hands and went their separate ways, relieved that a decision had been made at last.

The next two days were busy for the shopkeepers. Jed didn't want the emigrants to use many barrels—barrels moved around too easily when going up or down steep creek banks or in the rough ground of the mountains. Jed wanted extra-heavy sacks put over the regular flour sacks. Foodstuffs that would spoil if they got wet were wrapped in oilskin.

Each family went over their lists to make sure they didn't forget anything. Jed moved from wagon to wagon, checking to see if the loads were right. By mid-afternoon of the second day he was satisfied.

Jed recognized the growing excitement in the camp. It happened every year. Children got noisier. Husband and wives talked louder and there was an edge of anger—or fear—in their voices.

Jed began to tell Noah about the first year he went to Oregon. Noah interrupted. "I know I'm nervous," he said, "but don't give me any of your lectures. You're not fooling me by pretending to be calm. You've been pacing back and forth like a caged animal all afternoon."

Jed nodded. "You never get over it until you get down the road a ways. I probably won't sleep much tonight and you won't either."

The officers called for a final meeting of everyone in the train that evening. When supper was over, the people gathered in the center of the campsite. Jed began to talk about the next morning. His loud voice carried well in the cool evening air.

"We usually start the wagons rolling by seven o'clock, but because of so many green-broke oxen, it'll take longer to hitch up. Let's try to get started by eight. Noah checked out the Blue River crossing, and we shouldn't have any problems there. The livestock will have a chance to drink at the river, so we won't unhitch at noon tomorrow."

Sarge gave out the wagon assignments and people started gathering in their groups to discuss the arrangement. Finally the crowd quieted down, and Gil turned to Chet. "How about a prayer?"

"Good idea," seconded someone.

Chet took off his hat and bowed his head. "Dear God, as we gather together this evening, before our start on the greatest adventure of our lives, we ask You for divine guidance. Guide us and help us during whatever trials we may face. We ask for Your blessing on the long hard trail ahead. May we all have the faith and courage to do our part in making this journey successful. May we work together and help each other. May we share our blessings and our burdens. Help us to remember to live by the Golden Rule. Therefore, all things whatsoever ye would that men should do to you, do ye even so unto them; for this is the law of the prophets. Guide and direct us on this great venture to Oregon and we will give Thee the praise. Amen."

"Amen," echoed several voices.

Della's clear voice started singing "On Jordan's Stormy Banks," and they all joined in the chorus:

"I am bound for the promised land,
"I am bound for the promised land;
"O who will come and go with me?
"I am bound for the promised land."

Then, slowly and quietly everyone returned to their tents.

Still awake after an hour, Jed patrolled the fringe of the

quiet camp. When he finally unrolled his bedroll, took off his boots, and pulled a blanket over him, his mind continued to race. Did they have everything they needed? He went over the list again: medicine, splints, and bandages in the trunk. Letters from folks here that he was taking to Oregon. The company money. The train's constitution that had been adopted the night before.

The trunk was locked and only Sarge and Chet had a key to unlock it. Several men had complained that the company had too many supplies and that too much money had been spent. He hoped they didn't complain later because there weren't enough supplies.

Jed turned over to look at Noah's bedroll and there was enough light to see that Noah's eyes were open. Noah's smiled slightly and rolled over to look the other way. The next thing Jed knew it was morning.

4

When breakfast was almost over at Chet and Della's camp, Chet said, "Here comes Gil."

"Can't miss him," commented Noah. "He stands out like a cottonwood tree amongst plum bushes."

The tall bushy-bearded man came to them with his usual long-legged stride. Gil's back was slightly stooped and his clothes hung loosely on his gaunt frame. His clothes were rumpled and his brown beard was streaked with gray. It was often stained with tobacco juice as well. It had been a long time since a comb had passed through his hair. His small grey eyes beamed friendliness and most people responded warmly to him.

The ram-rod straight, neatly dressed Sarge approached from the other direction. After a short conference the men split up to make the final preparations.

Jed and Noah checked the supply wagon again and several boys went with them to retrieve the horses still in the livery yard. Noah rode to his aunt's house to say a quick good-bye and to pick up a letter she was sending west. Then he helped drive the horses to the corral that was now assembled at the camp.

Jed, Sarge, Noah, and another man planned to ride alongside the wagon train the first day in case they were needed. They would be using the well-trained horses and the most gentle of the newly purchased string. Jed knew that the first day would not be the time to be riding a green-broke horse. They might have to help hold a runaway yoke of oxen.

Gil would be riding behind the livestock to help the teenage boys, who were on foot, keep the stock together. Gil was determined that no critter was going to break away and run back to the campsite.

Jed and the other outriders rode back and forth along the wagons while the oxen, horses, and mules were hitched to the wagons. Finally, he rode up to the lead wagon. He stood up in the stirrups of the saddle, facing the oxen. He looked down the long line of wagons. It was 8:15, time to go.

He took off his hat and held it high, waving it above his head. "On to Oregon!" he yelled.

The cry was picked up by Sarge and Noah. A chorus of excited voices up and down the line joined in. "On to Oregon!"

The wagons started to roll. Those not in line found their place under the direction of the outriders. Sarge's nineteen-year-old son, John Lewis, walked beside his family's well-trained oxen pulling the lead wagon. His mother walked alongside the wagon carrying a rope that was attached to the long brake lever located near the rear of the wagon box. Jed had insisted that all wagons have a brake lever on each side of the wagons so someone else besides the driver could handle the brake in an emergency.

Jed could see Sarge and Noah goading some ox teams that weren't cooperating. He stopped and let some wagons pass by so he could check their spacing. He had ordered the drivers to stay eight to ten paces behind the wagon in front, in order to have a safe stopping distance. He was pleased with what he saw, although a few wagons seemed a little farther apart than necessary.

Jed knew how hard it was to keep so many green broke oxen in place the first few days. He noticed one lead yoke of oxen led by a father and his teenage daughter. The mother walked alongside the rear yoke with the brake rope in her hand. The smaller children were walking to the left of the mother and a few paces behind. Things were going suprisingly smoothly for the first day of travel.

Then he saw the boy Jimmy walking alongside his mother. His father was concentrating on holding his oxen in line. Suddenly Jimmy darted too close to the wheel.

"Hey!" shouted Jed. "Get away from there!"

The boy looked up, startled and ran to his mother, who gave Jed a dark look. "He's just a child!" she snapped. "Leave him be!"

Jed wanted to explain that he was just trying to protect the boy, but the woman's look silenced him, and he went on.

When the train got to the Blue River crossing, they stopped. One by one the wagons forded the hip-deep water. Ramps had been cut in the banks years ago. Periodic flooding had erased lower sections, but it was still easier to get down now than in the early years. Even though the stream was only a few yards wide, some folks used a raft that had been tied near the crossing. When the last wagon had crossed the river, the large herd of loose stock was driven across.

During the noon stop, the women prepared cold lunches. Many men refused to leave their oxen, fearing they might run away. In less than half an hour the wagons were ready to roll again.

Just before Jed gave the signal to start, he asked Della if she knew the parents of Jimmy. "Oh, that's Molly and Ben Adams," she said. "Real nice people. Kinda quiet."

Not real nice to me, Jed thought. At least she isn't.

The train followed him up a long hill, giving the animals a good workout. When they reached the top, the train moved from a northwesterly direction to almost due north. Jed turned to the west and looked back to see the wagons coming around the bend. They continued west for a short distance and then angled to the southwest, arriving at the edge of the little town of Westport.

Jed had ridden ahead of the train to mark off a circle near Mill Creek. With Noah's help, Jed directed the wagons to fill it in. The end of each wagon tongue was chained to the inner rear wheel of the wagon in front, so the tongue was nearly level. The chain used for the lead oxen was fastened to that same wheel about two feet higher and the other end fastened to the front of the wagon behind it. This made a corral for the livestock, and both the front and rear of each wagon was open to get at the supplies. Jed preferred this type of circle to one made by chaining the front wheel of each wagon to the rear wheel of the wagon in front. That made a much tighter and smaller circle, but left little room for the large number of livestock. The smaller circle left only one end of the wagon open to get to the supplies.

A gap about twenty feet wide was left in the circle and was closed off with ropes to hold the livestock in and to provide a gate. The cows needing to be milked that evening were tied to a wagon wheel before the oxen, horses, and mules were turned loose in the circle. Once the cows had been milked, the rope gate was opened on one side and the herd was let out to graze. The horses ridden during the day were used to herd the livestock. At the eight o'clock shift, fresh horses would be saddled for the night guard duty.

Fires were started to cook the evening meal and tents were set up. Several of the long narrow tables, similar to the one Jed gave Della, were filling up with pots of ham and bean soup and plates of biscuits.

When supper was over, Jed announced that Westport would be their last chance to buy anything else they needed on the trail. They could also mail letters back east if they wanted to. Noah would take them in.

Gil came at a trot from the herd looking worried. "Them horses grazed pretty good for about an hour," he said, "but now some of 'em are movin' around a bit. They's gonna be hard to hold when it gits dark."

Jed answered, "I think we better run all of the horses into the circle before it gets dark. There's some grass there and we don't want any of 'em going back. We've got about an hour before dark, so Sarge and I can help switch the riding horses and give the day horses some time to graze. We better put those four horses on pickets tonight outside of the circle—they had a good workout today." Jed's calm voice had a steadying affect on the other men.

Once the horses were in the circle, Jed picketed a horse near his bedroll. He wanted a horse close by in case he needed it in a hurry. Della handed Jed a cup of coffee as he joined Sarge, Chet, and Noah around the fire. Sarge asked how the herd was doing.

"All right," replied Jed, "but we'll have to have a little more help out there tonight. Gil planned on four riders and he's going out on foot to help until eleven. I told Gil I'd help from eleven till the two o'clock shift change."

Noah spoke up next, "I'll help from two 'til five. That's when the horses and mules should be turned out to graze." Sarge and Chet offered to help from five until all the stock could be brought in before the train left.

"That'll be an hour later than usual because we don't have a long way to go tomorrow," replied Jed. "We can give the livestock an hour more to graze on the short soft grass."

The next morning, the job of getting ready still went slowly. The oxen were called the same uncomplimentary names they had been the day before. A cold northwest wind blew dust into faces and down necks. Drivers and walkers switched sides, trying to escape it.

For the first few miles the trail went straight south. The midday stop was made about 11:30, when the animals were turned loose to graze and to drink in a nearby spring-fed creek. Noah caught up with Jed at the edge of the herd to report what he had found out the night before in Westport.

"From what I gathered there're enough wagons around there to get another train going in less than a week. They're waitin' for a few more people to show up before setting a start-up time."

"Hmmm," mused Jed, "from what we could see around

Independence, another train could be leaving there in a week or so. A riverboat man told me that he saw emigrants going on up to St. Joe. He thinks another riverboat load of Oregon-bound folks is coming to Independence pretty soon. A couple trains might be leaving St. Joe any day now. It's possible they'll be ahead of us on the trail when we get to the fork of the road. But even if there's a half dozen trains behind us, that's still a lot less than last year."

At 1:30 the wagons were rolling again and two hours later the stop order ran down the line, so people could rest a few minutes. They had to walk on the right side of the wagons to avoid the dust churned up by the wheels and blown around by a fresh west breeze. By the time the train arrived at the Lone Elm campground, the wind had gone down, and getting supper was not as difficult as cooking the noon meal had been.

The huge tree giving this stopping place its name looked bad. Limbs and bark had been cut off for firewood. This second night on the trail was more moonlit than the previous night. Some of the horses were hobbled and left outside to graze with the cattle. Others were left inside the circle. Gil and Jed had checked the herd about a half-hour before sundown and decided that three men on horseback could maintain order. The travelers were tired from fighting the wind and dust and turned in early.

The next morning things went a little smoother. The oxen were finally becoming trained. They were fed grain after they were yoked and the loose stock were driven out of the circle. The horses and mules that would be ridden or driven that day were tied to the wagon wheels and fed before they were hitched up.

Jed announced that they would be going up and down hills all day. There'd be plenty of firewood in the next stretch of the trail and the water supply would be good. Hunting wouldn't be good yet. Some of the eastern Indians had been moved west of the Missouri River by the government and had cleared out much of the game.

Noah rode at the front of the train that morning, so Jed had a chance to drop back and visit some of the families. He got off his horse and walked beside a man driving his oxen.

"Are they behavin' for you?"

"Some are, some ain't. They're a-learnin'. They better be!"

This year was like the other years, Jed thought. Some of the children looked at him with fear in their eyes and some looked at him like a hero. A few grabbed their mother's hand when he came near. Talking and joking with them for a few minutes usually helped calm them down.

Jed mounted his horse after the mid-morning rest stop and, seeing a wave of the hat from Noah, shouted, "All set!" It was time to roll.

Jed was at home on almost any horse. He'd been riding since he was four and had learned to think like a horse. He kept his mount still until a wagon drawn by four mules came alongside. The driver said he didn't like to drive oxen and hoped his six mules would see him through.

"If I have to, I'll buy some fresh ones at Fort Bridger or Fort Hall," he said.

A horseman named Zebelon was right behind the mule wagon. He had a tight line on his four horses, forcing them to move slow enough to keep the right space between his wagon and the one in front.

"I reckon," said the older man, "that it'll take awhile for my horses to slow down to an ox's gait."

"That time will surely come," said Jed. "It always has before." Zeb grinned widely and Jed could see several of his teeth were missing.

"Oxen and me don't get along very well, so I bought me four extra horses. I kin change 'em ever day. Beins I'm a bachelor, only loaded about fourteen hundred pounds of supplies. Course I started out with about five hundred pounds of oats and corn. I reckon that'll last a spell. I might just hang on to a few bags of oats when the grass gets good—save 'em 'til we have some poor pickens."

"You'll need all that and then some, Zeb."

"I wish I coulda bought those extra fine horses my neighbor, back behind me, sold in Independence, but I knew I didn't dare. I know him real well, and if he saw those purty horses get thin he would be hurt powerful bad."

Jed noticed that Zeb was a real horseman. His harness was adjusted to fit properly. The horses' forelocks were carefully trimmed, the manes combed out, and their hair curried smooth. The wiry little bald-headed man took pride in the way his horses looked.

Out of the corner of his eye, Jed saw Molly and Jimmy walking beside the next wagon. He circled around and dropped back to the rear of the train where Gil was walking beside his family. Gil's nineteen- and twenty-year-old sons, Will and James, were driving the two ox-drawn wagons. Gil's other teenagers and younger children were walking alongside, talking among themselves.

Gil's wife Emma was plodding along behind them, fanning herself with an extra bonnet. "Do declare, this is the hottest I ever been," she said to Jed in a raspy voice.

"After a while," he said, "you may remember this stretch as cool, compared to what's ahead."

"Humpf," she said, and did not return his smile.

A little farther up the line, Jed caught up with a family without young children. A girl of about eighteen walked beside her mother. When they turned to face him, he touched his hat and said hello to the family. He caught the sight of a charming face under the girl's bonnet.

Mighty pretty girl, Jed thought. Wonder why I haven't noticed her before.

It was a calm day, but after the wheels of forty wagons ground over one set of ruts, a powdery dust rose into the still air. Jed moved to the center of the line and told the driver it was time to form two lines. When the order to halt came, the driver should pull to the right about fifty feet and keep going until he was even with the lead wagon.

On his way to the front of the train, Jed heard a loud "Whoa!"

from the front of the second line. Jed hurried in that direction and found the lead wagon with a broken tongue. The right front wheel of the wagon had dropped in a hole and the jolt snapped the tongue. The train was halted.

The break was a long diagonal one, so it could be repaired. Henry, the blacksmith, brought an auger bit. The men bored three holes and bolted the pieces together. Then they pulled the spare reach from the floor of the wagon and lashed it to the bottom of the tongue with small rope. The tongue would last until a more permanent patch could be put on.

While the repairs were made, the men talked about Jed's insistence that the lead yoke's pulling chain be fastened to the rear of the tongue and not to the front, the way the wheel oxen's yoke is. Henry drove home the point.

"Dissen ground vas near flat, but if der tongue broke going up ein hill, und all der oxen vas a-pulling from der front of der tongue, der vagon vould roll backwards—gersmashen! Unless der brake vas pulled *quick—ja?*"

In half an hour the wagons were rolling again. When it was time for Jed to scout ahead for the evening campsite, he rode on at a steady lope for a half-mile and then let the horse walk. Finding a likely spot, he rode around the area and checked it carefully before dismounting.

He pried out a rock about the size of his head and rolled it out to where it could be easily seen. Leading the brown mare, he paced off 106 steps to the west. His three-foot-long steps measured the 320-foot width of the circle. He couldn't find another rock, so he dropped to his knees and pulled enough grass loose to make a pile he could see from several hundred feet away. Jed mounted and marked out a circle with the tracks of his horse, using the rock and pile of grass as guides. After he'd made two circuits, he rode away from the circle and dismounted where the grass was fairly high.

He took the bit out of the horse's mouth and let her graze until the wagons approached. The brown mare was one of the smallest horses in the string from Will's Livery. She was still a little green, but Jed found out she was quick on her feet and a smooth rider. When he could see the white tops of the wagons, Jed put the bit in the mare's mouth and checked the cinch on the saddle. He took a drink from his canteen and mounted to direct the circling of the wagons.

It was one of those warm, still evenings that sometimes come in late April. The smoke from the evening fires rose straight up. The evening chores were finished, and the horses—except for a few loose ones in the circle—were hobbled. Jed's horse was tethered about fifty feet from his bedroll.

When Jed returned to Chet and Della's fire after a brief conference with Gil, he found the families in the five lead wagons seated on the ground in a circle. Some of the women were seated on blankets, and most of the men were sitting cross-legged on the grass.

Chet spoke as Jed sat down between Noah and Sarge. "We thought it was such a nice night it'd be a good chance to get a little better acquainted. We always hurry getting ready in the morning, and the women are so busy during noon stops and at supper time, we don't have much chance to visit." The small man's freshly shaven face stood out in the circle of bearded and stubble-faced men. Chet's clothes fit his well-proportioned body neatly and his ability to keep his clothes clean was amazing.

"That's fine," said Jed. "By the time we get to Oregon, we'll know each other real well. You'll see everyone's good and bad sides. If somebody's got any secrets, they're usually known by the end of the trip."

The travelers were still a little shy with each other—except for Della and Chet, who seemed to know everyone. Sarge's wife Mary had kept to herself so far. She had worked the farm while Sarge was in the army and was tanned and strong, with powerful arms, yet she had a gentleness that reminded Jed of his Aunt Eliza, who had never done any more strenuous work than needlepoint. Mary's hair was dark, flecked with gray, and her soft brown eyes frequently twinkled. John Lewis, their nineteen-year-old son, seemed to be a good worker and loved to talk when his overpowering father wasn't around.

Josh was another young man in the group. He was driving the supply wagon. A slim young man, his thick brown hair hung below his cap. His features were a little rough but he had a pleasant smile. His folks, Caleb and Sarah, seemed to be weighted down with sorrow. Chet had told Jed that they had lost seven children to sickness. Only Josh and seven-year-old Nellie survived. Then there was the Adams family—Ben, Molly, and five-year-old Jimmy.

The travelers compared their day's experiences and discussed the weather. Someone asked Jed about the road ahead the next few days. After he had answered, Josh turned to Jed. "I guess I understand about why we have to changes places every day, but please explain just how it works so I don't mess up."

"Sure," answered Jed. "This system's always worked real well. If you don't rotate, the folks in back are always eating dust. By setting up in groups of five wagons each, people are never far away from each other and come to feel responsible for each other. It's best if Sarge and Chet are in the same group and Noah and I need to be in touch with them everyday. You're driving the supply wagon, which needs to be near Sarge, so your family's wagon has to come along, too. To fill out the group, we have Ben, Molly, and Jimmy, who joined us by chance just a few days before we started." He looked at Molly as he spoke and felt the same peculiar pain in his chest. Her gaze was no longer icy, but it was far from warm. He forced himself to look at Ben and smile.

Jed continued, "We painted the letter "A" on the first five wagons, a "B" on the next five and on down the alphabet. The last four wagons, where Gil's family is, are lettered "I". You're the lead wagon today, Josh, but it'll be forty-two days before you'll be in the lead again. Tomorrow you'll be in the fifth wagon and Ben'll be in the lead. The next day all five of you'll go to the rear and Ben's wagon will be the last one. Everyone in your group of five wagons keeps moving and at the end of five days, the last group moves ahead one notch. This afternoon we had two lines and some days we might have four lines or even more to get out of the dust.

"When it's time to circle, you all get back in your place in line. Sarge will supervise the lineup. Okay, Josh?" Jed had been watching the faces around the circle while he talked, but he turned to look at Josh for his answer.

"Yep," said Josh, "that explains it well enough for me."

His little sister Nellie had almost gone to sleep while she was leaning against her mother, so Sarah took her to bed. After a searching look at Jed, which he couldn't interpret, Molly took her son away. Soon the others headed for their last chores before going to bed.

Jed and Noah walked back to their bedrolls.

"Pat told Gil he didn't think they needed three herders all night. Said he wasn't gonna to do it," said Jed. "I've got the eleven-to-two guard duty tonight, so I told Gil I'd see that that Scotsman gets on a horse."

"He's a big man," responded Noah with a frown. "You better be careful."

"I've handled troublemakers before," answered Jed. "I always get them to do their part, one way or another."

Before falling asleep, Jed mused about the people in the five-wagon "A" group. Sarge'll be a good leader, he thought. Chet's solid—devout, too, but not real pushy. It's good he's the secretary-treasurer—he'll be as honest as they come. Della's a good cook and really kind, but very formal in a funny way. Calls her husband Chester, though he asks everyone else to call him Chet. She's got a beautiful voice, loves to sing, loves to read the Bible, too. Ben—can't tell yet, but he seems to be a good worker, quiet. Only two children with us—Jimmy and Nellie. Nellie may be a whiner, don't think Jimmy is. He took losing his dog real good. And Molly—Jed shook his head. There's some mystery there, he thought. Something's strange.

Sleep finally came to Jed. He awoke a little before eleven. Many years in the wilderness had taught him to wake up when he needed to. He pulled on his boots and jacket, covered his bed with canvas to keep the dampness out, and went to find the guard getting off duty.

When Jed met him he said, "Keep your gun belt on a few minutes until we make sure Pat gets to the job. Let's see if the man going off duty can get Pat going."

They didn't have to wait long. A slim young man—it was Josh—tied his horse to a wagon wheel and approached Pat's tent. Pat's family was in the tent, but he was sleeping outside. Josh called softly to Pat. There was no response. He reached down and touched Pat on the shoulder, then shook the man's shoulder. Pat suddenly struck out violently and the agile boy jumped back in time to avoid being hit.

"Time for guard duty," he said hoarsely. Getting no reaction, he kicked Pat's feet. Pat cursed but didn't get up.

Jed was at Josh's side. "Let me try," he said. "Pat, I know you're awake. It's your turn to ride, so get going."

Pat mumbled, "You don't need guards ever night. It's a waste of time."

"Every man takes his turn at guarding on this train and your turn is now," answered Jed steadily. When Pat didn't stir, Jed moved to the rear of Pat's wagon and filled the dipper from the water barrel. He brought it back and splashed the cold water on Pat's head. Pat jumped up and, brushing the water from his eyes and bushy eyebrows, clenched his fists.

He took a powerful swing at Jed's head. Jed ducked under the huge fist and struck the big man just below the center of his rib cage. He could hear the wheeze of air from Pat's chest. Jed cocked his left hand again and delivered a powerful punch to Pat's right cheek. Jed felt the pain on his knuckles as they crashed against Pat's face. The big man fell to the ground, took a few breaths, and got to his knees. Jed was standing close to the rear wheel of the wagon when Pat sprang at him with his head down. Jed jumped to one side and Pat's head crashed into a spoke of his wagon wheel. He sagged to the ground with a groan.

The half-dozen men who had gathered said nothing as Jed

reached again for the dipper. He refilled it and poured the water over Pat's head. Pat swore loudly and rolled to a sitting position, leaning against the wagon wheel.

Jed faced the big man and said again, "Every man on this train takes his turn at guard duty. You are no exception. The next time you want to play games like this, I'll come with a blacksnake whip and work you over with that. It'll be easier on my knuckles." Jed heard a snicker somewhere in the dark. He continued, "You've got exactly two minutes to be on that horse!"

Pat mumbled his displeasure and wiped the blood from his forehead. Jed replaced the dipper and spoke to the men gathered around. "Sorry to interrupt your sleep. I don't think this'll happen again—with anyone."

Jed took the pistol and gun belt from the early night guard, strapped it on, and turned to see Pat struggling to put on his jacket. Jed walked deliberately to the other side of the circle, checking the outside of the area for any sign of movement. He sat on the hub of a wagon wheel looking and listening. After awhile he walked slowly around to the other side. He could see the nearest rider, a few hobbled horses and cattle. When he walked farther down the line, he sat on a wagon hub and looked out over the herd. He could see that some of the cattle were grazing, but most of them were lying down.

Jed could make out all of the three riders, as they moved slowly around the edge of the herd. He recognized Pat on one of the nearest horses. Jed clenched the fingers on his left hand and straightened them out again. He could still feel the sting in his knuckles. He wondered if Pat's cheek felt any better.

The walking guard usually patrolled opposite the herd and Jed was no exception. The night guard always carried a five-shot pistol, but usually only three chambers were loaded and capped. It was to be used to alert the train if someone approached who didn't holler out a greeting from at least fifty yards. Several times during Jed's years of guiding a train a pistol shot had brought men running.

Jed had a lot of time to think while doing guard duty and thinking made the time go by faster. Tonight he mused about how well the trip had started out. Except for Pat, every man was doing his job without complaint. His mind drifted to the attractive girl he had seen while walking alongside the wagons. She seemed more mature than some of the other teenage girls on the train. Jed wondered if she could be twenty years old. For years he'd kept away from the young women in his wagon trains, because he knew that meant trouble. An old mountain man was not a good prospect for a husband anyway.

When Jed walked around the outside of the circle, he was pleased to see the thick grass. It looked like passing herds had not overgrazed it. There had been enough rain early this spring for growth.

The herd was corralled before midnight, when a soft rain began to fall. Bedrolls under the wagons escaped the worst of it. Those sleeping in the open scurried for cover. Sunrise was welcomed by the damp travelers. A few people changed into the dry clothes that had been stored under oilskins in the wagons, but most of them figured the damp clothes would dry on their bodies while they went about their chores. Wet clothes and bedding were draped over wagon wheels, chain fences, and anywhere else they could find.

That day the wagons rolled without any delays. Noah and a couple of other men rode off to try some hunting. The young blacksmith, Henry, was one of the would-be hunters. His partner Karl drove the ox team that day. The hunters took only two pack mules with them because Noah was not expecting a lot of game. They wanted to find out how well the mules worked. The wind was right for antelope.

Jed wouldn't have to ride far ahead today because tonight's camp would be along a creek fed by good spring water. They'd find plenty of water, firewood, and grass on the north side of the creek. Just after they stopped for the noon meal, it started to rain again. Everyone dashed to get in or under the wagons to escape the downpour. In about a half-hour they started off again sloshing through mud in their damp clothes.

"Dammit, I hate wet clothes," said Josh. "They itch."

"Well, I hate cussing more," answered Jed, "so let's have no more of it. There's ladies around, you know."

Henry was waiting for them at camp with two antelope, which had already been dressed and skinned and were draped over the mules. He was cleaning grouse as Jed approached him, his sleeves rolled above his elbows, his hands red with blood. His brawny arms had been scarred by sparks from the forge. The young blond blacksmith's thick neck tapered down to broad shoulders. He was a powerful man.

Hope I can keep Henry on my side, thought Jed. Looks like he'd be a good man in an emergency.

"Noah iss a gut hunter," said Henry. "Ven ve saw dese animals from far avay, he took us around ein hill and ve vas coming up from der utter side ven he stop us. He vas crawling to der top and den he vave us close. He put his shirt on ein stick and vaved it and got dem antelope so curious vatching that vaving, dey vas acoming right up der hill vere ve vas lyin' down und ve shot dem!" Henry laughed at the memory.

The other hunters returned with a few rabbits and birds, and the meat was distributed to as many families as possible. The next day's game would go to the next in line, until all had their fair share. This was the first fresh meat they'd had since leaving Independence. The air was filled with the smells of roasted antelope and fried rabbit.

Sarge's face parted in one of his rare smiles as he asked Jed, "You think you can find us this nice a spot to camp, every night, all the way to Oregon?"

Jed laughed. "Wish I could! I might be able to find half a dozen spots that compare to this one. You should know from your military campaigns, this kind of campsite doesn't come often."

The wind died down at dusk and the pleasant evening weather added to the enjoyment of a good meal of roast grouse and potatoes.

"Sure can eat a lot after walking twenty miles!" Someone said and the others laughed in agreement.

"Reminds me of a story," said Gil. "We got a new preacher at our church back in Kaintuck last year. It was only fittin' that we invite him to our place for a dinner to git to know our clan better. He was a really big man so Emma fussed that he'd probably eat a lot."

"Was he bigger than you, Gil?" asked John Lewis with a broad grin.

"Well, he wasn't quite as tall, but he was big—I mean really big!" Gil used his long arms to show the extent of his girth. The attentive crowd chuckled. "He was strong in the pulpit, too. You woulda liked his sermons, Chet. Our young chickens was just about big enough to start eatin' so we butchered a bunch of 'em. I don't recollect how many but with our clan it takes quite a few. Emma was busy a fryin' chickens for quite a spell and finally we gits to the eatin'. We was all hungry for that tasty tender food, so them platters of chicken soon disappeared and Emma brought out more.

"Well, that preacher was a mowin' away so much chicken I thought we might run out. We had always taught our younguns to go easy on the food 'til our company had plenty. We all held back a little, but that preacher kept right at it. When that platter came around the last time there was only a couple of wings left. James and Mark passed it by and the preacher took 'em both. Will took the empty platter, looking up at me like a bucket calf that just spilt all his milk.

"When we was done eatin' the preacher, my three big boys, and I went outside while the girls helped their ma with the dishes. There was a lot of chickens in our yard, and as I stood beside the preacher a big red rooster strutted nearby.

"'My,' said the preacher, 'that rooster acts proud.'

"I winked at my boys standing off to one side and said, 'He should be—three of his sons just entered the ministry in the last hour.'"

Gil was rewarded with hearty laughter.

The five lead wagons were about 150 yards from the spring. That was as close to trees as Jed wanted the train to get, especially if the trees were on an island and there were Indians around.

Sarge said that he and his son John Lewis wanted to go hunting with Noah the next day. Josh's parents reluctantly gave him permission to go with them too, if Sarge would be in the group.

Jed walked around the circle, saying howdy and noting each wagon's condition. A man called to him, asking him about the terrain ahead. When the man's wife handed him a cup of coffee, Jed realized that these were the parents of the beautiful young girl he had spotted earlier. He looked around and saw the girl washing dishes. Her father proudly told Jed about his children. The older ones had decided to stay in Illinois. It had been hard to leave them, but the promise of all that free land in Oregon was too much to pass up.

They had brought the three younger children. Jed guessed the youngest boy to be about sixteen and his older brother about eighteen—he had guard duty. The daughter's name was Martha. When Jed handed her the tin coffee cup, he was startled by her beauty.

That night, Jed couldn't get Martha out of his mind. She was one of the prettiest girls he'd ever seen. Even though he knew it foolish, he wanted to get to know her.

Jed awakened a little before two. The full moon illuminated the campsite, dimming the thousands of stars in the cloudless sky. As long as he was awake, Jed decided to check on the herd. He pulled on his boots, slipped on his jacket, and walked slowly to the side of the train where he could see the animals downstream from the spring. The herders were keeping the livestock far from trees, so they could watch them carefully. The shift changed. Jed was satisfied they were learning well and was glad they hadn't had a thunderstorm yet to spook the herd.

When Jed moved closer, he could make out the hobbled

horses. The tall horse, Blaze, was always easy to see because of his size and the white stripe on his head. Jed called out to the walking guard, "Everything okay?" and heard a "Yep, all's well!" in response.

He walked carefully back to his bedroll so he wouldn't wake anyone. He could hear snoring as he passed the tents. When he drew near Martha's campsite, Jed thought of her again and then laughed. You're like a lovesick schoolboy, he told himself.

The train would not be moving the next day, Sunday. The hobbles would be removed from the horses and the entire herd taken to the creek for water and then to a fresh pasture.

The morning was beautiful—bright sun shining on the dew-laden grass. The cool air smelled fresh and clean and the expectation for a day of rest were bright and cheery. The cows were lowing as they waited to be milked. There would be plenty of fresh milk for breakfast.

It's almost like a farm in Illinois, thought Jed. He looked up to see Gil walking toward him with his son, Will, by his side. Gil's face looked like thunder. Uh, oh, thought Jed. Trouble.

5

Gil handed Jed a horse hobble and said soberly, "Bad news, Jed. Blaze is gone and another horse, too."

"Oh, no," said Jed. "What happened?"

"I went out to hep Will bring in the herd—it was his fust time. Said I'd hep take off the hobbles. Well, the hobbles was there, but Blaze was gone."

"Tarnation!" Jed cried.

"I rode to the creek bank to check for tracks," continued Gil. "One horse crossed it without hobbles and the other one hopped across with the hobbles on. I don't know when them blame horses left, but they's sure gone now."

"Blaze was here at two o'clock," Jed said. "I saw him when I watched the changing of the guard."

They looked at the hobble carefully. It was the kind with only one buckle. This kind looped around one pastern, twisted several times, and buckled around the other front pastern. It looked as if it had not been twisted tightly enough and the horse had been able to get free.

"Drat it!" said Jed. "Blaze is one of the fastest and toughest horses in our string. We've got to get him back. I'd better take somebody with me—if he's not hobbled, he might be hard to catch."

"Can I go with him, Pa?" asked Will.

"If it's pleasin' with Jed, you kin, but you better git some breakfast in you fust."

Jed, who was in an angry mood by now, nodded his approval and got his horse ready. He tied a couple of neck ropes to his saddle and took a lariat along. The boy and the mountain man galloped down the same trail they had used the day before. They slowed down to a walk after about a half-mile, and Jed studied the ground for tracks.

"Nothing," Jed muttered between clenched teeth. He told Will to go to the left of the trail and he headed right. They angled away from the trail and then slanted back again. When they were about two hundred yards apart, a yell from Will brought Jed over, and Will showed Jed the tracks he had found.

Jed remarked, "Good! Looks like the horses are headed back to Westport. I hoped they'd do that."

Will gave a whoop of satisfaction.

"Hey, Will, this is Indian country! Let's keep it quiet. Most of the Indians around here are friendly, but let's not announce that we're here anyway. When you want to signal me, just wave your hat. I'll be watching."

Will nodded and they rode steadily along the trail. After a couple of miles, Jed said, "Let's take it slow over the crest of each hill, so we don't startle them." At last they saw the horses going up a knoll. Blaze was free, but the other horse was still hobbled and was hopping along behind Blaze. Blaze stopped for a minute to graze.

Jed studied the terrain a few seconds and said softly, "Let's drop back a little and go around this hill far enough to the right, so Blaze doesn't see us."

When Jed judged they had gone far enough, they turned to

the left and went up the hill. As they got to the crest they saw the horses at the bottom starting up the grade. Jed told Will what to do and as they approached, the big horse detoured to the left of them. Will cut him off. When Blaze turned back, he was met with a well-thrown loop of a lariat. His freedom was over.

Jed and Will put a neck rope on him, positioned a loop over his nose, and went to meet the hobbled horse. Jed swore as he took the hobbles from the sore pasterns. The horse had worn the hair off his hide just above the hooves and that area was burned raw.

"You stupid excuse for a horse!" said Jed. "You're going to pay for this. You'd never have made it back to the States this way—if that's where you were going. Indians might have found you in time. Otherwise, you'd be wolf or coyote feed." Jed tied a horse to each of the saddle horns and pulled his rifle.

"Whatcha gonna do with the gun?" asked Will.

Jed answered, "Didn't you see the antelope off to the south, just as we turned back there?"

"Nope," said Will.

"Well, it looks like they're headed this way. If they didn't see us, I might be able to get one on foot. The wind is blowing in our faces, so they couldn't get our scent. You stay on your horse and hold on to mine. Keep a sharp lookout for Indians because they'd love to have this bunch of horses. If you see any, just head out in my direction as fast as you can. Don't worry about making noise, the more you can make, the better!"

Jed checked the load in his rifle. He inserted a cap and eased the hammer down so his gun would be ready to fire when he cocked it. Will watched Jed walk in a crouch to the top of the hill and then saw him crawl out of sight. Will searched the horizon, as Jed had told him to. For the first time on the trail, he was alone, all alone in Indian country, sitting on an Indian's most coveted possession—a horse. And there was not only his horse, but three others. He bet that an Indian brave would do almost anything to get those horses. He felt the hairs on his neck prickle and sweat rolled into his eyes.

It seemed forever before he heard the rifle shot that meant Jed had shot at an antelope. It was the signal to head that way, because he'd get only one shot.

Jed smiled at how quickly Will came with the horses. He decided not to tease him. The boy looked really scared.

Jed gutted the antelope and loaded it behind the saddle of Will's horse. The brown gelding he was riding didn't like that at all. Jed quickly pulled his saddle and put it on Blaze, who didn't mind being bridled.

Jed and Will rode leisurely back to the train. "This is Shawnee country, Will," explained Jed, "and they're not all warriors, you know. They're farmers, too, because wild game is mighty scarce around here. They raise corn, potatoes, beans, vegetables, same as us. It seems odd that we found antelope here. They must've drifted into the area this spring—we usually don't see any around here. The Indians'll have them all hunted before very long."

They dropped the antelope off to a family that hadn't gotten meat the day before. Jed then took the horse with the raw legs to the supply wagon and smeared the sore pasterns with a generous amount of salve. "You'll be mighty stiff in the morning," he told the horse, "but you'd better keep up if you don't want to end up inside a wolf."

The gentle south breeze brought the sound of a fiddle and hymn singing to Jed's ears. Chet had told him last night they planned to have a service this morning. The worshippers gathered about halfway from the spring on the south side of the circle. There was no preacher on the train, but Chet had said he'd lead the service. They sang some well-loved hymns—Della's warm contralto could be heard over the rest of the voices— and Chet read from Psalm 24:

> "The earth is the Lord's and the fulness
> thereof; the world, and they that dwell therein.
>
> "For he hath founded it upon the seas, and
> established it upon the floods.

"Who shall ascend into the hill of the Lord?
or who shall stand in his holy place?

"He that hath clean hands, and a pure heart;
who hath not lifted up his soul unto vanity, nor
sworn deceitfully.

"He shall receive the blessings from the Lord,
and righteousness from the God of his salvation."

When the service was over, Jed showed Gil the sores on
the hobbled horse. Gil shook his head. "What would make a
horse hurt hisself like that? Fool thing."

"Will was a big help in finding them, Gil," Jed said.

The tall man grinned at Jed's kind words. Then he grew
serious. "How we gonna keep this from happening again?"

"Who was on guard duty then?"

Gil shifted the chaw of tobacco in his left cheek. "I don't
know 'em too good," he said. "Two of 'em is brothers and the
other is their brother-in-law. Should I put 'em on different shifts?"

"Not yet," answered Jed, "but I'll watch them close. Just
remind me when their next turn will be."

Sunday afternoon was spent hunting, washing clothes, baking,
mending, visiting, and even sleeping. Mary had brought dried
pumpkin, and she and Della made several pumpkin pies, filling
the air with their aroma. Sometime during the day all of the
wagon wheels were greased, and Henry put shoes on a yoke of
oxen. The hunters returned laden down with meat. The good
mood lasted into the evening. Jed could sense a feeling of
contentment as he moved around the campsite.

"Right nice day," Zeb told him. "Couldn't ask for better."

"Where are goin' tomorrow, Jed?" someone called out.

"Tomorrow we're going by Blue Mound," said Jed. "You
might want to climb it, but I suggest you save your energy.
There's a lot more interesting hills coming up. We've got to
make time while the weather's good.

"We'll also cross the Wakarusa River. This won't be a
problem, unless we have rain. It's usually not very deep, but

the banks are pretty steep."

Darkness closed in and the travelers began getting ready for bed. As Jed headed for his bedroll, he was startled to see a couple in an embrace. He was positive that the boy was Gil's oldest son and the girl was Martha.

Well, he thought philosophically, that's one decision I won't have to make now. Still, he felt a little sad.

The next morning Jed rode around the inside of the circle about fifteen minutes before start-up time. Most of the oxen were already yoked up, and the last of the tents had been packed away in the wagons.

Sarge was talking to a man with a spade in his hand. Jed slowed down as he passed them, then stepped down from his horse to tighten the cinch on his saddle, eavesdropping shamelessly. The man had evidently been arguing with Sarge, so Jed stayed to the left of his horse and listened.

The man addressed Sarge. "I don't reckon we need to fill all the privy holes when we ain't coming back this way."

Sarge's answer was forceful. "Other trains are following us, maybe tomorrow, maybe in a few days. We're gonna act like civilized people, even if we're on the move. It takes only a minute or two to fill that latrine hole with dirt. Look, I'll give you a choice: You can fill that hole in right now or I'll throw you in head first."

Jed mounted up, grinning. The man with the spade reluctantly turned to his chore. Jed was satisfied that Sarge could keep order in the train. A man had latrine duty about one night out of ten, which wasn't bad. And at least it didn't take long.

The weather was clear and warm. The wagons rolled on past the Blue Mound and turned north to the Wakarusa River. The south bank of the river rose so steeply that the wagons had to be let down the incline with ropes. An inch rope was tied to the back axle of a wagon and snubbed around a stake driven in the top of the riverbank.

Once several of the lead wagons made the crossing, Jed got another group started at another ford to speed up the process.

Before all of the wagons were across, the mud on the north bank had become so churned up it was difficult to get out of the shallow river. A yoke of oxen with a twenty-five foot chain was brought in and hitched to the stragglers to pull them out.

The wagons circled on the broad bottomland on the north side of the river. The grass there was tall enough for a good feed, so the herd was taken north for their early grazing and brought back close to the circle before dark.

Jed gave the signal to roll before seven the next morning. The animals, now full of grass, were easier to hitch than they had been during the first days out of Independence. The five wagons designated "A" were at the rear of the train and the "B" wagons were in the lead.

The weather was ideal, and the wagons moved over the flat grassland, lush with spring wildflowers, in a northwesterly direction. Jed hoped to make more than twenty miles that day. They moved into rolling hills, traveling almost due west.

The next afternoon they arrived at the Kaw River crossing. Jed had ridden ahead to see if the ferries were ready. Joseph and Louis Papan greeted Jed cheerfully and, yes, they were ready for the train. This would be their first train of the year. Their big dugout canoes, connected by platforms, could carry two wagons each, and the animals swam across. Jed had told the emigrants earlier that they could count on the two ferry operators to treat everyone fairly year after year and to charge only one dollar per wagon.

The wagons were all across the river before dark. The river was not as high as it had been, and Jed wondered if that meant dry weather and short grass to the west.

The next day the wagon train headed more west than north, over fairly level ground. The wind was nasty, so the wagons formed four lanes about twenty paces apart. That kept the dust down a little.

When the circle was made that night, the milking done, and supper eaten, Jed made his usual rounds. At Gil's campsite he hunkered down next to Gil.

"Gil, I've been telling the folks they're going to have to be gathering cow chips pretty soon. There won't be enough wood to keep forty campfires going from now on."

Gil nodded. "They bin warned. I don't think they'll be too finicky. Emma don't like it none, but she'll do it. Say, tonight's the night for them boys who let Blaze get away to be on guard duty. Names are Bill and Randy."

"I'll watch them," said Jed. "Maybe they learned a lesson from the last time. If not, they'll get an education tonight. That hobbled horse that followed Blaze is still so sore we can't ride him."

"Seems to me," said Gil, "we shouldn't be usin' hobbles any more."

"Right," agreed Jed. "The horses are tame enought now to stay around. Still, Blaze is tethered near me tonight, so I know he won't get away."

Jed turned in after asking the eleven-to-two guard to call him when he went off duty, in case he didn't get up. But when the night guard approached him at two, Jed was already awake and waved him on. Jed lay on his back for awhile looking up at the stars. He had done that so often that he could tell time accurately by the position of the Big Dipper.

The brothers had just started their shift, so Jed waited a while before going to check on them. His years of sleeping outdoors as a fur trapper had taught him to stay awake when he needed to. Many times his life had depended on it. Keeping his mind busy helped him to stay alert. He searched the heavens for other constellations he recognized—Orion, Taurus, and Gemini.

He was pleased that Pat, the big Scotsman, had taken guard duty without complaint the second time around. So far it looked like this group would be the best one he had guided to Oregon. Except the first. Quickly he pushed that thought from his mind. No time to think about that.

Jed had learned that Martha and Gil's oldest son, James, planned to be married soon, although it was still a secret from the train. They had known each other since they were children. Jed's mind turned to some of the other young girls on the train. It wasn't uncommon for a man of thirty-four to marry a girl of sixteen or seventeen, but he didn't think that was right. Then he wondered why he was thinking of marriage, when he wasn't settled down enough to live in a proper house with a wife.

Jed's keen ears heard the distant rumble of thunder. The sky was still clear. We've been lucky so far, he thought. He pulled on his boots and saddled Blaze, leading him carefully to the rope gate on the side of the circle where the herd was. Then he mounted up.

Jed watched intently as a rider approached in the darkness. When the rider was close enough to see him easily, Jed rode out to meet him. It was Randy. They rode together about a hundred yards before Jed could make out another horse, without a rider, on the other side of the herd.

When Randy noticed Jed's interest, he said nervously, "Maybe Bill's in trouble. I better go see what it is."

Jed reached out and grabbed the rein of Randy's horse and said sternly, "We'll both go. And quietly too. You follow behind me and don't make any noise."

When Jed got to within twenty yards of the prone figure, they stopped.

"Maybe my brother's hurt! I'll go git him!" exclaimed Randy.

Jed stepped down from the tall horse, handed over the reins and said, "Stay here and be quiet. I'll check on your brother. You know dang well he's asleep, not hurt."

Jed moved quietly toward Bill, who was snoring loudly. One of the reins was tied around his wrist and his hat was under his head. It was easy to see what had happened the night the horses had run off.

Jed watched Bill for a few seconds, then he moved very slowly to the horse's head. Taking his knife from the sheath on his belt, Jed cut the rein close to the bridle bit. He carefully laid the rest of the rein on the ground and slowly led the horse back to Randy.

"Your brother's asleep," said Jed, "just as he was when the horses got away. You stay here and hold the horses. I'm going to give Bill an education." He walked silently back to the sleeping man, the way the mountain man had learned to do years ago. Then he stepped astraddle of him and dropped to his knees on Bill's arms. At the same time, he drew his knife and held it about six inches from Bill's face.

Bill awoke with a snort. He could see nothing but the knife. He shrieked so loudly Jed's ears hurt and he clapped a hand over Bill's mouth to stifle his yell.

"I could be a Pawnee brave taking his first scalp and eager to steal horses," Jed hissed. "You're lucky this time. Don't you ever forget there are women and children depending on you to stay awake—some of them are yours!"

Bill sputtered, trying to speak.

"Don't worry," laughed Jed. "I'm not going to scalp you. I'm just going to give you a haircut. If you try to fight me, my knife might slip and cut more than your hair, so be still."

With his left hand holding Bill's hair, Jed cut a strip a few inches wide from the front of his hairline past the center of his head. He made the cut as close as possible to the scalp without drawing blood and then pocketed the lock of hair.

Jed stood up and said loudly enough for his brother to hear, "If this ever happens again, you're both in for a lot of trouble. People could die because you're asleep." The brothers listened to Jed's angry words in silence.

Noticing the clouds gathering in the west and a sudden streak of lightning, Jed added, "Now round up the herd and bring them in. A storm's coming." Jed mounted Blaze and rode away for camp. He was was headed for the rope gate, when he saw Gil striding toward him.

"The gate's open and the walkin' guard, who woke me, is wakin' all the men with Noah's help," shouted Gil. "He's sure we're in for a big one."

"I think so too. It's coming up real fast."

"I heard a awful scream," said Gil. "Did you scalp

somebody?"

"I just gave a man who was taking a nap a little haircut," answered Jed, holding up some of the hair. Gil laughed appreciatively.

"I doubt if he goes to sleep on the job again. His brother knew he was asleep, so he's just as guilty."

A streak of lightning and a clap of thunder put the two men into action. Jed rode out to help bring in the approaching herd and Gil trotted back to the circle to man the rope gate when the herd was gathered in. All over the campsite, tents were being erected and staked down by the light of lanterns and the lightning. Several tents were lashed to the bottom of wagon wheels. Deafening thunder alerted everyone to the storm's progress. Jed saw that Noah had rolled up their bedrolls and thrown them in the supply wagon.

"My family's ready," called Gil. Streaks of lightning lit up the large sheet of oilskin he had draped over his shoulders and tied under his chin.

"Hey, Gil," shouted Noah. "You look like a ghost!"

"What about the rope gates, if the herd stampedes?" asked Sarge. "I've seen storms that make them crazy."

"We'd better put up another rope or two," answered Jed, "and two men ought to be close to each gate. If the animals are already stampeding when they come to the ropes, they'll probably go through anyway, but if they just drift up, we might be able to scare them back to the center."

"There are four of us here," said Gil, "maybe two of us kin take each side."

"Tell your families first," said Jed, "so they'll know where you are. Noah and I'll circle around to the other gate. We'll get some more rope from the supply wagon."

The wind had picked up and was blowing near to a gale by the time the extra rope was put up. The wagons rocked dangerously as the wind caught the canvas. Jed saw that most people had crowded into their wagons rather than staying in tents. Ox yokes and extra chains were anchoring the guy ropes of the tents.

After a few minutes of increasingly strong winds, the storm struck. The men guarding the gates ran for the sheltered side of a wagon, checking on the herd during the flashes of lightning. Marble-sized hail peppered the campsite, followed by a driving rain that came down in sheets. The wagons swayed, but stood— each carried nearly a ton of weight.

The men shouted to each other over the din. "Grab the bucket, Noah!"

"Here comes a washtub—I'll try to catch it!"

"Watch that sheet of oilskin, Jed! It'll be gone to hades if it gets away from you!"

At last the wind began to slacken and the rain lessened. The herd had not panicked but had stayed in the center of the ring with their heads down. A few distant flashes of lightning showed up the night guard approaching. He reported that one tent had blown down but the family had moved to his wagon, where there was enough room for them. The faithful guard was the toothless bachelor Zeb, who drove the horse-drawn wagon.

With the danger past, the men could all take shelter for what little night was left. Jed and Noah went to the supply wagon where their bedrolls and sack of extra clothing had kept dry under oilskin. They lit a lantern and shed their wet clothes, grateful to have dry ones.

"Man, I haven't seen a storm like that since 1834 in Illinois City," said Jed. "Came up so fast!"

"Least we didn't get no twister," said Noah.

They decided to stay in the wagon on top of the saddles and supplies. They figured it wouldn't be long until daylight anyway. Rain still misted through the canvas top, but the cover of oilskin kept them nearly dry.

When the cold gray morning arrived, it was still raining and the sky was dark. A group of men gathered near Sarge's wagon to discuss the best way to start the breakfast fires.

Jed said, "I think the rain'll be over in a few hours. We ought to go ahead and milk the cows, yoke up the oxen, and start traveling. If it doesn't stop raining, we'll have to unhitch somewhere and let the livestock graze. But if we're lucky, we'll get across the Red Vermillion before the water raises too high. I think we should roll as soon as possible." An affirmative nod around the circle confirmed Jed's decision.

Emma disagreed, however, and said to Jed, "I ain't walkin' through no mud."

"Well, you'll be staying here by yourself then," he said. "The rest of us are moving on."

She sniffed and turned toward her wagon. "Worst mess I ever saw," she said. "Mud ever'whar you look."

A damp and quiet group started on the trail that morning. Children rode in the wagons to keep out of the rain, still chewing on dried beef or apples. They all had a chance to drink fresh warm milk before the train started to move. The wagons were hard to pull in the old trail ruts, so four lines were formed on new sod whenever possible. By the time eight or ten wagons had rolled over the same track, two strips of sod were almost destroyed. The herd that followed trampled the soft ground. Anyone following would know that wagons had passed in the mud.

The Red Vermillion River had not risen as much as Jed feared—the water didn't even come up to the wagon boxes. The rain had stopped before they reached the river, so the teams were unhitched as soon as they forded the stream. It was eleven o'clock.

The hungry livestock were turned loose to graze and drink down the river from the ford. Crosscut saws were put to use felling dead trees in the river islands. The soaked men worked quickly to get the fuel ready. When a tree trunk had been sawed in lengths, axes split the wood into smaller chunks. Branches were trimmed off with axes and children were kept busy carrying the wood to the fires. These were not the usual noon cooking fires, but much larger ones which were also used to dry out the wet clothes and bedding.

The children who had jounced in the wagons for five hours were ready to move about. Jed noticed little Jimmy Adams running back and forth from the growing pile of wood to his dad, carrying as much as he could. By the time the women had the meal ready, a good supply of wood stood beside each campfire. Clotheslines had been strung from wagon to wagon and the smell of drying wool mingled with the aroma of fresh biscuits and fried bacon.

Once the ravenous appetites were satisfied and the clothes were drying, spirits rose and laughter was heard again. Already the night's storm was becoming part of the lore of the trek—something that would be written about in letters and diaries.

Jed dozed by the fire after lunch. The noon sun felt warm and a soft breeze was blowing. He was anxious to get the train rolling, so reluctantly he pulled himself up and began to pass the word that they'd start traveling again in an hour.

Jed told the travelers that since wood would be scarce up ahead, they ought to bring as much as they could. Josh came by to tell him that the river had risen more than a foot since they crossed.

"I guess it was worth it then to push through the mud this morning," said Jed. "But it sure didn't feel like it at the time."

Most of the clothing was nearly dry when the wagons started moving. The wheels rolled easily across the almost-firm ground. Tiny pink, yellow, white, and violet wildflowers covered the ground, waving in the afternoon breeze.

They were in Indian country now. They could expect to see Kaw and Pawnee. Jed reassured the emigrants over and over. They shouldn't have trouble with Indians—they were too busy fighting each other. Still, they would be cautious—and grateful that there was enough game for all. Noah had been successful again. There would be fresh antelope that evening.

6

After the cows had been milked that evening and just before the livestock were turned out to graze, Jed saw the unmistakable sign of a cow about to give birth. Gil quietly helped Jed move the big horned cow to the far end of the circle.

Will and Josh quickly steered the other animals away from the cow, driving them out of the gate. Despite the slight confusion, the birth of the calf was rapid. Almost immediately the mother started licking it and nudging it until it shakily began to stand up. Pleased that everything had gone well, Jed continued on toward his meeting with Sarge.

Suddenly a woman screamed. Jed whirled to see a small boy, about two years old, toddling toward the calf, delightedly calling "Goggie!"

At that moment the cow started for the boy. Jed ran for the child, knowing he couldn't reach the cow first. Hollering like fury to distract the cow and with a flying leap, he grabbed the boy before the cow reached him. Together they rolled away as far as they could. Each time they rolled, Jed carried the weight of his body and the boy's on his elbows.

Then the cow charged them. Jed doubled up his knees until they pressed against the child. When the cow's lowered head was close enough, Jed kicked with all his strength and the heels of his boots caught the cow in her nostrils, stopping her for an instant. The force slid Jed and the boy a good six feet on the green grass.

Gil and Josh were there then with a club and a blacksnake whip and drove the cow back to her calf. Jed rose to his feet, shifted the screaming child to a better position, and started toward the wagons. The distraught mother ran to her child, who had almost stopped crying by the time Jed handed him to her.

"Thank you," she said simply. Her brimming eyes showed her gratitude.

The boy's father appeared about the same time. "We're much obliged," he said. "I saw what was happening, but I couldn't get here fast enough."

"I was the closest man there," answered Jed. "I did what anyone would have." He looked up and recognized the man's haircut.

Bill stuck out his hand. "Thanks," he said.

Jed took it, pressing it tightly, and nodded.

Early Sunday morning Noah formed a hunting party. Before they left, Jed warned them to be on the alert for Indians. Noah was armed with his long rifle and a five-shot revolver. The other men had rifles and shotguns. Jed was paired up with Will, and almost as soon as they left camp they bagged several geese along the Big Blue.

"Hey!" said Jed suddenly. "Pawnee sign!" Will froze. When Jed proposed that they head back to camp, Will needed no convincing.

That afternoon about a dozen braves rode into camp. Jed met them, welcoming them in sign language. Jed motioned to the emigrants, who formed a circle around the visiting braves. Sarge was the first to step forward to the chief, handing him a packet of needles.

"I got plenty of tobacky," said Gil. "And I sure would like some a them moccasins." He quickly made a trade.

The Pawnee wanted horses but Jed told them emphatically that the white men needed all their horses to keep moving. Their next request was no surprise to Jed. They wanted "whiteman bread." Jed knew several women in the group had baked bread that Sunday, so he asked Chet to see what he could find. He returned with four half-loaves.

While the Indians were smacking their lips over the fresh bread, some of the bolder children ventured near, getting their first look at real Indians. Jimmy, peeking out from his mother's skirts, seemed fascinated with the nearly naked Indians, their feathers and beads, and dark flashing eyes.

Finally satisfied, the Indians rode away. Jed hoped they could see that the train's herd was guarded by three boys on horses and eight men with guns. Nonetheless, he decided to post extra guards that night.

When Noah and the rest of the hunters returned, their three pack mules were laden with game. A few rabbits were hanging from the saddles. It looked as if everyone would feast that night.

After supper, "A" group gathered together, as had become their custom. They found it easy to talk to each other now, and the visit from the Indians was on everyone's minds.

"Mercy," said Della. "Those Indians were nearly naked! How can they stand the cold weather? It changes so fast here!"

"They can take the cold better than we can," said Jed. "I've seen a Sioux hunting party start out on a frosty morning with no more clothes on than these Pawnee. They're mighty tough and can take pain like you wouldn't believe."

Josh asked, "How long have Indians been using horses? Their horses look different from ours."

Sarge straightened his large mustache and his furrowed brow reflected his concentration. "This is the way I heard it. There were no horses when Columbus came. When Columbus made his second voyage in 1493, he brought both mares and stallions with him. The Spanish didn't geld any of their stallions at that time, so naturally they had foals.

"The Spanish eventually found gold in Central America—

lots of it. It didn't bother them to kill a lot of Indians to get whatever they wanted. Well, ships kept arriving with supplies, including horses. Some of the conquistadors traveled by horseback all over Central America and into Mexico in search of gold. By the time they had worked their way up to California and Santa Fe they had long supply lines. A lot of horses ran off or were stolen.

"Naturally the Indians wanted to imitate the Spaniards. Why should they walk when they could ride? So within a hundred years or so, the Apaches and Comanches were on horseback. When Lewis and Clark explored the west over forty years ago, they found that Indians everywhere were using horses.

"Getting horses made a big change for Indians. They could hunt buffalo easier and haul the meat and hides back to the villages. Using the travois, they could move their villages very quickly—which they liked to do when the game gave out or if someone was after them. They got real good at using horses when they were fighting, too, whether against other tribes or white men."

"Indians are the best riders I ever saw," said Jed. "The Sioux can ride bareback over the roughest ground as fast as their horses can go and not fall off. They can cling to a bucking horse like they were glued on."

John Lewis asked, "How do they put up feed for their horses in winter?"

Sarge looked at Jed for the answer. "They don't put up anything," he said. "The horses have to graze all winter. They can paw through the snow for the grass if the snow isn't too deep, and there's usually grass underneath. They feed them some willow shoots or other small trees in an emergency, so they can chew the bark off. Cottonwood bark makes the best emergency feed. During hard winters, their horses get mighty thin and it takes a few weeks of spring grass to get them going again."

"What about fur trappers?" asked Josh. "How did you feed your horses?"

"About the same as the Indians," answered Jed, "only it was worse a lot of times. If we holed up for the winter in a safe place for us, wasn't always the best place for the horses. I'm glad I'm not trapping anymore. I hated to see what happened to the horses. Some just plain starved to death."

"Lord, what a waste!" declared Josh.

Two days later the wagon train arrived at Alcove Spring, a place many of them had heard about. The name, Alcove Spring, had been chiseled on the ledge above the alcove two years earlier. The tree-lined nook had been a pleasant interlude to a group destined for tragedy—Alcove Spring was named by the Donner Party.

The travelers were then faced with crossing the Big Blue River. Jed was relieved to find that the water level was lower than usual. They could ford the river this time. In past years, they'd had to raft the wagons across. The wagons moved down the shallow banks and entered the sluggish stream briskly, to keep from bogging down should they meet quicksand.

After crossing the Big Blue, the train headed northwest. Just before the train moved on again after lunch, Mary approached Della and said, "Jed was wrong for once. He told us less than a week ago we'd see fields of wildflowers for days, but they're most gone. Just a few left now."

"I think maybe we'll joke Jedidiah at the supper table," said Della. "He's right most of the time and I think he'll just say there wasn't enough rain here this spring."

"They were the most beautiful sight I think I've ever seen. It's wonderful to think that no human hand had any part of it."

Della smiled broadly. "Jedidiah told us we'd have to go through hell up ahead but he didn't tell us we'd go through a heavenly garden to get there!"

When the train camped that evening, Jed announced that two wagon trains were ahead of them. They had crossed the Big Blue farther north. While Jed's outfit had been the first to leave from Independence or Westport, these trains had evidently started from St. Joe, which was a shorter route to this point.

That evening, as "A" group sat around the campfire, Noah asked, "Jed, how many wagons are in those groups?"

Jed answered, "The first train passed about a week ago, with about forty wagons pulled with oxen. They have some loose stock but not enough. The second train, of about twenty-six wagons, has only twelve wagons pulled with oxen and the rest with unshod horses. Their loose stock is pitifully short—maybe fifteen cattle, mostly milk cows and a few horses. They're about two days ahead of us now, but unless they've got a lot of money to buy more livestock at the forts they won't make it to Oregon."

Josh, who was seated across the fire from Jed, asked, "How in blazes can you tell so much about two trains you haven't even seen?"

Before Jed could answer, Sarge spoke up. "Josh, Jed lived in the plains and the mountains for years. He can read signs on the ground like some people read a book. He can tell from the trampled grass and the look of cow manure how long ago they passed by. I bet he counted the places where the wagon wheels sank in the ground overnight and the number of campfires they had—that's what I'd do. The campfire spots aren't as accurate because some families share a campfire. When he looked at the tracks made by the loose livestock following the train, he could tell about how many animals were in that herd."

Ben said, "That's amazing, Jed! How'd you learn to do that?"

Jed shrugged. "Part of the job," he said. He was glad to hear Ben join in—it was the first time he'd said anything in days, although he seemed friendly enough. Just quiet, I guess, thought Jed. Molly and Jimmy weren't at the campfire that night. In fact, they often went to bed early, as Sarah and Nellie did. Twenty miles a day was a long walk for a five-year-old. Caleb was another quiet one. Well, thought Jed, I'd rather have two quiet ones than one who yaps all the time.

The next morning the wagons rolled through grass-covered hills on their way to Rock Creek. The creek was not deep, but its bed was a jumble of rocks and the east bank was very steep. A long rope tied to the rear axle of each wagon and held by twenty or more men and boys eased the wagons down the slope one by one. When the wagons had crossed and the loose stock had been driven up to the crossing, a few oxen raced to reach the water.

A young ox slipped in a hole and broke a leg. The owner, a man from "C" group, felt the animal should not go to waste and offered it to all of the train. It wasn't long before the meat was distributed and was cooling.

That evening there was fresh beef for supper along with the cornbread. Some of it had been cut thin and was fried, some was boiled, and some cut in chunks and roasted over an open fire. Leftovers were salted and smoked over a fire of green branches. Those chunks would keep for days.

On Jed's nightly walk through the camp, he reminded the emigrants, "From now on we'll have to depend on prairie fuel. You've already picked up dry cow and ox chips from last year's campsite. You've learned to use them just fine. We won't have firewood for a long time now so we'll have to gather chips everyday. You ought to keep a sackful in the wagons because if it rains wet chips are worthless. When we get near the Platte we'll see lots of buffalo chips."

"Don't worry, Jed," Mary called out to him. "We can do it—some of us women been shoveling cow chips out of barn for years."

About midway in his patrol, Sarge approached Jed with a somber face. "The Witherspoon girl is sick, very sick. Her forehead's burning. I gave her laudanum and calomel, but—" He shook his head.

Jed frowned. "You don't think it's the cholera?"

"I don't," said Sarge, "and I've seen plenty of cholera. But some of the folks do and they're scared. Frankly, if it was cholera, as small as she is—only six years old—she'd be dead by now."

The next day the train traveled in a northwesterly direction over gently rolling hills about two or three miles from the Little

Blue. They stayed that far from the river because its many the little feeder creeks presented formidably steep banks as they neared the mainstream.

They camped at the Little Sandy that night. The atmosphere was glum. The little Witherspoon girl was so sick and weak that everyone felt she wouldn't last much longer. A guard woke Jed about three-thirty in the morning with the news that she had died.

Jed woke Sarge and Chet, so they could arrange the burial. Then he went to visit the parents. The mother was so grief-stricken she couldn't let go. Jed looked into her vacant eyes and his heart hurt for her. He had done this many times and it always saddened him deeply. He remembered with a pang when it had been his turn to be comforted, and how the comfort had never come.

"Ma'am," he said gently, "we've got to make a decision right now. We're going to have to leave your little girl here. We'll make it as easy on you as we can."

She nodded and he signaled to Sarge. In the pre-dawn light, the men began taking turns digging until the grave was ready. As soon as breakfast was over, the emigrants gathered around the grave. The small body, wrapped in a blanket, was placed on the mound next to the grave. A man from their group read several passages of scripture and Chet offered a prayer. Della began singing, "My Faith Looks up to Thee" and others joined in for the first verse. Della continued, her rich voice bringing comfort,

"While life's dark maze I tread
"And griefs around me spread
"Be Thou my guide.
"Bid darkness turn to day,
"Wipe sorrow's tears away,
"Nor let me ever stray
"From Thee aside."

Then it was quiet except for a few muffled sobs. Jed saw Molly and Sarah standing together, their hands locked. He searched the crowd for Ben, but couldn't see him. The lines from two horse harnesses that had been placed under the body, were lifted and the body lowered into the grave. Chet moved forward and reached for a handful of dirt mixed with ashes. As he dropped it into the dark hole, he said, "Ashes to ashes, dust to dust; and the spirit to the God who gave it."

Then it was time to move on. As the emigrants prepared to leave, Jed supervised the filling of the grave. Earth was mixed with campfire ashes. Only a slight mound was visible when the work was completed. The father had carved a crude marker, "Jenny W., b. 1842, d. 48." Sarge stepped off fifty paces due north and drove the sharp end in the ground.

"Indians won't find this one," he muttered.

When the wagons rolled northwest, each passed over the grave so that its exact location might not be found by coyotes or wolves. It was generally agreed that Jenny had not died of cholera because no one else was sick.

Jed rode ahead of the train most of the day, checking the area for signs of Indians, but he found none. The train moved along the broad level bottomland of the Little Blue.

Once Jed had selected the evening campsite, he dismounted and let his horse graze. This gelding was one of the two he owned. The other horse was a better night horse—he wasn't afraid of shadows and didn't startle easily. And he quickly adjusted to the different riders on guard duty.

Jed had purchased these horses at Fort Laramie on his return trip in the winter and had stabled them at the livery. He often wondered where this one had been before he bought him. The horse's legs were scarred, which meant he'd been ridden on rough mountain trails or where there weren't any trails at all. The only white hair on his back was covered with the saddle. Jed wondered if he had been used with a poorly built pack saddle by a careless mountain man or with a poor riding saddle without a blanket. Jed knew he had half-starved him last winter and perhaps he had been starved before, the way he grazed whenever he could. He was a steady horse. If his reins were on the ground, he might move them a little to get more grass but he'd never run away.

Jed rode the green broke horses most of the time and they were working better every day. They would soon be well trained.

The west wind blew hard the next day. Every step was an effort. Before the wagons circled that evening, Noah and his hunters arrived with the three pack mules heavily laden with buffalo meat.

"We were lucky to get this because there weren't many buffler in the herd," said Noah. "That wind kept our scent away or we wouldn't have been so lucky."

Feasting on roast buffalo that night helped raise the spirits of the train. Voices returned to their normal level and a few chuckles were heard up and down the line.

Jed was working on a tender rib, when Noah remarked, "With all that fat in your mustache and beard, you're a greasy looking codger!"

"Noah, you should talk. What color is your beard supposed to be? I thought it was red. If you stuck your head in the Blue right now, you'd muddy the waters for all of the trains on down the line."

Noah laughed. "Maybe we oughta go down to the Little Blue and get ourselves cleaned up."

"That sounds good to me," said Jed. "I've probably got two pounds of sand in my hair."

They each grabbed a chunk of lye soap and headed out.

The wagons rolled in the morning under a clear sky without much wind. They were traveling almost due north. After seven or eight miles, the trail turned to the west and the rest of the day they stayed fairly close to the Little Blue.

Riding ahead of the train, Jed let his mind wander, although his eyes were continually searching the horizon for anything out of the ordinary. Except for Jenny's death, things were still going pretty well. The folks were working together well. They could hitch and unhitch very quickly and they took directions from the leaders. It was a well disciplined, modest-sized train. He didn't like a big one.

Late in the afternoon Jed moved on to check out a good campsite along the Little Blue. To his surprise, he saw a circle of white-topped wagons as he approached the area. They must be in trouble, he thought. It was the train that had been two days ahead of them. It looked like all the wagons were there. Could it be the cholera?

He moved forward, his eyes darting left and right. He saw nothing except the small circle of wagons and a small herd of cattle nearby.

Horses, thought Jed, where are the horses?

7

There were no horses in sight. Jed knew that this train had been nearly half horse-drawn. His eyes searched the riverbank and beyond, for where the horses might be, but he had already guessed what had happened. As he neared the wagons, members of the train scrambled to meet him.

"Indians," said the first man to reach him. "They stole all our horses except the four we had corralled inside the circle."

"And where are they now?" asked Jed.

"Four of our men took them across the Little Blue looking for the ones that got stole."

As the people crowded around Jed, the desperation of the situation was evident in their faces. They look pretty pathetic, he thought. This could slow us down real bad.

"D'ya think they'll come back? They could all be dead by now," said a mournful man with sandy hair.

Jed answered, "They'll probably come back, but not with the horses. If the Indians had a good start, they'll never be found."

"Has your train got any extry animals?" he persisted.

"Our train will help you if we can, but I don't know how much. The members'll have to decide that, when they get here."

While Jed was still talking, a shout went up that the riders were returning. All four men were leading horses that were in a pitiable condition. An even worse looking horse was being led by a rope tied to one of the saddles. The men looked as exhausted as their animals. The only horse they found was one evidently too slow to keep up the fast pace of the Indians.

A man who introduced himself to Jed as Hiram also asked if extra stock would be available from Jed's train. Then he muttered angrily, "From now on I'll shoot every damn redskin that gets within my rifle range."

Jed clenched his jaw, but merely said again that they'd just have to wait and see. He hurried back to his train and notified Sarge, Chet, and Gil to gather at once in front of the lead wagon. They could talk more freely there. As soon as they were assembled, Jed told them what he had found. They immediately agreed to help the train, but didn't want to hurt their own chances of success in reaching Oregon.

"Got any suggestions, Jed?" asked Chet.

"Some of them'll have to return to Missouri," said Jed thoughtfully, "because they can't take those horse-drawn wagons without horses. If they've got the money to buy extra oxen at Fort Laramie, we can let them borrow our oxen for a while, but I'd guess they don't. Some of them barely have enough money for the tolls."

They walked in silence for a while. Once they reached the campsite, Jed mounted his horse and guided the train to its circle position. After the teen-aged boys had driven the herd to the Blue for water and grazing and the men had gathered in response to Jed's call, Sarge described what Jed found in the other camp.

"I feel it's only right to help them out," said Chet. "We can't just drive by and ignore them."

Most of the men nodded. "But," said someone, "we don't have too much to share—we're cuttin' it pretty close to the bone as it is. We sure can't give 'em any of our livestock."

"I don't think you should give them anything—sell, maybe, or lend, but not give," said Jed.

"Well, that makes things a mite different," said Caleb.

Plans for making an offer of assistance were discussed and

finally an agreement was reached. Sarge, Chet, and Gil asked Jed to go with them. As soon as they arrived at the other camp, Sarge made their offer to the expectant faces around him. It was met with both joy and disappointment. Jed studied the faces of the men in the light of the campfire. It was obvious that some of them wanted more help, with no strings attached.

Sarge asked Jed to explain how much oxen cost at the forts ahead and to list the tolls they'd have to pay along the way. Many were surprised at the cash outlay to come. Some of the those who had lost their horses were distraught.

"I don't have that kinda money," said a middle-aged, heavy set man. "I feel like I'm stuck here—can't go forward or backward, neither one."

"Maybe it's best to sleep on things and take a go at figuring it out again in the morning," said Sarge.

When the four were walking back to their camp in the dark, Jed told them about Hiram's earlier outburst. He was their so-called leader, and he'd never been over the road before. The train had used only one guard at night and when the four o'clock guard took his shift, he found the other guard asleep. The sleeping guard was Hiram.

"If that group joins our train, Hiram better not be with us. He's the worst kind of troublemaker," said Jed. "No self control."

Sarge called for a meeting the next day at first light. When breakfast was over, Gil, Sarge, Chet, and Jed returned to the troubled camp with a little more generous offer than the first one. Several more families had offered to loan oxen. Shortly after eight o'clock the final offer was accepted.

Chet explained the written offer: one yoke of good oxen owned by the company would be sold to the now nearly horseless train. They could use the oxen to pull a supply wagon back to the states. They could also pull another wagon with their four remaining horses and still have one to ride. Eight oxen would be loaned to pull wagons to Laramie. They'd be replaced at Laramie by good, well-rested oxen, or the owners could take back the ones they'd loaned, whichever the owners preferred.

All of the ox-drawn wagons could join Jed's train as far as Fort Laramie. At that time, they would have a choice of waiting for another train or permanently joining Jed's train all the way to Oregon. If they made that choice, they would be required to buy into the supply pool and to pay their fees from that point into Oregon. Jed and Noah would not charge them from this point to Laramie.

Along the way, they'd have to take their turns at guard duty and live by the rules spelled out in the constitution of the train. Noah, Sarge, Gil, Jed, and Chet would inspect all of the wagons and supplies today, before starting off. Newcomers to the train would get a more rigid inspection before leaving Fort Laramie. Spare stock would be required from that point on.

When the four men went back to their own train, they called the members together to tell them of the outcome of the meeting. Sarge told them the stock could be turned over to the other train at any time.

"There's going to be some wagons and a lot of supplies abandoned," he said. "You might want to buy some. They might even give you some things, but I don't want to hear of anyone trying to buy something at an unfair price. These people have suffered enough without being cheated."

A half hour later, the officers went to check the ox-drawn wagons and supplies. Some of the wagons didn't have enough dried fruit to suit Jed, but they were able to get more from those who were abandoning their horse-drawn wagons. A couple of battered wagons were traded for some of the wagons that were going to be left behind. When the livestock had been turned over and the bartering among the train members was finished, Sarge gave the word to his train that they could start trading.

Gil and his oldest son, James, bought a good wagon and some supplies. James wanted to get married as soon as he was twenty-one—which would be in a few days—and this looked like a good chance to make preparations. After loaning one ox to the other train, Gil still had seven reserve oxen, so they could use four of them on the new wagon. They had enough extra cash to buy more oxen at Laramie.

Everyone felt sorry for those who would be returning to the states. They had gotten a bad deal. Hiram, their leader, hadn't even read the trail books that were available in the river towns where trains started. Even though Jed didn't agree with all the information in the books, they did report the ferry tolls and the high price of oxen and supplies at the forts. He wondered why others in the train hadn't heard anything about the expenses on the trail.

"Guess they just read the letters in the newspapers back home," he told Noah. "Nobody says anything bad about the trail there."

About fifteen men were in the group returning home, and Jed advised them to have their guns displayed most of the time. He was sure a band of Indians wouldn't attack a well-armed group of that size. If necessary, they could use a couple of milk cows to help pull a wagon. Jed explained how to double their teams and use a rope to climb the steep bank of the Wakarusa River. He pointed out to them that they had lots of time, good grass, water, and wood, so they shouldn't have problems.

Jed suggested that the folks going home could leave their wagons and supplies for another train to use as it passed by. Many intended to, but Hiram shook his head.

"I'll burn my wagon before I leave it. Nobody's going to get anything of mine for free, especially them thievin' redskins."

"You can do that if you want to," said Jed as calmly as he could manage. Then he continued with an edge of anger to his voice, "I heard you threaten to shoot every redskin that came within rifle shot. You just might have a chance, on the way home, to do that. Some of 'em might pay you a visit. If you take your hate out on a few, you could rile the whole Pawnee nation, and not one of you'll ever get back home. Think about that. Just keep your guns in sight and you won't have to use them. And have night guards that can stay awake, and you all should get back to St. Joe."

Jed could see that his remark about staying awake infuriated Hiram. He glared at Jed for a few seconds, then turned and walked away without saying a word. Another man gave Jed a black look and followed Hiram.

The sandy-haired man approached Jed and said quietly, "I'm glad you talked to Hiram like that. We'll be watching him careful and won't never leave him alone at guard duty again. We'll probably vote him out as leader before we start back. He lost that job when he let our horses be stole. At least we're getting rid of Ezra Baines—he's going with you. Watch out!"

Jed guessed that the angry man who followed Hiram was Ezra and felt a momentary sense of dread. Then he wished the wagon train well and returned to Della's campfire for dinner. Sarge had hoped the train could get underway before two o'clock, but it was after two-thirty before the train pulled out of its circle. Gil's son James, with his newly purchased wagon, followed his father's wagons.

Those oxen used to a yoke chafed at the harness tugs that rubbed their hind legs, but Jed knew they'd get used to it. The fourteen wagons from the other camp brought up the rear. Jed told them they could make two groups of five and one of four at the evening stop. He'd letter their wagons J, K, and L on Sunday.

Noah went ahead to scout for the evening campsite because Jed wanted to stay with the newly organized train. Gil had an extra ox yoke with him, but he had to buy a set of horse harness for the other two oxen on his son's wagon. They could use the harness on oxen by turning the collars and hames upside down.

The train now consisted of a long line of fifty-nine wagons. This was more than Jed preferred to have, but he figured things would work out. There wasn't much else they could do. The newcomers had no spare animals except milk cows.

Jed dismounted and walked beside the teams of oxen in harness. One driver had never driven oxen, and the oxen had evidently never been harnessed, so it wasn't going well. Jed handed the reins of his horse to the young man, took his whip and drove the oxen for a mile or more, coaching the new driver all the time.

"I've driven as many as eight yoke on a freight wagon," he told the novice. "Sometimes you have to holler pretty loud to get their attention. You need a long whip with that many, but you don't have to cuss at them all the time the way some old bullwhackers do. Just talk to them, so they get used to your voice. That helps a lot."

The circle that night was much larger, with fifty-eight more cattle to corral. Jed wondered how the two groups would mix. He hoped they'd work together to form one train. He was uneasy because the more people on the train, the greater the chance for trouble.

The next day the train moved along the rolling hills beside the Little Blue. Jed told them that when they left the Little Blue, they'd be about two full days from the Platte. When that time arrived, they didn't stop long at noon or unhitch the animals. They gave them buckets of water filled from the barrels on the sides of the wagons. The travelers ate a cold lunch—bacon on biscuits—and a handful of dried fruit. Then they started out again for the Platte.

Jed warned them that the water in the Platte was muddy and sandy. "Don't dig a hole in the sandy banks and let the water seep into it. The water might look better, but it'll be more alkali.

"The best way is to dip it up, let it settle, carefully pour off the top three-fourths, and throw the rest away. Straining it through a cloth will help get rid of the fine sand."

After they crossed the last sandy hills before getting to the Platte Valley, they drove through deep gullies. The rain had washed out the many ruts made by the wagons of earlier years. There were no trees on the south side of the Platte, so they'd be burning buffalo chips for fuel.

The train moved slowly over the barren land between the rivers. Finally, as they crested a slight ridge, a shout went up. "There she is!" It was the Platte River, a braided, sinewy complex of watery strands that rose in the Rockies and debouched in the Missouri River. There were trees on the islands in the river, but none on the banks.

Jed rode ahead of the train in the afternoon and was surprised to find a small group of soldiers in the campsite he wanted.

The young officer in charge said, "The main body of men will be coming in a few days to build a new fort near here. They're abandoning the old Fort Kearny near the Missouri."

"Whatcha going to build it with?" asked Jed.

"I guess," said the soldier, "we'll use the sod we're standing on and some cottonwood from the islands in the river."

"We have an old soldier as our wagon train leader, a Sergeant Yeager," said Jed.

"Sergeant Yeager?" a middle-aged sergeant spoke up. "I served under a Sergeant Yeager for several years when I was a private. He was a real good man—saved my life once! He was tough but fair—he'd never ask his men to do anything he couldn't do himself. Some men learned the hard way to not pick a fight with him. Sure like to see him again."

Jed answered, "Sounds like our Sergeant Yeager all right, and you'll get to see him soon. In an hour we'll be camping near here." The sergeant grinned.

When Jed told Sarge an old army buddy was camped nearby, Sarge hurried to the soldiers' camp where he spent the evening reminiscing.

"We had some close calls," he told Jed later. "Some victories, but the worst times were those long, dry marches, when we thought we'd die of thirst. We've got to keep our water barrels filled on this trip!"

Jed agreed. "Water's more important than gold, more important than food, even."

That evening Jed told the emigrants that if they could travel at least twenty miles the next day, they might be able to find better water in a small creek. However, the next day's travels proved there wasn't enough water in the creek for everyone's use, so Jed picked a spot near the Platte to camp. The next night they arrived at Plum Creek, where there was a better water supply. This was an unusually good buffalo hunting area because the hills were close to the river.

That evening Jed thought it was time to cut up the antelope hides that had been dried and made into rawhide. Noah and Jed had honed their knives to make them razor sharp. About a dozen helpers gathered around. When the legs of the hide had been trimmed off and one side of the hide was squared up, they were ready to cut it into thongs. With the hide held firmly by two men, they cut off some wider thongs. It took steady and skillful hands to keep the narrow strips even. The rawhide strips were extremely stiff, but after being worked with bacon grease or other fat, the thongs became somewhat pliable. Some were supple enough to become shoe laces.

"Lookit how soft my hands are, boys," said Josh. "This grease is just the thing to make you purty!" The others laughed with him.

Ben said, "We're doin' women's work, you know. No Indian brave would be caught doin' this. Right, Jed?"

Jed nodded. "That's right—Indian women do all the tanning and working with animal hides."

"I'll be sure and tell Molly what she's missed," Ben said.

As Jed was pulling on his boots the next morning, he looked up to see Gil and George from the new group "J" approaching. His heart dropped and for an instant a frown crossed his face. Then he straightened up and smiled. "You're visiting early today, Gil."

George looked grim. "It's my wife," he said. "It's time. . . ." He shuffled his feet uneasily and looked into the distance. "With the first two, it was hard. I—" His voice cracked.

Jed sighed. After a moment he spoke. "Let's talk to Sarge and Chet to see if we can hold the train for a day."

"Thanks!" George said and hurried back to his wagon.

"Shoot!" said Jed. "I hate having babies born on the train, even if it does go all right. And if it doesn't—" Jed threw up his hands in a hopeless gesture and shook his head.

A minute later Gil watched the frown disappear from Jed's forehead. The cheerful tone of his voice returned. "Let's make good use of the day. I know buffalo are close by. Noah and a half-dozen other men can start hunting soon and a bunch of us can get wood from the islands. We can dry buffalo meat today to use when we don't have fresh meat."

When Sarge and Chet were consulted, they agreed with Jed. Gil said, "Being an old family man myself, I know you're doin' the right thing. I've heard tell of some trains goin' on ahead and lettin' the wagon catch up later, but I don't think that's right."

"I wouldn't permit that," said Jed. "It's too dangerous in Indian country. Hurrying on right after the birth and traveling after dark is crazy."

The word about the delay spread through the train, and plans were made for the day. When the hunters had ridden south and the herd turned out on the good grass, the other men gathered axes to get wood from an island in the Platte.

Suddenly a knot of newcomers approached Jed. A man shouted angrily, "What the hell are we stopping all day like this for? It's good traveling weather and we ought to make fifteen to twenty miles. It ain't right to hold us up!"

Jed's anger glinted in his dark eyes when he answered. "We didn't ask you on this train, Ezra. You could have gone back to the states with the others, and when I hear you talk like that I sure as the devil wish you had. A lot of people went out of their way to help you and now you're going to go by our rules. I have the responsibility of getting you folks to Oregon and I intend to do that. If it means stopping a day to save a life or two, I'll do it. Your stock is getting good rest today and we might get a lot of good buffalo meat dried if we don't waste all day standing here belly-aching."

Ezra glared a moment and turned away. The woodcutters headed for the river.

By mid-morning the hunters returned loaded down with meat. Under the direction of skilled butchers, the women and youngsters began cutting it into very thin slices. Because the meat was so fresh, it was hard going. If it had hung overnight, it would have cut easier.

Drying meat was a complicated process at home. On the trail it required ingenuity. Fires were lit and large forked stakes were driven into the ground close by each one. Long slender green branches were placed on top of the stakes. Small nails were then driven through some of the branches and the meat strips hung on the nails. Sometimes thorny branches could be used instead of nails. All kinds of racks were improvised to hold the meat the right distance from the fires. Normally, the sun would help dry the meat, but this meat had to be cured in one day. Fires had to be kept going all day and into the night.

Mary moved around the camp, watching the fires. She had overseen meat drying for years. It was important that the fires not be high enough to cook the meat, but hot enough to drive out the moisture. Ovens of the few sheet-iron stoves along worked well, but there weren't enough. A few roasting fires were also kept going to cook chunks for a late noon meal. Men and boys moved back and forth from the island for wood to keep the fires burning.

At the "I" group campsite, Jed saw Aaron lying in the shade of a wagon and hurried to his side.

"You all right?" he asked.

"Sure," Aaron said with as much force as he could muster. "Just resting a minute."

"He'll be fine," said Annie, coming from the group's fire. "The smoke just bothers him a little."

A little later Jed asked Will if Aaron was really doing all right.

"Most of the time," Will said. "When he ain't, we just all pitch in and hep out. It's no problem. Even Ma don't mind."

Jed smiled and nodded toward Emma, who was muttering to her daughter about the heat of the fires.

About the time the sun had reached its zenith, a baby's cry was heard. Soon the announcement spread around the circle: A boy had been born.

Jed kept busy all afternoon supervising the drying. He moved from fire to fire with Mary, giving advice and explaining how to test the meat to see if it was ready. "If you don't get it dry enough," he warned, "it'll spoil and all of your work is for nothing."

By mid-afternoon, many of the strips were dry enough to be stored away. There was more fresh meat to put on the racks, so the fires were kept going.

With the layover, the women had time to prepare a filling evening meal. Beans—"whistleberries," Gil called them—had been soaked since morning and there was plenty of time in the afternoon to cook them. A supper of beans, biscuits, buffalo meat, and sauce from dried fruit was enjoyed by the three men at Della's long narrow table.

The meat drying continued over many of the fires until after dark. It was about dusk when George, the father of the new baby, approached Jed.

"Just wanted to thank you, Jed," he said. "Sure do appreciate it."

"We needed to stop a day to dry meat anyway and today was sunny without much wind," answered Jed.

"I heard," said George, "about your set-to with Ezra this morning. My wife was feeling mighty poorly for a few hours after the baby was born but she feels right well now. She can travel in the morning. I think it would have darned near killed her today." He cleared his throat. "Wouldya like to see our son? My wife wants to thank you."

His voice was so earnest, Jed couldn't refuse, so he went with him to the opening in the tent where the mother and child were. At George's urging, Jed reluctantly peeked inside. He saw the pale smiling face of a young woman and the dark haired, wrinkled, red-faced baby she was holding. The rays of the setting sun shone on the baby's glossy black hair.

"Jed," she said weakly, "we sure do thank you for not leaving us behind. We'll never forget you for that."

Jed answered, "It was a good day for us—we have lots of meat to show for it. What did you name the baby?"

"We have two boys already, so we had a girl's name picked out this time."

George laughed. "A little change in the plans," he said.

His wife continued, "We hope this boy grows up to be as strong, brave, and kind as the man we named him after. His name is Jedidiah. We named him after you—Jedidiah Oregon Starbuck."

Jed was surprised and he felt himself blush. After a moment he stammered, "Well, I'm sure honored. And he looks like a strong little pioneer, too."

He heard a woman's voice behind him. "It's an honor you've earned, Jed."

When he turned, he saw it was Molly with the two young boys, who had come to say goodnight to their mother and new brother. Molly had kept them in tow all day and was keeping them in her tent for the night.

Jed thought, what made her change her mind about me? Still embarrassed, he said goodnight and slipped away to check on the drying meat. It was late when the last of the meat was packed away in the wagons and Jed spread out his bedroll.

The night was warm. Jed left his blanket and canvas top rolled up at his feet. He removed his boots and made sure his gun belt was within easy reach. Then he stretched out and looked up at the stars. So, Molly doesn't hate me any more, he thought. Wonder why? I wish I didn't care what she thought. She's a married woman.

The next day the wagons rumbled westward on the flat land next to the Platte. The valley was so broad the train could form four or more lines to get away from the constant dust churned up by the wheels. When the rigs spread out in the valley, the fifty-nine wagons and their loose stock made a caravan nearly a quarter-mile wide and over a half-mile long.

There were complaints about the water in the Platte, most of them from Emma, and with good reason. It flowed brown with mud. It was full of critters. Every bucketful had more sand than water. Folks said the sand aided the digestion. But it was the only water available.

The grass was not as tall here as it had been in the valley of the Blue. The women were getting used to using buffalo chips for fuel. They had discovered that the chips worked well if the fire was fed right. They made a lot of heat and there was absolutely no odor.

The train had several small tent latrines that were lashed to the side of a wagon in the daytime and set up over a shallow hole in the ground at night. During the daytime stops, they were seldom used. Jed's train used a routine practiced by most Oregon-bound travelers. As soon as the train stopped, several men grabbed a spade and turned a little earth on one side of the wagon.

That side was for the women. About a dozen or more women and older girls would stand close together in a line a few feet from the freshly dug holes. Their long dresses made a solid shield, offering privacy behind the linsey-woolsey and gingham wall. The boys and men used the other side of the train for their needs with very little modesty.

This Sunday both Noah and Henry were busy most of the day shoeing oxen. Many animals did not have shoes and it was time they did. By now most of the oxen were so tame a child could lead them. However, the minute the farrier raised a foot to nail a shoe, there was trouble.

Two procedures were used on the trail, where a holding chute was not available. Neither was easy. In the first, an ox's head was tied to a front wheel of a wagon and the hindquarters tied to a back wheel. One hoof at a time was raised with ropes. When that one was shod, the next was picked up.

The other way was to throw the ox on his side with all four feet tied together. A rope was tied to each foot, one at a time, and pulled up by passing the rope over a stake that had been driven into the ground. When all eight shoes had been nailed on, the ropes were removed and the animal set free. If the travelers were lucky, they might not have to repeat the job for nearly two months. Horses were much easier to shoe. Most stood docilely and let the smith raise one foot at a time.

While the oxen were being shod, wagons wheels were being greased, clothes mended, and pies baked. Small groups of men who had finished their chores rested in the shade, smoking pipes. Laughter could be heard erupting from a group listening to Gil tell his tales of life in Kentucky.

Jed returned to the supply wagon with the clothes he had washed in the river. He had just finished draping them over the wagon wheels when he heard a loud shout, "Wagons a-comin'!"

All activity came to a halt. Jed joined the others searching the eastern horizon and could see nothing. Sarge called to him, "You're looking the wrong way! They're coming from the west."

Jed switched sides and could make out two-wheeled carts piled high with pelts pulled by mules. A few four-wheeled wagons, loaded with buffalo robes, were pulled by oxen. A half-dozen shaggy looking men walked beside their animals.

Jed walked out to meet them. A tall man on horseback held up his hand to stop the train. "Jed!" The ragged, hairy creature jumped from his horse and stuck out a dirty hand. The emigrants stared at the men before them.

"Well, I never!" said Della.

Their clothes were so greasy and dirty it wasn't clear if they were cloth or animal skins. Their long hair and beards were matted with grease and dirt. The emigrants quickly stepped back from the stench of the fly-covered hides.

"Jed, you old son-of-a-gun, you done look civilized—waugh!" the creature said.

"Well, Zeke, I sure can't say the same about you," Jed replied with a laugh.

Zeke slapped Jed on the shoulder, nearly flattening him, and joined his laughter. "We gotta get these here hides to the Missouri before they spile and start to stink." After a few minutes of banter, the odd-looking caravan moved on to the east.

"Whew!" Sarge said. "Which stunk the most, the hides or the men?"

Jed answered, "I was too close to Zeke. I couldn't even smell the hides."

"Where'd all them buffler robes come from?" asked Gil.

"I can't rightly say, Gil, but you could see a lot of them were dry. They might have bought a bunch from last year's wagon trains. All trains shoot buffalo for eating along the way, of course, like we do. I didn't ask Zeke about the green hides that are fresh off carcasses this year."

"There's only one train ahead of us," said Sarge. "That wouldn't make many hides. I reckon they killed buffalo just for hides."

"Sure, they did. They had a lot of wolf pelts, too. Wolves follow the buffalo and if there are a lot of buffalo carcasses around, they'd get a lot of wolves, too. You can't tell what these old mountain men are doing now that the beaver business is done with."

"You knowd that Zeke feller and one more of 'em—did you know the rest, Jed?" asked Josh.

"Aw, I probably saw 'em somewhere. I knew Zeke from rendezvous days. They all have a lot of stay-alive savvy, that's for sure."

That night around the campfire, Josh asked Jed about his days as a mountain man. "Well, I'm not much for story telling," he said, "but some of those old guys really knew how to spin a yarn—like Gil, here."

He paused a moment, gathering his memories. "Guess you've heard of Jim Bridger?" Josh nodded. "He was the greatest of the mountain men—old Gabe, they called him. I met him once at a rendezvous."

"He's got a fort now somewhere out west, doesn't he?" asked Sarge.

"Yep. Just west of South Pass. Don't reckon we'll see him, though—he's hardly ever there. Doesn't like company much, anyway."

"Who else did you know?" asked Josh.

"Well, there was Jim Clyman. There's a lot of stories about him, maybe you've heard 'em. In the fall of '23 he and Jedediah Smith were in the Black Hills, a hundred fifty miles or so northwest of here. They surprised a grizzly bear in a tight canyon and he mauled Smith mighty bad. Well, Clyman sewed him back together right out there in the wilderness—sewed his ear back on and his scalp together. Jed woulda bled to death if it weren't for Clyman."

"Golly!" said Josh. "Wonder what he used for a needle and thread?"

The group laughed. "I'm sure it wasn't embroidery thread, Josh," said Mary.

"You never know what a mountain man carries in his possible sack," said Jed. "I always carried a bone needle, and sinews from small animals aren't hard to come by. Old Jedediah could have been part rabbit or squirrel for all we know.

"Jedediah Smith was a devout Methodist, like you Chet," continued Jed. "Didn't smoke, drink, or cuss."

"What happened to him?" asked Chet.

"He was killed by Comanches along the Santa Fe Trail, long

time ago."

"See what happens iffin you're too holy, Chet?" laughed Gil. "Better to take a nip now and then. You'll live longer."

"And James Clyman?" asked Josh? "What happened to him?"

"He was a surveyor before he came west, so he was real interested in the land he saw. He kept a journal—like Noah here does—maybe someday I'll get to read it. Once when he was out in the wilderness alone he was short of bullets, so when he shot a buffalo, he'd dig out the bullet and reshape it with his teeth."

Sarge whistled. "That ain't an easy thing to do!"

"Not only that," added Jed. "He walked all the way from Independence Rock to Fort Atkinson on the Missouri River. He almost starved to death—badgers were about the only things he found to eat."

"Ugh," said Josh. "Badgers."

"He went to Oregon in '44," continued Jed, "to California in '45, and back east in '46. Haven't heard about him since."

Sarge stirred the dying fire and announced that he was ready to call it day. The others nodded and moved toward their wagons.

8

The next morning Gil called to Jed as he was about to
mount his horse. "Hey, Jed! Gotta talk to you."

"Okay, Gil, what's on your mind?"

"Mebbe you heard that my oldest boy, James, aims to get
hitched when he turns twenty-one? Well, that's the day after
tomorrow. We thought a night weddin' would be the right thing
because we don't want to hold up the train."

"That's all right," said Jed. "I can find a campsite along
here so we can stop an hour early, or even sooner. That won't
be a problem."

"We do have a mite of a problem, Jed. We ain't got no
preacher, but we thought if someone would give 'em their vows,
they could get married again by a preacher once we get to
Oregon."

Jed had an immediate answer. "Chet does a good job of
filling in for a preacher. He can do it."

The usually talkative Gil was having trouble saying what
was on his mind, so Jed waited for him to continue. "The problem
is," stated Gil, "the bride's father says that even though Chet
is good with words and everythin', he's got no authority to
give the vows. He says the only man on the train that he'll
allow has that authority is you. The captain of a ship can do it

98

and he says you're the head man on this train."

"Oh, no!" cried Jed. "I couldn't do that!"

"Why not?" asked Chet, who joined them. "You do a good job of speaking to the group. You don't have stage fright, do you?"

"No," said Jed, "that's not it." For a moment Jed looked confused, almost like a boy. "I can't really say. I just don't have good luck with weddings. Sarge is the wagonmaster—he'd be the one to do it."

"Well, yes," said Gil slowly, "but Sarge *won't* do it. He won't even think about it. He says for 'em to wait till they get to Oregon. Jed, you're their only hope. Those young lovers are goin' to be sick if you say no. I told 'em I thought you'd hep 'em out. All three of my older boys know you good and they think of you as a man who ain't afeared of nothin'. They sure would be disappointed if I tell 'em you can't hep us out."

"But—" attempted Jed.

"Now, listen. Chet'll write out the vows, make up the prayer, and mark the verses to be read from the Bible. All you have to do is read. That shouldn't be hard for a man who kin read good and has a strong voice like you."

Gil's plea was too much for Jed. Refusing now would put the whole Maddox family friendship in doubt.

"Oh, all right," he said, resigned, "but Chet'll have to help me or I'll make a mess of it."

"Thank you," said the smiling Gil. "I knowd you're a man with a lot of ability. You'll do a right smart job of it. Now, we're all friends on this train. People won't 'spect a great show, just a simple ceremony."

Chet added, "I'll have it all ready by tomorrow night and go through it with you."

"Just one thing," said Jed. "Let's not tell anyone ahead of time who's doing the knot-tying. If they know now, they'll be laughing at me for the next two days."

That evening Jed wanted to be alone for a while, so he left the circle and walked out into the darkness. In his mind's eye, he saw a bride in a calico dress with wild roses in her hair. She smiled up at him and then was gone. For five years he'd kept that memory away, and now it threatened to swallow him up.

The next morning Jed told the train they'd try to get more than twenty miles in that day so they could do less on the day of the wedding. Dust was the worst they'd seen and the heat increased with each step. At the noon stop, flies swarmed over the food and into the faces of the emigrants. Tiny gnats buzzed into their eyes and ears. Emma scowled as she batted at them and even Della waved them away with irritation.

"Remember Job," she said to Mary. "Just remember Job."

"Hope we don't get boils next!" said Mary, picking flies out of the cornmeal mush.

That evening, camp was set up an hour later than usual. The wind had died down and mosquitoes kept up a constant attack. Chet started a green-grass fire, hoping the smoke would keep them away.

After the evening meal, Chet gave Jed a copy of the wedding vows and prayer. He had written everything out carefully, so it would be easy to read. Jed looked at the pages and was surprised to feel only a small pang of sadness. They're only words, he said to himself. Only words.

The pages in Chet's Bible were marked by a string and the verses were marked with pencil. Jed read them slowly, feeling a strange comfort he had never allowed himself to feel before. Then he read the vows. I can do it, he told himself with relief. I can do it.

There was excitement in the camp the next morning about the upcoming wedding. People hurried their chores and the wagons rolled a little earlier than usual. The oxen were not unyoked at noon and everyone ate a cold lunch so they could get started again.

The circle started forming at three-thirty, and by four o'clock the tired and thirsty oxen were drinking their fill in the muddy Platte River. Chores were completed rapidly. The women had first chance at the river to bathe away the dust of the trail and to wash clothes—laundry that dried quickly in the arid climate of the High Plains. Then the men took over. Water was heated for those who shaved. Whiskers and the beards were lathered with soap and scrubbed vigorously.

When Noah got into the river, he remarked to Jed, "The sand in this stream should scour the dirt off, even if the water isn't too clean."

When Jed had the last of the soap out of his beard, he told Noah, "At least for tonight, I won't be able to tell where my buffalo-hunting friend is just by the smell!"

Noah grinned at the old mountain man and replied, "I reckon even you are clean enough so the ladies won't faint dead away if you try dancin' with 'em." Jed put on the only clean clothes he had, after rinsing out the dirty ones that had been soaking in the shallows.

Even before supper was finished Della began baking a cake. John Lewis had found a dozen prairie chicken eggs, and all the women in "A" group contributed a cup of superfine flour and a half-cup of white sugar. She used a light sheet-iron plate that Jed had given her before they left Missouri. It was crude, but practical—made of a piece 16" x 22", with a handle on each end. The blacksmith had also made a roaster oven, 14" x 20," which had a handle on each end as well.

Cakes could be baked on the trail either of two ways. One was to lay the flat sheet on the cooking grill or set it over the fire on rocks. The big roaster was used as a cover. Another way was to put a cake pan in the roaster, set it over the fire and cover the top with the flat lid. Either way, the heat could be controlled by sliding the cover to one side and letting the excess heat escape. They would place a small rock under each corner of the pan, so the cake wouldn't burn on the bottom. The big roasters were usually nine to ten inches deep—big enough to roast several pounds of buffalo meat. They were also used to render buffalo tallow, heat water for washing clothes, and bake a big batch of biscuits or pies.

The evening of the wedding, Noah and Jed gathered a pile of buffalo chips for Della's oven. When the roaster was placed on the grill and the four flat-sided rocks placed in the roaster, she put the cover on and carefully fed the fire to keep the heat even. After the oven was hot and the cake inside, she added one buffalo chip at a time to the fire. She sang "A charge to keep I have—a God to glorify!" softly to herself while she worked. After a few verses, she put another chip on the fire and started another hymn. Her singing was used to time the placing of the chips to maintain an even heat for the cake.

Jed marveled at the way emigrant women could make do. He'd seen them meet the challenges of trail living time and again. He got his piece of comb from his bag and started working on his black hair and beard. Della went to the wagon and brought out a mirror with a handle on it. She didn't say anything, but smiled as she handed it to Jed and kept on softly singing.

"Haw! The way you're fussing tonight," said Noah, "a feller'd think you were the one getting married."

Jed decided it was time to pull rank. "Noah, you go help Gil's family with the cleaning up the wedding site. Pick up the manure and get the table set up."

"Okay," said Noah half-heartedly, and he was off.

Within moments Chet approached Jed carrying a fine-looking dress shirt and string tie. "From Sarge," he said.

Sarge was several inches shorter than Jed, but was strongly built, so the shirt was just large enough. It had been freshly ironed by Mary and smelled good, like clean wash. After he'd put it on, Jed felt like a preacher or a judge. Then he muttered as he tried awkwardly to tie the black tie in a bow. Chet came to his rescue, tying it neatly. At last Jed looked at himself in the mirror and smiled. Not half bad, he thought. Then he felt his wrists tingle. "Nerves," he muttered.

After looking over his lines again, it was time to go. As Jed stepped over the wagon tongue, he saw Della wearing a dress he had never seen before.

"You sure look mighty pretty, Della," he said.

She smiled. "It always makes me feel like a girl to get dressed up for a party."

Della picked up the cake—it looked perfect and smelled even better—and the three of them started for the wedding. Chet asked, "Would you like me to carry the cake, Della?"

"No," she said. "As hard as it is to bake a cake here, I don't want you dropping it along the way. If I drop it, I'll only have myself to blame."

Almost everyone in the train had already gathered. When they reached the line of long narrow tables, Della placed her cake on one, smiling proudly, and joined the crowd. With the assembly facing north and Jed facing south, the setting sun would not be shining directly in anyone's eyes.

Chet and Jed walked to the fiddler, Phineas Ardmore, who was sitting in the center. The bridegroom, James, approached from the other side and joined them. Chet nodded to the fiddler and then disappeared. When Jed turned to face the crowd, he saw James' grin and he smiled in return. Looking out over the crowd, Jed saw Noah, who was staring at him with his mouth open. Then he saw the bride. She was aglow from the last rays of the sun and from her own happiness.

The fiddler started a slow version from "Sweet Betsy from Pike" and the bride proceeded slowly toward them, hanging on the arm of her father. Jed was struck by her beauty, and he heard the collective sigh of a dozen admirers. Her long dress was dark blue and full-skirted. The tightly fitted bodice emphasized her loveliness. Her golden hair hung in curls below her shoulders. Her smiling eyes never left the man she loved.

James took a half step to meet her and took her hand. They both turned to face Jed. He opened the Bible to the first sheet of paper. His hands were trembling slightly. "Dearly beloved," he began, "we are gathered here in the sight of God to unite this man and this woman in holy matrimony."

The service proceeded without a flaw. Joy spread like a warm blanket over the crowd. "Colossians 3: 18 and 19," Jed read. "Wives submit yourselves unto your own husbands as is fit in the Lord. Husbands love your wives, and be not bitter against them."

Gil, standing in the front row, reached for Emma's hand and beamed at her. She managed a small smile in return.

Jed said, "Repeat after me: I, James, take thee, Martha, to be my lawful wedded wife."

And, "I, Martha, take thee, James, to be my lawful wedded husband."

When the vows were completed, Jed finished the ceremony in a commanding voice easily heard by all of those present. "And now by the power invested in me as supreme commander of this wagon train, I now pronounce you man and wife. What God has joined together, let not man put asunder."

Phineas started playing his fiddle, tears were dried, and the couple promenaded through the rows of onlookers.

"Hoo-hah!" cried Will. "Let's us have a party!"

The crowd gave a collective cheer and headed for the cake and coffee. Chet put his hand on Jed's shoulder and then stuck out his hand. "Fine job," he said. "You might make it into Congress yet." They walked together to stand in line to congratulate the happy couple.

Jed started to shake the bride's hand when she reached up and kissed him lightly on the cheek. "Thank you, Jed," she said.

He ducked his head. "I wish you well—you're going to need good wishes, married to this lunk!"

James grinned. "Thank ye, Jed. You made a right fine marry-er. We'll name our firstborn after you."

Jed groaned. "Maybe it'll be a girl," he said.

The women, supervised by Della, kept brewing coffee over the smoldering fires. Everyone exclaimed over the cake.

"Best brown sugar icing I ever tasted," said Zeb with a toothless grin.

After a while, pipes were lit, hands clapped in time with the music, and stories were told about other wedding nights. A jew's harp joined the fiddle and voices sang along.

"Time to dance!" Gil called out.

The groom bowed formally to the bride and then took her in his arms. After they circled the yard once, others joined in. One enthusiastic couple started a reel. "This is the way we do it in Missouri," the wife said.

The bride danced rather timidly, and Chet explained why. "She was raised a Methodist like me, and we don't believe in dancing. Martha's twenty-one now and she can do what she wants to. Della and me won't be dancing, though, and neither will Martha's folks." He gestured to a beaming middle-aged couple surrounded by their friends from "C" unit.

Jed saw that Sarge and Mary and even Caleb and Sarah were joining the reel. Caleb and Sarah were smiling and seemed more full of life than Jed had ever seen them. He could see the tall Ben standing alone. Molly, pretty as a picture, was dancing with Josh.

Noah waved at him from across the circle and he walked toward him, accidently bumping into Josh.

"Oh! Thank you, Jed, for cutting in," Molly said, moving quickly into his arms. "Josh nearly broke my foot," she whispered, laughing.

Jed was surprised to feel Molly's lightness—she was very quick on her feet and kept up with him at every turn. He wanted to say something important, something she'd remember, but couldn't think of a thing. Instead, she started the conversation.

"You did real well, Reverend Jed," she said. "Sounded like the real thing to me."

Jed ducked his head. "Well, Chet gave me the words," he said.

"I think it was the Bible gave you most of them," she said with a smile.

Jed smiled in return and felt his heart open as it hadn't in five years. But he couldn't let that happen. "Why aren't you dancing with Ben?" he asked.

"Ben?" she echoed.

"Your husband."

"Oh," Molly's smile dimmed. "He's not feeling good."

Jed felt a tap on his shoulder and reluctantly relinquished Molly to Sarge, turning to Mary.

Mary smiled, her face flushed with pleasure. "Having a good time, Jed?" she asked. "I just love parties!"

"Sure," he said absently. "Me, too."

After a dance with Mary, Jed asked Sarah to dance and found her as light and quick as Molly had been. Toughened by walking on the trail for hundreds of miles, the dancers didn't tire easily. When Jed took a break, he saw Noah again and waved.

"I would have joshed you real good if I had known you were going to do the knot tying," said Noah. "You sure surprised me and you did a right good job of it. I won't ask you to do my wedding when we get to Oregon, but I'd be honored to have you stand up with me."

"I'd be just as honored to do it," Jed said warmly.

"Supreme commander!" continued Noah. "I don't know whether to salute or bow."

"It wouldn't hurt you to do both," retorted Jed.

The music started again and Jed made his way through the crowd to Molly and asked her for another dance. It seemed that she had been in his arms for less than a minute when again he felt Sarge's tap.

"Never knew you were such a dancer, Jed," Sarge said.

Mary was dancing with Caleb and Jed decided he'd had enough dancing. He looked around. The several units and the two trains were mixing well. Everyone was having a good time. Jed was sure a bottle or two was passed around in the semi-darkness of the outer circle, but he decided not to investigate. The tables were cleared and the crowd was diminishing by twos and threes.

When the music stopped, Jed could hear Noah. "Hey, James! It's time for your eleven o'clock shift of guard duty. Don't be late now or we'll report you."

"Right!" A circle of the Maddox brothers surrounded James. "Time to go, brother!"

James groaned. "Oh, no!"

Noah took pity on the young groom. "Aw, I'm taking your shift tonight. I know you got more important things to do. Haw!"

The couple ran off to their new wagon pelted with handfuls of cornmeal and followed by laughter. After the couple left, the fiddler yawned and said, "Time to turn in." Gradually the revelers returned to their campsites and low murmurs replaced whoops of laughter. The fire died down and the tables and lanterns were packed away. The moon drifted high in the cloudless sky, and a breeze brought the edge of a chill.

Jed walked back to Sarge's wagon, removed the dress shirt and tie, and hung them in back. He found his rumpled shirt and made his customary tour of the wagons because he wasn't at all sleepy. He circled the camp, noticing with satisfaction the well-guarded herd. Then he headed back to his bedroll, feeling restless, frustrated, and lonely.

He lay awake, watching the stars. A good wedding, he thought, James and Martha will be good for each other. A happy night for so many people. And for me? Well, I had happy plans once, too, for Caroline and me. And the memory didn't hurt as much as it once did.

Holding Molly in his arms tonight had made him realize how much he missed a woman and how much he wished she wasn't married. Just thinking that made him feel guilty, so he thought about the trip ahead and drifted off to sleep.

Just then he heard a movement and was instantly awake. A teenaged girl from the new part of the train stood in front of him and then dropped to her knees at the edge of his bedroll. He almost jumped up, out of her way, but didn't want to awaken anyone.

He whispered, "What in tarnation are you doing here?"

"Can I lie down beside you and talk for a little while?" she whispered back. The sweet smell of vanilla almost engulfed Jed.

"Thunderation, no! Get yourself back to your tent, girl. If anyone found you in bed with me, they'd hang me without a trial. Would you like to see that happen?" he pleaded.

"No," she said sadly, "I just wanted to be friendly." She stood up and silently walked away.

Jed was wide awake. My God! he thought. Did anyone see her come? He turned and looked at Ben and Molly's tent, twenty feet away. Ben was sleeping outside, as many men did, but Jed couldn't tell if Ben's eyes were closed. I wonder, thought Jed, why Ben sleeps outside when he's got a wife like Molly?

9

The train continued to inch its way across the flat land of the Platte River valley. Early one morning Jed decided he wanted to go on a buffalo hunt. He figured that if he was really going to settle down after this trip, this might be his last chance. He also asked John Lewis, as well as a boy and a man from unit J—Peter and Harry—to go with him, and told Noah to stay with the train.

The evening before, Jed had spotted a large herd in the distance. The four men rode out to the southwest right after breakfast, leading the pack mules. They let the animals lope for about a half-mile and then slowed them to a walk.

"Are we gonna shoot buffalo on the run?" asked Peter.

"Some people do it that way," answered Jed, "but that's hard on the horses and dangerous, too. The buffalo would be scattered over a big area when they fell, and we'd have to go get them. Indians hunt them on the run, and they lose horses to the stampeding herds. We don't have any horses to spare."

When the hunters reached the rolling hills away from the river, they stopped on top of a mound. Jed pointed to faint dust clouds to the southwest, but no buffalo were in sight.

"That must be them down there," he said. "Nothing else makes that much dust."

After ten more minutes of riding, John Lewis saw a few buffalo on a rise. Jed took the hunters south and then west. When he reckoned they were only a mile or so east of the herd, they stopped to eat. As fast as they could, they downed a few biscuits and bacon, ate a few dried apples, and slurped a drink of warm water from their canteens. Then they tightened the cinches on their saddles and rode on west.

Jed pointed. "See that hill? That's where we want to take a look."

Once they reached it, he dismounted and went around the crest until the others lost sight of him. When he returned, he called out, "Yep, they're there! One man's gonna have to stay here with the horses. We can't afford to lose 'em."

"I'll stay," said Harry. "I ain't much of a hunter anyway."

John Lewis and Peter took the big buffalo rifles from the scabbards. Jed got his rifle. The three of them moved around to the south side of the hill.

"We're in luck," said Jed. "They're down there right in front of us. We won't have to crawl up on them the way we usually do."

As the buffalo moved by, the hunters watched, waiting for the right ones. Jed pointed to what he thought was a young cow without a calf. He touched John Lewis, who was on his knees beside him. John Lewis watched the front leg move forward, exposing the "sweet spot." He took careful aim and touched the hair trigger. The buffalo staggered for about twenty feet before dropping. A few nearby buffalo jumped out of the way and moved on. The fallen buffalo didn't scare the other animals away, but Jed knew if the wind switched so they got the scent of humans, they'd all be on the run.

John Lewis backed away and silently disappeared around the point of the hill. Jed waited a minute or two until the right buffalo was near the fallen one and then gave a signal to Peter. He fired, but the buffalo kept on going. Jed handed Peter his rifle, whispering in his ear, "Just think of it as a big rabbit. Aim careful and squeeze the trigger slowly."

His next shot found its mark and there were two buffalo down. By this time, John Lewis was back with the big gun loaded and ready to shoot. When he had his buffalo, Jed picked one and there were four animals ready to be butchered.

"I'd like to try another one," said Peter. Jed shook his head. "We have all we need, but if a cripple comes along, you can have it to put it out of its misery. We'll wait a bit." They moved back to where they could reload their rifles. Jed watched Peter closely. He'd seen times when the excitement of the hunt had made boys careless.

Peter carefully loaded the big gun. "This is the best gun I've ever used. I learned on Grandpa's flintlock and later Pa let me use his gun. It was much smaller calibre though."

"These Hawken .50-calibre rifles pack quite a wallop," said Jed. "The buffalo we just dropped were only about a hundred yards away, but they'll do the same thing at a hundred fifty yards. If you take good care of these guns, they'll work real well. With a .50-calibre bullet in their lights, buffalo don't go very far."

Jed was getting eager to butcher the animals, but he'd promised to wait. At last a young bull limped into range. It looked like he had a broken leg. Peter took aim with the big buffalo gun and in seconds a wolf's dinner was on the ground.

For several hours the four hunters skinned the buffalo and cut up the meat. John Lewis' skill with the knife pleased Jed. The lad told Jed he started helping his mother and neighbors butcher when he was very young. The three pack mules were loaded first and the rest of the meat was tied to the saddles of two horses. The hunters would take turns riding until they arrived at the campsite.

Jed took them toward where he thought the night camp would be. When they were clear of the hills, they could see the wagons to the northeast and Noah waiting for them. Everyone greeted them excitedly. It was good to have so much fresh buffalo meat, but Jed cautioned the travelers to eat biscuits and other food too. A diet of buffalo meat alone would send them to the latrine every few minutes.

After the train had passed the confluence of the north and south branches of the Platte, they set up camp. It was a warm night without a breeze and the mosquitoes were relentless.

The next morning dawned hot and still. By the mid-morning stop, the weather was sultry. The hot travelers drank thirstily from the barrels of warm water, their dirty faces dripping with sweat. Children cried from the heat and some smaller children were allowed to climb into the wagons to ride.

"This is twister weather," said Caleb to Sarge. He nodded.

When the four lines moved on, the going was not any easier. Gnats swarmed around them and flies droned in their ears. Mothers fanned their babies constantly to keep the insects away. Children who had begged to ride found the wagons stifling. Raising the canvas sides on the wagons provided more air, but dust poured in as well.

The oxen were black from the swarms of flies on their backs. Their tails were in constant motion, but they couldn't reach a fraction of the insects. In pity, drivers used their long bullwhips to chase the flies away, but they always returned. Those walking alongside threw sand on the oxen, which gave them some relief from the stings.

Jed realized that a sea of buffalo had been on the trail there a day or two before. The grass had been trampled for several miles along the river. The thousands of hooves on their way to water had pulverized the sod until it looked almost like a plowed field, and the dry banks had eroded into the river.

The dust that had plagued the train all morning became almost unbearable by mid-afternoon. Without wind to blow it away, it hung like a cloud. Lips cracked, eyes smarted, and coughing echoed up and down the line. Most of the travelers had covered their noses and mouths with bandannas, but still the dust seeped in.

The four lines moved farther apart and then formed eight lines to try to escape the dust. After about a half-mile over the barren ground, Jed called a halt. The livestock were turned loose to drink in the river and slowly the dust settled. The travelers ate their noon meal hastily. The heat, flies, and gnats made them short tempered and their throats were so dry no one felt like talking. The livestock didn't venture far from the shallow river and the grass that grew along its banks.

Just before they started west again, a few clouds appeared on the horizon in front of them. They were not the heavy, moisture-laden clouds familiar to midwesterners. The travelers heard a few rumbles of thunder and, seeing a few streaks of lightning in the distance, hoped for relief from the heat.

Jed turned to Noah, "This looks like it could be a dry thunderstorm—the kind that starts prairie fires."

A half hour later the clouds were closer and the thunder louder. Smaller clouds drifted by to the northeast. A bright streak of lightning and a loud clap of thunder followed.

"It could of hit on the other side of the river," said Jed. Soon they could see some smoke and in a minute or two, the flames of a fast-moving prairie fire.

"It might burn itself out at the river," said Noah. "It's good for us that it struck on the north side."

They turned their horses and rode back to the head of the train. Jed called to the anxious driver, "Don't worry! The fire won't jump the Platte."

Once ahead of the train, the men dismounted and walked for a while, scanning the sky. Lightning flashed and thunder boomed, but there was no hint of rain. Then a tremendous flash illuminated the plain.

"'Bout two miles ahead, maybe three," shouted Noah. "Looked like a real fire starter."

"This side of the river, too," confirmed Jed. They mounted up and rode back to the wagons in a gallop. They saw Gil and Sarge riding toward them.

"Get 'em into the river fast!" hollered Jed, and the four men spread out to warn the drivers.

Whenever Noah's horse stepped in a soft spot in the river, she became nervous. He turned the horse around and urged her as near as she'd go to that spot. Then he thrust a pole in the sand as far as he could. The soft spots were soon marked with poles. At last he found enough solid bottom more than a hundred feet from shore to support the two lines of wagons. He waved to Sarge, who signaled the two approaching columns. Noah, joined by Jed and Gil on horseback continued to test the bottom.

Before they returned to the wagons they could see two groups of men working furiously, sloping the steep banks of the river. When Jed and the others rode up the bank where the train might exit from the river, they could see the fire was far enough away so they had enough time.

"How could green grass burn so fast?" called Josh. "It never would back home."

"The grass looks green," answered Jed, "but it's been dry for so long there isn't much moisture in it. This area wasn't grazed very short last fall and it hasn't been wet enough to rot. But don't worry. When the fire gets to the area the buffalo trampled, it'll go out—unless the wind changes to the north.

"Looks like there's been a lot of prairie fires along here. There's no trees on the river banks, just on the islands," said Sarge.

Before the fire got any closer, the two lines of wagons entered the knee-deep water and faced upriver. The wind was blowing parallel to the river. Jed was afraid that if it switched to the south, the smoke would spook the animals, so he ordered each lead team of oxen be tied to the wheels of the wagons in front of them. The oxen from the lead wagons were unhitched and tied to the wagon wheels. The loose stock was corralled between the two wagon lines. Guards watched them closely.

Lightning continued to crash around them—blazing bolts crackling down to the grass with deafening blasts of thunder, starting still more fires. The emigrants nervously waited as the fires raced to the east. The wind held steady, so most of the smoke stayed across the river from them. Enough light smoke drifted their way to make the animals restless, but the guards held them in line.

It was a relieved group who watched the danger pass by and continue on east, where the flames gradually died out.

"Praise the Lord," called out Della.

"Amen," sang a hundred voices.

The wagons pulled out of the river. Several of them had settled into the sandy bottom, giving the oxen a hard pull. Horses and mule teams struggled as well. The interlude was good for thw hweels, as felloes swelled to tighten the iron tires.

It was hazardous traveling over the burned ground. Buffalo chips were still burning, and the wheels churned up the fine ashes, which filled the air and choked the travelers. It seemed like hours before, exhausted, they finally camped for the night. A mile beyond the blackened area, they found adequate grazing.

The next day's trek proceeded smoothly until they arrived at a river crossing which looked to be more than a half-mile. The sight of Noah riding toward them in knee-deep water convinced the emigrants they could manage it.

The order for the crossing was given, and the train got underway with Noah leading the procession of ox teams. Jed stayed on the south bank until a dozen wagons were halfway across, and then he rode out to the middle of the river to direct the traffic flow. Sarge and Gil stayed on the south bank until everyone was across, plus the livestock.

The water was cool, and the children had to be urged to move quickly across. Most wanted to take off their shoes and play in the shallow water. Jimmy held his mother's hand and splashed in the water with glee. Sarah scolded Nellie when she tried to join in the fun, giving Molly a stern look as well.

An early camp was made close to the river. In the distance, the hills to the southwest were dark with buffalo.

"This herd is large enough to cause trouble. They don't smell us yet," Jed said to Sarge. "There must be ten thousand there."

"They might not cross the river," said Sarge. "They might just string out along the riverbank for a few miles getting their fill of water. Of course if they do decide to come this way, we could be in big trouble."

Jed decided to go on a scouting trip after supper, looking for the buffalo. He knew that if they crossed and drifted north to Ash Hollow, they'd eat the grass and spoil the campsite.

"There's no sign of 'em wanting to cross the river," he said when he returned. "I think we can sleep easy tonight."

"We'd better sleep easy," said Noah. "Tomorrow's Ash Hollow."

The great hill leading down to Ash Hollow was notorious for its steepness. Most of the emigrants had read letters about it in their hometown newspapers. The hollow itself, they knew, was beautiful. But getting there was going to be demanding, of their muscle and will.

The next morning they were rolling soon after six. The animals had a hard pull for a while and then easy going in a northwesterly direction. It was hot and the noon stop was short. After lunch the train pushed on, rolling slowly across the high plateau.

The dryness chapped their lips and hands, but it was even harder on wagon wheels. By the time they'd mounted the steep hill on the north side of the South Platte, the humidity from the river was gone, and the wood wheels began to shrink from the iron tires. Teamsters jammed shims inside the iron, in hopes the tires would stay on until they could be made smaller.

After an hour or two, Jed, atop Blaze, stopped ahead. When the lead wagon reached him, the travelers saw why.

"Lordy!" shouted Gil. "Look at this hill!"

"It's a lot steeper than I figured," Ben told Sarge. "This is gonna be tough."

Emma moved to the brink of the hill and turned on Jed. "Only a crazy man would bring us to this cliff! How many people did you send to their deaths here? I ain't goin'."

"Now, now, Emma," said Gil. "Jed knows what he's doin'. He ain't been wrong yet. He'll git us down."

In fact, the trail appeared to go straight down, with nothing to break the descent. Jed began directing the wagons at one set of ruts and Noah at another. The emigrants were told to secure the supplies on their wagons so they wouldn't fall out the front of the wagon as they started down. Many of them lashed things down with rope and tied the front canvas opening shut.

The lead yoke of oxen was taken off of each wagon because they would be in the way going downhill. When a wagon was ready it was driven to the brow of the hill. Chains were wrapped around the rear wheels several times on the front side of each wheel just above the ground. The wagon was driven forward until the chains were under the wheels.

The front side of each wheel was chained to the wagon box. Then the rear wheels were chained to the front wheels, and the men were told to tie each hook on the chains with rawhide or bolt each chain together so no chain would shake loose on the way down. A rope was tied to the head of each ox, and a man walked about twenty-five feet to each side to keep the animals in check. The long rope was necessary, so that if a wagon tipped over, the men would have a chance to get away and not be crushed.

The oxen strained to move the locked wheels until the wagons were on the steep downgrade. From then on there was very little pulling. The sliding chained wheels tore at the earth and dust filled the air. The men on the ropes of the oxen struggled to keep their footing on the steepest part of the hill, but the chains under the wheels kept the wagons from going down too fast. Shorter ropes bristled from each wagon, and women and children hung on, ready to add their weight.

At the steepest grade, Jed gave the signal and the twenty men and boys holding onto a 300-foot rope tied to the rear axle of a wagon dug in to stabilize it. When the others saw that this method worked, they hurried to get their wagons ready for the downhill slide. Three pack mules were led down the hill to carry the chains back uphill.

"Now I see why Jed told us to mark our chains," said Caleb.

"Yep," said Ben. "So we'd end up with our own after this."

Once the system started working, it was possible to keep

the wagons going downhill, one after the other.

"Look at these ruts," Jed remarked. "It won't be long 'til new trails will have to be started. These two are getting pretty deep."

John Lewis, Josh, and several other young men did double duty, taking the place of older men, who found leading the oxen down the steep grade the hardest work of the trek thus far. Some of the older boys were given the job of leading the extra yokes of oxen down the hill. The women and children who weren't holding the short ropes picked their way gingerly down the hill. They took a longer path that seemed less steep, but still some of them stumbled and slid to the bottom.

When all the wagons were at the base of the hill, the loose stock were driven down. As the wagons were being unchained, the women took those few minutes of rest to try to straighten out the upset items in their wagons.

"Lordamercy, look at this mess!" called Della.

"Can't tell a basket from a box," said Mary. "And I'm not sure I want to look inside one!"

"Can you tell me," shouted Emma, "why we ever let that fast talkin' trapper talk us into hirin' him? It'll be an hour afore I git things to rights."

But already Jed was calling for a start-up time in five minutes. The wagon train had several miles to go before it would get to the spring-fed creek where they would make camp. The animals were ganted up and ready for the water and grass they found. After traveling in the bare Platte Valley, this campsite looked lush, with large trees and the cleanest water since leaving the Blue.

"About time we had a nice place to stop," said Sarah. "I've had enough sand to last me a lifetime."

The wagons didn't move the next day. Noah and a few men left to hunt. There was water to wash dishes, clothes, themselves, and their children.

"Sure feels good to get the sand washed out of everything,"

Della told Chet and Jed at noon.

"Don't get too used to it," said Jed. "It'll be back to North Platte water pretty soon. And North Platte water isn't much better than South Platte water—it's just barely wet."

Della groaned.

Henry spent the day shoeing oxen. Hooves were getting worn down. Jed shod his own two horses as well as Blaze. It was easier to shoe horses now that their hooves were worn down enough that they didn't have to be trimmed much. If the shoes were the right size they could just be nailed on.

That night after supper, families gathered around campfires and compared stories about the prairie fire, the buffalo, and "the Hill," as it was called.

"About that fire," said Chet in his good-natured voice. "I sure do respect the way Jed and Sarge gave the orders to get things done. There was no time to lollygag around. We sure were fortunate no one got hurt."

"The folks worked together, that's what counts," said Sarge, stroking his mustache. "A few years ago we were in a bad fire south of the Santa Fe Trail. The Comanches might of started it—we never knew for sure. If we'd of had a captain like Jed, instead of a greenhorn who wasn't hardly dry behind the ears, we would of got out of it better. It was open country, with no streams nearby. After standing around lookin' at the dang thing for a while, we finally got a back burn going. Then we had to kill a mule and split him in half—got horses to drag the two halves to put out the backfire. They didn't want to do it any more than we did."

"What happened then?" asked Josh.

"We got out okay, but we were almost too late. Prairie fires move like lightning."

There were a few moments of silence while they thought about Sarge's story, then Molly asked, "Any more hills like that, Jed?"

"Yep," said the mountain man. "You'll see one on the Barlow Road that'll make this one look like an anthill. It's so steep that nobody's ever gone up it, only down. But that's a long way from here. We got plenty of time to get ready for it."

John Lewis asked, "How'd you get to be a mountain man, Jed?"

"I reckon that's his business, son," said Mary. "Don't be nosy."

"I don't mind tellin'," said Jed. "Probably not too interesting, though. I was born in southern Illinois, not far from you folks. I grew up like everybody else—hunting, fishing, swimming when I could, doing farm work—lots of farm work. I liked to trap, but Pa always said schoolwork came first, my Ma thought so, too. So I learned to read and write and do arithmetic—don't regret it, either.

"When I was sixteen Pa died and I took over the farming with the help of my kid brother. In the fall of 1836—guess I was about twenty-two then, a fellow named Bill came back from the mountains to visit his folks, who lived nearby. He'd been gone about five years, but I remembered him pretty well. He told me about how he'd been trapping beaver in the West. That sounded pretty good to me. His partner had just died, so he asked me to go back with him."

"Did his partner get killed by Indians?" asked Josh breathlessly.

"Nope," answered Jed. "He got killed 'cause he drank too much whiskey and got into a fight with another trapper during the rendezvous. Got stabbed. He lived long enough to give his traps and rifle to Bill. Well, Bill got a job driving a mule wagon loaded with furs back to the States. After he dropped 'em off in St. Louis, he came on down to the farm.

"The more he talked about the West, the more I wanted to go. My brother was old enough to take over the farm then, so Bill and I left for St. Louis in the spring. Don't have to tell you, my Ma didn't like me going. From there we each drove a load of supplies to the rendezvous site. I drove a mule team first, but then I took over a wagon pulled by oxen and became a bullwhacker in a hurry.

"After the rendezvous, Bill and I waded the streams and trapped beaver until the ice got too thick. Then we holed up for the winter. We worked at first thaw until it got so warm the pelts weren't good anymore."

"Why'd you quit trapping?" asked John Lewis.

"Well, that's a story for another day," said Jed. "But I can tell you this—it's a whale of a lot of work and misery. There just isn't enough pay in it to make it worthwhile. Not for all those cold, cold nights, for the wind, and the terrible loneliness. Not enough money in the world."

Jed looked at the faces around the fire. Josh and John Lewis were watching him intently. He noticed that Molly looked interested, too.

"Time to get to bed," he said abruptly. "We've got a long day tomorrow."

"First, tell us where we are exactly," said Josh.

Jed said, "Best answer I can give you is we're about 460 miles from Independence."

"Independence," said Della softly. "It seems a lot farther away than that."

10

The wagons left the peaceful grove of Ash Hollow the next morning and continued across the plains. Most were carrying a supply of firewood, cut the day before, and casks of clear water from Ash Hollow spring.

The animals were full and well-rested, After traveling nearly one-fourth of the way, they were still in good flesh. The people, too, were in good health. Along the North Platte the nights were cooler and the grass was shorter and drier.

That night a guard woke Jed about one-thirty. A quarter moon was shining but wasn't giving enough light to see clearly. The guard whispered that the herders thought they had seen Indians spying on them from a distance. Jed moved quickly and was soon on his horse and out by the herd. The herders had wisely gathered the animals in a tight cluster, close to the train.

As Jed's eyes became used to the darkness, he recognized Gil's son James. Jed rode toward him. When they were close enough to speak without being overheard, James said softly, "They're just over my shoulder."

Without appearing to look in that direction, Jed could make out two shapes on the ground that appeared to be large rocks. "Looks like kids," murmured Jed. "One of 'em just slapped a mosquito. No brave would do that—it'd give him away."

The two horsemen rode a few feet away, as if they were patrolling the area. "Let's move the herd in. It's too risky to leave them out here," decided Jed.

"I'm willing to do that, " agreed James, "but some of the fellers thought we ought to rough 'em up a bit. Show 'em who's boss."

"It'd be stupid to shoot boys that young. I'll stay here and watch them. Go tell the others and start moving the animals in."

The forms in the grass didn't move, and it wasn't long before the herd was in the circle and out of their reach. When the rope gates were up, some of those who were awakened by the commotion came to see what was happening.

Jed explained that the Oglala Sioux had decided to pay a visit. Ezra, who was to go on duty as a guard the next shift, spoke up. "Let's go run them Injuns down and shoot 'em. We oughta teach 'em a lesson about stealing horses from white men!"

Jed looked at the irate man and said, "I've told you what to do in a situation like this and we're not changing that now. If we shoot those boys, some white folks are going to get hurt. If not us, somebody else. The four of you can patrol the outside of the circle close to the wagons, and I'll ride out a little farther to see if the boys are gone."

Jed found that the boys had already left. As a precaution, he rode a wide circle for an hour. Then, leaving orders to turn the herd out, he returned to his bedroll.

The next day Jed rode out ahead a little earlier than usual. Instead of hunting, Noah agreed to stay close to the train. Jed wanted to scout farther south and west, to see if he could see any sign of hostiles in the area. Della fixed a lunch for him and he headed out ahead of the train.

He started early, traveling slowly because he had plenty of time. When he'd gone southwest about ten miles, he rode to the top of a hill and looked around for signs of Indians. He found nothing, other than the tracks of two ponies headed southwest. The boys had probably left their mounts about a mile away and walked to the herd the night before. Jed assumed the Oglala were camped along the South Platte.

From the top of the hill, Jed went on to the north. He looked around methodically, spending most of the day fruitlessly checking out the area. About an hour before the usual stopping time for the train, Jed was about four miles southwest of where he thought would be a good campsite. He let his horse walk slowly to the crest of a hill. He saw nothing at first, but in a minute or two felt a shiver up his spine.

There, coming over a crest of a hill was a band of Oglala. They were about a mile to the south, galloping to the northwest. They must have seen him, too, because they immediately turned and began racing toward him. Jed let Blaze walk slowly to the northwest until he was out of sight of the Indians. Then he turned the big horse to the northeast and let him lope down the hill, wondering why the Oglala were coming his way. He touched Blaze gently in the flanks and they started a long, loping stride down the hill.

"We can't stay around to see what they want with us," Jed said to his horse, "so now's your chance to prove how good you are."

Jed wasn't expecting trouble even though they were in Sioux territory. He had met some of their minor chiefs earlier and the relationship had been cordial. A few braves had even approached one of Jed's wagon trains in prior years, and Jed had traded with them.

There has to be something mighty wrong for them to come after me this way, he thought.

Blaze, now on a dead run, was swiftly covering the ground, and Jed urged him on to his top speed. Now and then Jed turned to see if the Oglala were still in sight. They were. He judged he was about a mile and a half ahead of them. There looked to be about thirty braves, but this was not the time to stop and count them.

His blood pounding in his veins, Jed thanked his lucky stars he was riding the fastest horse on the train. Blaze had been raised by a breeder who made a business of raising horses just for the trail. He got his mares from Indians and used stallions from cavalry stock. The foals were fast and much larger than Indian ponies. Blaze was five years old, so he should have as much stamina as any horse.

Jed searched the eastern horizon as they raced forward. At last he saw the white canvas tops of the train. As he got closer he could see Noah riding far out in front, just as he'd hoped. He took his hat and waved it frantically in a circle. He saw Noah's horse turn and then smoke from Noah's pistol. He'd gotten the message.

Jed turned Blaze and headed toward the wagon train. When he saw the wagons starting to circle in response to Noah's shot, he pulled on the reins and slowed Blaze down to a lope. No use ruining a good horse when there was so much distance between him and the Oglala.

When Noah returned to the wagons, which were nearly a half- mile behind him, the circle was almost complete. He passed them by at full gallop. As he reached the rear of the train, Gil joined him. His long frame was bent over the horse's neck and with every jump the horse's head touched his long beard. The men nodded at each other without a word.

The herd was about an eighth of a mile behind the train, with only one mounted herder. Two boys were walking alongside. Gil uncoiled his black snake as they rounded the rear of the herd. They yelled as they moved toward the loose stock, "Giiit! Gayaaah!" The animals bellowed mightily in response.

If a critter didn't move fast enough, Gil snapped his whip and a tuft of hair flew from the laggard's back. The herd was moving quickly, and the boys were running as fast as they could. Noah and Gil each reached down and pulled a boy up behind him.

The animals were so used to going into the circle that they rounded it and entered the gap at a dead run. One ox ran into a rear wagon wheel and shoved it a few feet inside. Just then Jed rode into the circle on the lathered-up Blaze.

"Whew!" said Jed. "Sure am glad to see you folks!"

"What in the blue blazes is goin' on?" called Gil.

"Yeah, did you start an Indian war or something?" asked Noah.

Jed shook his head. "Don't know what the devil's the matter—but I reckon we'll find out shortly."

Drivers hurried to unhitch the wagon teams, which were turned loose with the yokes still on their necks. Chains were hastily put up and the rope gates were soon in place.

"Jed! They goin' to attack us?" hollered Sarge from across the circle.

"Don't think so," Jed struggled to make his voice heard above the confusion. "But keep your guns in sight! Hear me? *Keep your guns in sight, but don't use 'em!*"

Both men and women had fear in their eyes, despite Noah's assurances that Jed could handle the situation. "Don't worry," he told them. "Jed knows Indians."

Suddenly the hostiles were there. The braves slowed to a lope and then rode slowly around the south side of the circle. After they had circled to the north, where Jed and Blaze were plainly visible, they stopped in a line just beyond accurate rifle fire. Their horses looked exhausted with legs spread apart and heads down. Their sides were heaving. After a minute or two, the chief rode forward about hundred feet and raised his arm, palm forward.

"That means he wants to talk," Jed explained. "Nobody is to shoot," he repeated emphatically. *"Nobody."*

Jed rode to meet the minor chief in front of him, stopping before he got there and motioning him to come closer. The emigrants behind Jed were watching silently. Even the children were quiet.

Ezra moved off the side, his rifle loaded. When he started to pull the hammer back, he felt the muzzle of a rifle against his neck. Gil whispered in his ear, "You start to aim that gun and my rifle barrel is acomin' down on your head so hard you won't know for a long time what's goin' on. Don't you have any brains? You shoot the chief, and Jed'll have a dozen arrows in him in a few seconds. Be better to shoot Jed.

"But if you shoot anybody, I kin promise you one thing. When the fight's over, we'll raise a couple of wagon tongues and hang you so's you'll die real slow. Think about that!"

Ezra slowly lowered the hammer on his rifle. Jed and the chief began to speak to each other in sign language, their hands moving rapidly. When Jed turned back to the circle, Noah opened the rope gate. The chief and his braves turned their horses westward and slowly rode away.

All eyes were on Jed. "Three boys were shot through the head, so the chief says," he told the crowd. "One was his son. I told him we saw only two boys last night and didn't shoot either one. I asked him about them and he admitted that they had returned soon after dawn.

"Two other boys brought three bodies into their camp when the sun was just past the highest point of the day. I reminded him I had guided trains through this land for years and never had trouble with them. I scolded him for chasing me. But there's no reasoning with him now. He's out for revenge. They won't return to their camp until they find someone to pay for the loss of those boys!"

Someone hollered from a distance, "Will they come back here, Jed?"

"I don't think so. They could see our guns and how quickly you circled up, but I think we better make sure they don't camp too close."

Shortly, mounted on fresh horses, Sarge and Jed rode from the circle and headed west. They could see the Oglala leaving the riverbank where they had watered their horses. Jed rode close to the river looking for a spot where braves might be hiding. Finding none, they watered their horses one at a time and then loped them to get a closer look at the band ahead of them. When Jed thought they were close enough, they slowed their horses to a walk. The Oglala were far enough from the river that they could not run to the low bank without being seen.

Sarge and Jed followed the Sioux warriors until they were satisfied that they were at least ten miles from the wagon train, then they returned. Della had hot coffee waiting.

Sipping coffee from a tin cup between bites of dried buffalo meat, Jed told the nervous emigrants gathered around him more about his talk with the chief.

"He wanted to trade for Blaze, and I'm sure they'd like a lot more of our horses. Their horses are tired out now, so a few of the braves might run back on foot to try their luck. I think we better put our horses in the circle and have extra guards tonight."

"The wagon train that was about six days ahead of us, where the St. Joe trail comes in, is now leading us by only two days. They're the only train ahead of us, so I suppose they're the ones who shot the boys. God help them if this band catches them by surprise."

Sarge asked, "Don't you think they'll be extra careful?"

"Maybe, if they know Indians—but if they really knew Indians, they wouldn't have shot the boys in the first place."

"That's right," agreed Sarge. "The most stupid thing you can do in Indian country is to shoot some of their women or kids. They'll get their revenge one way or the other."

During Jed's guard duty from two to five, he wasn't sure that all of the coyote howls he heard were actually made by coyotes. But he didn't mention his feeling to anyone else, not wanting to make the emigrants even more nervous. He didn't see anything unusual, and the horses and mules were let out to graze as soon as there was enough light to make sure it was safe.

The next day both Jed and Noah scouted ahead of the train. Jed rode far ahead to the west and Noah stayed to the south. As the train moved to the west, the travelers could see massive rock formations on the horizon. At the noon stop, Josh asked how far away they were. Sarge told them they'd be about four miles from their campsite that evening. That was where Jed met them when the train circled for the night. He moved from wagon to wagon with the disappointing news: There'd be no going to the Courthouse and Jail rocks that evening.

Josh said, "Aw, darn it, Jed. You're too jittery."

Jed explained, "If the Sioux haven't found other whites to satisfy their revenge, they could slip up behind those rocks any time without being seen." When he saw the crestfallen faces, he added, "We're only about fifteen miles from Chimney Rock. We'll get there early tomorrow and you can climb that one."

Oregon-bound travelers marveled at these well-known landmarks along the Platte. The largest rock looked like a two- or three-story building to early travelers and so was called "the Courthouse," usually the grandest building in a midwestern town. The other one was about the right distance away to be a jail. It was smaller and looked solid.

Jed went to bed early and woke up at eleven when he heard the night guards changing shifts. He watched as the new guard went to the west end of the circle and turned to the south, the side the herd was on. Gil thought it best to keep the herd away from the riverbank, so the guards could watch them better.

Jed put his boots on and strapped his gun belt around his waist. He thought he should check the north side. As his eyes became more used to the dark night, he slowly walked around the northwest part of the circle. When he had gone a little short of the rope gate, he stopped suddenly, stepping next to a wagon wheel so he wouldn't be seen easily.

It was a little too far away to see clearly, but something was out there. He motioned for the guard to come. It was Zeb, the toothless bachelor.

"Do you see anything out there?" asked Jed.

"Indians?" Zeb whispered.

"I'm not sure," answered Jed, "but I aim to find out. If you stay here I'll play a little Indian myself and crawl out close enough to see."

Jed checked his pistol and made sure there were several caps in place. With his gun back in his holster, he dropped flat on the ground and slowly crawled forward. By the time he'd gone about fifty feet he knew they weren't Oglala.

How stupid can you get, he thought. He stood up, but the couple didn't notice him. He walked back to Zeb disgusted.

"They're spoonin'," he said, "and a lot more than that."

"My gosh!" exclaimed Zeb. "Don't they know how dangerous that is out there?"

"I guess," said Jed, "that they aren't thinking about that. I think I'll try to scare them a little."

He sat on the hub of the wagon and waited for the couple to come his way. When they finally returned, giggling, to the circle, Jed went to meet them. They stopped when they saw him and started to run away. Jed held up his hand.

"Don't run, I want to talk to you." The girl was clinging to the boy's arm. Jed recognized her. She was the lonesome girl who had tried to creep into his bedroll "to talk" two weeks ago.

"Do you have any idea what could have happened to you out there?" he asked them. "Indians could have crept up from the river and your folks would have found your naked scalped bodies in the morning."

The girl shivered and the boy began to gulp an excuse. Jed stopped him. "I know what it's like to be young, and I don't care. My job is to see that you get to Oregon alive, not to bury you along the trail. If you're going to play with fire, it'd be safer to do it under your own wagon. You're lucky you didn't get scalped and you're even luckier you didn't get shot—by me!"

Jed turned and walked away.

The fear of Indians had almost evaporated the next morning in the excitement of being close to Chimney Rock. The emigrants could see the tall spire in the clear morning air and watched it loom larger as they approached. Jed stayed close to the train in the morning, but in the afternoon he rode Blaze far ahead.

Blaze was as spirited as ever after a day's rest. He was so well-trained that Jed preferred to ride him, rather than any of the others. Jed circled Chimney Rock and checked the south side before heading north on the west side of the unusual formation. Jed always found it as fascinating as everyone else did, but now he was searching for danger. He found none.

He knew the young people would like to climb the sloping cone of the base until they reached the nearly vertical column that looked like a huge factory chimney. The tip of the spire was hundreds of feet above the base, and folks often teetered backwards as they stared up, awestruck. Hawks swooped and lit on the top.

They'd probably carve their names in the soft stone, too, the way others had done. Jed grinned as he recalled doing the same thing in 1843. He guessed that the rain had probably washed his name away by now. Then he remembered helping Caroline up the base of the spire—that was the first time he'd held her hand. He shook himself back to the present.

People had been arguing for years about how high the tip of the spire was from the valley floor. Jed guessed that it was somewhere between four to six hundred feet. He wished he'd had more schooling. He knew there was a way to calculate the distance using a stick, but he couldn't recall it now. Too bad, he thought.

He turned to his job. He figured the best spot to camp would be northeast of Chimney Rock, close to the river. He expected to see a grazed-off area there and remains of a campsite from the wagon train that was two days ahead of them. He didn't. Instead, he saw something that made his skin crawl and his stomach wrench. He let the reins go slack and Blaze was off toward the burned-out debris of a wagon.

"Oh, my God!" he said. Blaze was reluctant to get close to the burned smell, so he dropped the reins on the ground and slipped hobbles on him. He tied his bandanna around his head, covering his nose with the two thicknesses. Then he walked slowly toward the wagon. Tears came to his eyes and rolled down his face to be soaked up in the bandanna. When he had seen all he needed to see, he returned to Blaze. The stench was still in his nostrils when he mounted and rode back to the spot on the trail just north of Chimney Rock.

Whipping off the bandanna, he checked out the banks before marking the campsite and riding back to meet the train. Noah took one look at his face and asked, "What?"

"The Indians got their revenge," Jed said.

As soon as the circle had formed, Jed called Noah, Chet, Sarge, and Gil together. "We'll need a few volunteers for burying detail," he told them. "And Ezra. Be sure he's along."

As soon as the detail had been formed, they walked to a spot about fifty feet south of the burned wagon and began digging. A yoke of oxen had been brought along to pull the two dead, bloated beasts a quarter of a mile off the trail.

"The smell of the fire must have kept the wolves away," said Sarge.

"There must be another pair somewhere," said Jed. "Gil— see if you can find 'em."

The men worked diligently digging the large grave, changing off every ten minutes. When the grave was finished, the bodies of three adults and an infant were rolled onto blankets.

"See that, Ezra?" asked Jed icily. "That's what Indians do to people who shoot at them."

Ezra responded by rushing to the bushes to retch.

It was easy to figure out what had happened. A pregnant woman had gone into labor. Obviously, the train had gone on without them. Another woman had stayed to help. The baby had been born, and then the band of Sioux had appeared, looking for killers. It didn't matter that the new mother was not one of them.

"They got their revenge and are probably back to their tribe by now," said Jed, "with scalps tied to their lances. I'm sure they won't be bothering us anymore."

When the bloated and scalped bodies had been buried, ashes

and rocks were placed on top of the grave. Then the men walked silently back toward their camp, heading for the river to wash the stench from their clothes. Gil and James found the two live oxen and drove them to the herd.

In the distance, young people scrambling up Chimney Rock appeared as black specks on its face, their shouts of laughter ringing in the air. They were oblivious of the horror below. At camp, the men sat silent, turning away from the supper before them, and thinking of how close they'd come to death.

The next morning the wagon train stopped at the gravesite. Chet said a few words about paying respect to all fellow human beings, whether or not their names were known. He offered a simple prayer for those who had died alone on the trail. Those who had brought the ashes from their campfires dumped them on the grave before they left. In a melancholy mood, the travelers continued west. One by one, the wagons rolled over the mound, flattening it forever.

The noon camp was not far from Castle Rock, which was about two miles south of the trail. It was a long afternoon before they arrived at Scotts Bluff. They had read about the castellated towers, the battlements, the embrasures, and the other castle-like formations in the walls of the towering bluffs.

"Jed!" said Henry excitedly. "Dey look like der castles in the Old Country! *Ja!* Joost the same."

Many of the emigrants wanted to go exploring, but Jed turned the train to the south. There was no way to pass the bluff south of the river—they had to go south of the bluff instead.

As they continued west, days were warm, but the nights were cool and the mosquitoes were not as hungry. After another few days of traveling, Jed announced that they were only about three hours away from Fort John, which most emigrants called Fort Laramie. "That means," he continued, "we're about one-third of the way to Oregon—the easiest one-third."

"That means," said Chet evenly, "that we have a difficult road ahead."

Ben pushed his hat back a little and said, "We haven't seen too much of hell yet. I reckon it's comin' up."

Since leaving the States the emigrants hadn't seen anything resembling a town, so they were excited about seeing Fort John.

"Don't expect too much from that old fort—it's not like Independence!" said Jed. "You'll be lucky to find nails!"

"Can't we buy provisions?" asked Caleb. "We're all out of spuds."

"You can get flour, whiskey, maybe some sugar, and buffalo or antelope meat—that's it," said Jed.

"I want potatoes," Sarah said crossly. "I'm tired of biscuits ever' night, and sick to death of bacon."

"Remember, Sarah," said Molly pleasantly, "Jed made sure we had plenty of provisions before we left. He never told us we could buy food along the way. You should have stretched your potatoes out a little more. Tell you what—I'll trade you a few of our potatoes for some of your pickles or jam. We're almost out of both."

The offer made Sarah a little happier and she agreed to the exchange first thing in the morning.

The train had to cross the Laramie River before getting to Fort John. It was lower than it had been in previous years, and Jed wondered if that meant a dry trip all the way to South Pass. The water was below the wagon boxes as they rode through the swiftly flowing river.

"Least it's got a solid bottom," said Gil.

Once on the west bank of the river, they could see a dozen wagons on the plain to the west. Three riders were approaching from that direction at a gallop. Jed and Noah rode to meet them and stopped when the other three reined in their horses.

"Hello, Jed," said a bearded man, who was the first to speak.

"Well, howdy, Dave," answered Jed. "It's been awhile since I've seen you. How be ye?"

"Tolerable, I guess," Dave replied.

The man beside him interrupted. "Did you pass a family

with a new baby?" he asked urgently. "I supposed they'd join up with you. Isn't that your train comin' yonder?"

"Yep, that's our train coming," said Jed. "Did you have any trouble with horse thieves along the way?"

"We might of," the man answered, "but we shot three thievin' redskins before they got the job done."

"I warned 'em—" broke in Dave.

"You have to teach 'em a lesson," the man continued. "You can't put up with that. I'm the wagonmaster and I ordered 'em shot where they was lyin' in the grass."

"We found your family," said Jed without emotion. "The parents, the baby, and another woman—scalped and bloated from two days in the sun. The wagon had been burned and two oxen shot with arrows."

The wagonmaster gasped. Dave moaned, "Oh, no."

Sarge's rage was evident on his face and in his voice when he turned to the other wagonmaster. "What kind of a miserable excuse for a human being would leave a family behind? And a baby—you think that baby could defend itself? Why didn't you listen to your guide, who knows Indians?"

The wagonmaster clenched his teeth and his face turned red, but he kept his mouth shut. The two men glared at each other in silence.

Then Gil asked, "Were there any other younguns in that family? And what about the family of the other woman?"

The third man answered. "There are two young children, a girl and a boy. They've been with my wife and me for the last few days. Their mother was my wife's cousin. We can keep the children. We'll make a home for them. The other woman was the father's mother. They have no other relatives on the train except my wife and me."

Sarge had cooled down enough to respond. "We found the other two oxen and they're in our herd. I think the family who takes the children should have those oxen."

"We can give them to you as soon as they cross the river," said Jed.

The wagonmaster said coldly, "We're ready to leave right now. As soon as we have the oxen we'll get out of your way."

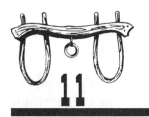

11

J ed turned toward the wagons crossing the river and Gil followed. Sarge stayed on the west bank to line up the wagons in four rows. Before all the wagons were on dry land, Noah returned to help the herd across. With the help of a few boys, he brought the oxen belonging to the slain family across the river. The three men waiting hurried on west with them, and it wasn't long before their train was going up the hill to the north.

As the rest of animals entered the river, they stopped to drink. It was the best water they'd had since leaving Ash Hollow. Jed didn't want to leave the river until the last of the loose stock had forded it, so Noah rode ahead to pick a campsite, and Sarge started the wagons moving after him. Several dozen Sioux tipis were clustered around the fort—the wagon train would have to go beyond them. Noah picked a spot a little west of where the other train had camped. The herd would be grazing a little to the northwest of the campsite on higher ground.

For the rest of that day and far into the next, the camp was busy. Noah and Henry were shoeing and reshoeing oxen and making repairs. A few tires needed to be set, so they were taken to the blacksmith shop back at the fort. The work could be done more easily there than in camp.

There was a good selection of oxen at Fort Laramie. The thin, foot-sore beasts that had been traded to the fort last year now were sturdy, and their feet were in good condition. They looked to be ready for the hard road ahead.

Those who had joined the train a few weeks earlier after their horses had been stolen wanted to become full partners of Jed's train. This kept Chet busy with bookkeeping details. The newcomers had to pay two-thirds as much for the company supplies as those who started out at Independence. Chet would use that money to pay ferrying fees across the rivers and tolls for the road over Barlow Pass. Those starting out from Independence wouldn't have to pay as much, now that the train was larger. The latecomers paid Noah and Jed one-half of their fees for the trail ahead.

Jed found time to wash his clothes and dirty blankets in the river, laying them on bushes to dry. Most of women were down at the river, too. He passed Molly and Emma on their way back to the camp.

"Water's too cold to wash anything proper," said Emma.

"Howdy, Jed," said Molly with a smile. "Water seemed just fine to me—I was just glad to get wet!"

Finding a secluded spot downstream, Jed quickly undressed, jumped in, and washed off as much dirt as he could reach. Then he put on his buckskins. Just before dark he saddled up and rode into the adobe-walled Fort John. Several Indian women and children and some half-breeds were in the fort. The women were married to the white "squaw-men" who worked there.

Jed could see that the horses were kept in the yard. The fort's oxen might graze a long way away, but horses were always brought inside the walls at night. Jed found a place to tie his horse and looked up old Misseaux, the company storekeeper. He had stopped here both coming and going for several years and knew Misseaux well.

A son of one of the founding families of St. Louis, Misseaux had bolted the traces in 1824 and come to the mountains with the young Jim Bridger. Tiring of the rugged life outdoors, he took on the storekeeper's job at Fort William in 1839 and then moved to Fort John. If Misseaux had a first name, no one remembered it.

"This calls for a snort of whiskey," Misseaux said, as he reached into a cupboard.

"Oh, none for me," said Jed. "I need to keep my mind clear."

"How 'bout some coffee then?" asked Misseaux. Jed nodded.

The men talked about the old days, when beaver were the main attraction in the mountains. "Now it's the Oregon Trail," said the Misseaux.

Jed said, "Looks like Fort Kearny's goin' to be moving farther west on the Platte."

Misseaux bent close. "I heard that the army's goin' to take over this fort. It'll be called Fort Laramie, run by the gov'ment."

"Just about everybody already calls it that, so they might as well," said Jed. "There might be problems with Indians if more soldiers come," he added. "I never had any worry with Indians until this year. The train that just left here today had bad trouble and people died, but they were plain stupid or it wouldn't have happened."

Misseaux nodded. "I heard about it," he said solemnly.

Jed said, "We got to show 'em we're strong, but friendly. No point in being belligerent."

"Got no argument with that," said Misseaux as he refilled their coffee cups.

"There's gonna be fewer trains this year," said Jed.

"Yeah? How ya figure?"

"When we were leaving the states, some trains were forming in Independence and Westport, but if there's going to be more than four coming, we sure didn't see them. A couple of them should be along in a few days. The St. Joe people who joined up with us don't think there'll be more than two trains coming from there in the next week or so."

Misseaux shook his head. "Dang it. Don't make my time hardly worthwhile."

Jed continued, "If there's going to be many trains, they'll

come later than usual. The next two weeks should give you the answer." Jed offered to pay for his coffee.

"Nope," the storekeeper said, "you bring me business, so the treat's on me. We sold some oxen today and maybe a few more tomorrow. You generally pay me purty well when you trade your skinny horses for good ones on your way east in the winter. Of course, your people don't buy near enough flour and supplies from me. That's 'cause you make 'em bring everything but the piana!"

Jed laughed and then said, "This might be my last time through here. I might stay in Oregon."

Misseaux cackled. "Naw! You mountain men allus talk of quittin', but you never do 'til you're so stove up you can't climb on a horse. You're young yet—you wouldn't be content to stay in one place. If you don't lead wagon trains, you'll go to Californy or somewheres else.

"Or maybe you have a woman on the wagon train who wants to marry you and settle you down. Is that it?" The storekeeper laughed again.

"Nope," answered Jed. "Not much chance of that." After a pause he said, "It's time I checked on things at the train so I better say thanks and goodnight. See you tomorrow."

"Sure you don't want some of my white lightnin'? It's fresh made," said Misseaux.

"No, not tonight, pal," Jed said, and with an affectionate pat on the storenkeeper's shoulder he left.

Jed was let out through the fort's gate, which was always closed at dusk, and he rode toward camp. He could hear dogs barking in one of the Indian camps not far from the fort. They reminded him of Jimmy's dog, left back in Independence, and of the dogs he'd had as a boy.

The stars seemed extraordinarily bright that night and the air was cool and fresh. The wind had died down a bit. Misseaux's comment about a woman after him to get married had stabbed him with a loneliness that made his heart ache. Would he ever find another woman to love? Would he ever have a family again?

Teen-aged girls who giggled and looked at boys like Josh with cow eyes were all that were available. His mind went to Molly. How nice it would be to have a mature woman like her for a wife. You fool, he thought, don't even think about a married woman. Think about the chores to do.

Jed circled the herd and tethered his horse near his bedroll. He lay awake for a long time, feeling sorry for himself because there was no one to love him. I'll always be alone, he thought. I'll never be really happy.

He tried to pray, but the picture of the lovely Molly stayed in his mind—her gentle blue eyes, her smile, her silky brown hair, her warmth. "Lord," he said at last, "lead me out of temptation and let me lay by the still waters."

At last he drifted off to sleep. A few hours later he awoke suddenly and raised up, sweating and shaking. He'd had a nightmare. He worked to slow his breathing, dropped back down, and thought about the dream.

Noah was accusing him of something terrible, something so terrible he could hardly let himself remember it.

He'd killed Ben!

They were hunting in the dream, but it was very dark and fuzzy. Were those Indians in a deep ravine? Jed knew that Ben couldn't see them *yet he sent Ben toward them.*

Jed cringed at what he had done—even though it was only a dream. Ben had been killed and Molly, weeping, had turned to Jed. Oh, no, he thought. Would I do that? Betray a friend? Kill someone? Noah had known the truth—that Jed sent Ben off to die, just as King David had sent Uriah to be killed so he could have the alluring Bathsheba.

Noah would never be his friend again. If Molly found out, she would hate him. Jed lay awake, sweating in the cool air, for hours.

Soon after the morning chores were finished, a party of Sioux rode into camp. Jed had told everyone to expect them, and not to be afraid since they were so close to the fort. The Indians expected food, especially bread or biscuits. Any flour used would be replaced from the company stock, so the women had baked more than usual. Della used her Dutch oven to make a big batch of biscuits. While the biscuits baked, many emigrants traded with their visitors. The Indians liked needles, hand mirrors, and steel knives. Emigrants chose moccasins and deerskin jackets. A few green buffalo hides were traded for the supple, tanned Indian buffalo robes, which would be put to good use in the freezing temperatures ahead. Many of the white folks were impressed with the Indians' fine workmanship.

Jed interpreted for the two groups when he could and helped with the trading. Sarge and Noah kept a sharp lookout, watching for anything unusual and steering the Indians away from the horses and wagons. When the biscuits were ready at last, the Indians accepted a pile of them with delight.

After the Indians had gone, Jed and Noah began inspecting the latecomers' wagons as they had promised to do. Most of the people didn't mind the inspection, but a few resented having their supplies checked out. Ezra was one. He didn't say much, but it was obvious he was unhappy.

One wagon needed a couple of tires set, so the driver hurried off to the blacksmith at the fort. Jed found that most of the oxen looked all right, and there seemed to be enough of them. He wouldn't know until later that Chet and Gil had each bought an ox for a family short of money. When Jed learned that George, the father of the newborn baby, had only one extra ox, he gladly loaned him enough money to buy another one.

Gil bought a few more oxen for his own family. "Cain't never have enough!" he hollered. His son James traded a harness for an ox yoke.

During supper Jed told Chet what a good job he was doing at handling the money and the bookkeeping.

"It's a lot more than I'm used to," admitted Chet. "I've done more work in the last two days than I did in the last two months!"

"I know," said Jed, "but from now on it won't be so bad. Of course, we do have to pay for the ferry crossings."

"We'll do it," said Chet, as he finished the last of the cornbread and gravy from his plate. He smiled at his cheerful wife Della as she handed him a piece of freshly baked dried apple pie.

Noah took a bite of his pie and said, "Della, there might be a lot of good cooks on this train, but they's sure none as good as you."

Della smiled. "Thank you, Noah. By any chance were you looking at that last piece in the pan when you thought of that?"

Chet said with a chuckle, "He's just telling the truth, Della, but I'm going to use my authority as your husband to reserve that piece to eat just before going to bed."

"Noah's right, Della. You know, I'm not much for saying thanks I guess, but it don't take apple pie to make me feel obliged to both of you for all you've done for us," said Jed. "You folks have made Noah and me feel like part of the family and that's real nice."

"That's right," added Noah. "Real nice."

As Jed was getting up from the table, Sarge strolled by.

"Jed, that other guide, Dave—what did he used to do?"

"He was a bull whacker on a freight train I was on," said Jed. "He seemed like a decent guy, a good worker if somebody told him what to do. He freighted as far as Fort Bridger and he might've gone on to Oregon on an emigrant train, but I'm not sure. On the freight train he let some pushy men insult him. I stood up for him once. I don't think he's strong enough to handle a wagon train. He should never have let that stupid wagon boss on the other train have his way."

"That's just the way I had him pegged," answered Sarge.

Jed moved on. He thought of how Sarge had taken responsibility for the train, but always listened carefully to his suggestions. He allowed Jed to make a lot of decisions that some wagonmasters would object to. Jed hoped he wouldn't make a mistake to destroy Sarge's trust.

Jed passed Ben and Molly's wagon on his way to visit Henry. Jimmy ran out to meet him. "We had pie for supper," he said.

Jed stopped. "That's good, Jimmy. You like pie?"

"Yep. Did you have some, Jed?"

"Yep, apple." He looked over Jimmy's head. Molly and Ben were watching him, smiling. He nodded and managed a weak smile back.

At Henry's campfire, Jed stopped and hunkered down.

"Tired, Henry?" he asked.

"Ach!" Henry replied. "Everyvere on mein body iss tired. So much vork. Iss gut, no?"

"Iss good, yes." said Jed. "Hope all the shoes are on tight because we'll be going over some rocky ground before we get to the North Platte crossing."

It was nearly dark when Jed returned to his picketed horse. He saddled him and led him out of the circle and rode the half-mile to the fort. He felt the urge to see Misseaux again.

After he was let in the gate, he secured his horse, bought a pot of coffee and found some others from the train to join him. He chatted with the fort blacksmith, who stopped for a cup before going to his late-evening meal and his Indian wife.

When Jed left the fort there were still a few emigrants there. He buttoned his jacket against the penetrating cool night air as he rode west. He made up his mind he wouldn't think about Molly tonight, even if it meant he'd have to concentrate on every mile of road on the way to Oregon. Jed thought he'd ride around the herd before he unrolled his bedroll, so he rode slowly in that direction.

He recognized Ben—he was herding tonight. Seeing him alone in the dark reminded Jed of his dream, and his stomach clenched.

"Howdy, Jed," called Ben warmly. "Got a minute to talk?"

Jed felt his throat close up. "No, Ben, sorry, not now," he said gruffly. "Talk to you tomorrow." He rode off, despising his coldness.

Ben's long legs kicked his horse in the flanks and he rode alongside the departing trail guide. "Whoa, Jed, this isn't like you at all. Seems like you been avoiding me, Jed, and I need to talk to you."

"All right," Jed answered glumly, "but I'm not very good company." He suddenly had a crazy idea that Ben knew what he was thinking, could see through him. He started to sweat.

They rode for a few minutes in silence. Then Ben spoke. "What I have to say isn't easy, but I have to say it anyway. First off, Molly isn't my wife. She's my sister. Now before you ask questions, please hear me out."

Jed felt like someone had hit him with a lightning bolt. For a moment he couldn't breathe and then his heart felt like exploding.

Ben was looking off at the herd while he spoke. "Molly was married to a fine man, but he died real sudden when Jimmy was about six months old. My farm was about a half-mile away so me and my wife helped her some. Our younger sister lived with her and did some of the work."

Ben paused a minute, then continued, his voice rough. "About two months later my wife died in childbirth. The baby, too. The world was not a very nice place for either of us then. Molly sold her farm and she and Jimmy moved in with me. We did the best we could—for Jimmy mostly. But it was hard."

Jed nodded, remembering his own grief and the loneliness that had clung to him for so long.

"Well, six months later a widower wanted Molly. She didn't want him or any man yet. And she didn't have to take any man, as long as she lived with me. More than once I had to interfere to protect her. We both thought we wouldn't get married again. So when we pulled up and moved farther west, we just let on that we were married. It was my idea—a stupid one, I guess—to protect Molly.

"We never outright told folks we were husband and wife, they just assumed that we were and we didn't argue. Then we got the idea to go to Oregon. We planned to be honest when we joined the wagon train, but on the riverboat up from St. Louis we heard so many stories of all the unmarried men going to Oregon. We knew it wouldn't be easy for a widow woman, especially one as pretty as Molly, so we just kept up the deception."

Jed could understand only one thing: Molly wasn't married. *Molly wasn't married!*

A herder from the north end of the herd approached them. "Is there something wrong?" he asked. "You fellers are sure talking a lot."

"No," said Jed, "everything's wonderful!"

"Wonderful!" exclaimed the young man. "What's so wonderful? We have to ford rivers, fight off insects, sweat like the devil, get soaked when it rains, and nearly die of thirst when it don't. Now we got mountains, deserts, and God knows what ahead. What's so wonderful about that?"

"What I meant," said the embarrased Jed, "is that our livestock are in good shape, our supplies are holding out, and our wagons are still hanging together. We're not behind schedule and nobody's sick—it could be a lot worse!"

The young man turned his horse around and headed back to his position, shaking his head and muttering, "Ain't my idea of wonderful."

Ben was grinning at Jed. "I had a feeling you'd think that way. I felt you were sorta building up some anger at me."

Oh, if you only knew, thought Jed. Waves of relief rolled through him. Anger, jealousy, self-pity—all the things he'd been struggling with for so long evaporated, and he grinned back.

"Ben," he said. "You're about the best friend a man could want."

He went to his bedroll and made ready to sleep. He looked at the tent where Molly and Jimmy were sleeping and wondered if he had a chance. She'd been nice to him, but she was nice to everybody.

Oh, Lord, he thought, Your wonders never cease. Thank You for lifting the burden from my heart, and show me the right path to follow.

The camp came alive the next morning in preparation for their continued long trek west. Before breakfast, Gil brought bad news to Chet and Della's table. Pat wasn't with his wagon. His wife Maude was sure he was still at the fort, drunk. She said he didn't get drunk very often, but when he did, it took a long time for him to sober up.

Jed told Gil not to worry. They'd find someone else to drive Pat's wagon. "Sarge and I'll find him and catch up to the train later. Noah'll take over for a while."

When breakfast was over, Jed and Sarge headed for the fort with an extra horse in tow. Sarge told Jed, "I've helped get a lot of drunken soldiers to their post in my day. They're all the same—sick and stupid."

The men found Pat lying under a table. "At least he's still got his boots on," commented Sarge. "Let's go."

They pulled him out and heaved him up to a sitting position. "Hey, Pat," said Jed. "It's time to go."

"Go?" mumbled Pat. "Where we goin'?"

Sarge shook his head. "Let's get him outside."

After struggling with the big man for what seemed like hours, they got him on a horse and headed west. He was not the singing, happy man he had been the night before. Instead he held on to his throbbing head glumly, in silence.

Just in time for the mid-morning stop, they reached the wagons. Pat was slumped in the saddle, held up by Jed and Sarge who were riding on each side of him. When they got to Pat's wagon, his wife halted the oxen.

"I see you've did it agin, Mister Patrick," she said angrily. "Forget about us, why don't you—just think about your own good time. Here we are a thousand miles from home and you're still playing the drunken fool."

Pat groaned and Jed tried to hide his smile. There was no seat in Pat's wagon, so the men struggled to get him between the boxes and sacks. Then the train jolted on in the bright sunlight.

Laramie Peak now seemed very close. The Oregon-bound

travelers had watched it looming larger for days. Some bluffs looked chalky, and evergreens were growing from the cracks.

"How do they do that?" asked Josh to no one in particular.

"Never saw anything like it," said Gil.

Soon they came to the steep Mexican Hill. It was much shorter than the hill leading to Ash Hollow, but still some precautions had to be taken. The hind wheels were rough-locked and when every wagon was safely down, the train continued at its usual pace.

By late afternoon, Pat—still pale and silent—was driving his own wagon. Before the afternoon was over, the wagons passed a great gray bluff covered with the signatures of previous travelers.

It wasn't far from the North Platte River, so the wagons went a little west and found a good campsite. Once they were settled, most of the emigrants hiked to the big rock to look at the many names carved there.

"Hey, lookit this!" exclaimed Gil. "Remember Dick Martin from Owensville, James? He went out in '45 and here's his name!"

"Here's one I know," called Della. "Millie Henderson! Right there—Millie Henderson, June 9, 1844!"

Before the evening meal many of the travelers had chiseled their own names in the soft sandstone.

There was good grass for the animals in this valley and by dark they were full and contented. After supper Jed headed for Gil's wagon. As he passed Molly and Ben's wagon, Jimmy ran out to him, shouting, "My name's on the big rock!"

"That's fine," said Jed. "There are lots of names there. Pretty soon we'll go by another big rock and you can write your name there, too."

"Will you tell us so we won't miss it?" asked Jimmy.

"Don't worry about that! It's so big you can't miss it," said Jed with a broad smile.

Jimmy turned to his mother and said, "Do you hear that, Mama? Another big rock!" Jed looked up to see Molly's smiling face. He smiled briefly, feeling a little embarrased, and walked on toward Gil's wagon.

The next day the wagons had to lumber up and down the sandstone hills, because the bluffs came so close to the river there was no room for passage there. The sandstone was already rutted by the weather and thousands of wagon wheels, and the pull was hard. The wagons made it to Cottonwood Creek a couple of miles from the North Platte for camp that evening. Several creeks ran from the Black Hills to the river, some with good water.

That evening Jed and Noah decided the train should stop for a day and dry another supply of buffalo meat.

"Once we pass the Sweetwater, we probably won't find many buffalo. It'd be better to dry some here," said Jed.

The next evening Noah and his hunters came into the circle with the pack mules and several horses loaded with buffalo meat. A dozen people ran to help them hang the meat on the spare reaches of the wagons, which could be raised seven feet off the ground. The nights were chilly enough to cool it overnight.

Jed made his rounds that night contently, satisfied that the trip was going well. Whatever happens next, he thought, we'll be ready.

12

Early the next morning Noah and four others left again to hunt. The rest of the train went to work cutting the thin slices of meat and setting them on the rack to dry. The meat that had cooled overnight was easier to cut thin than fresh meat. Younger children considered too small to wield a knife helped to keep the fires going. Jed was glad the wind had dropped off. Strong winds helped dry the meat, but blew the flames from the fires in all directions.

About midday the hunters returned. Two men were walking, leading the loaded horses. Ezra was the first to enter the circle. He was scowling and muttering, his face red and swollen. Not far behind was Sarge with a large bruise on his cheek.

Sarge ordered the hunters to a halt and said in a thunderous voice, "Ezra is my prisoner. I charge him with attempted murder." The crowd gasped. "What happened?" cried a dozen voices.

Noah, Josh, and Henry stepped down from their mounts. Jed waved to Gil across the camp to come immediately. Chet joined the huddle and after a few minutes Chet announced to the group, "Ezra here is charged with attempted murder, a serious charge, so we have to follow our constitution—he'll have a fair trial. He's not going anywhere, so we'll have the trial at two o'clock, after dinner. Let's get a lot more of this meat cut up before then."

A dozen men moved toward the loaded pack animals and took charge of the meat. John Lewis asked Josh what had happened.

"Ezra made the stupid mistake of attacking your dad with a knife!"

At two o'clock, the men formed a semi-circle around Chet. Women, girls, and boys under eighteen were not allowed. Chet cleared his throat and spoke, "Our constitution calls for a trial like this to be conducted by our wagonmaster, but he's the one bringing the charges, so someone else has to do it. I say we ask Jed. What do you say?"

"Aye!" called several voices.

"Are there any that say no?" questioned Chet.

There were none. Jed walked to the center of the circle. "Sarge has brought the charge of attempted murder against Ezra Baines," he began. "This is a serious charge, so let's get the story of what happened. We'll hear all of the witnesses.

"Josh, you're first. It's important to tell the truth, exactly like you saw it."

"Well, we was ahunting," Josh said carefully. "We found good hunting. Noah had Henry shoot the first buffler. Then Ezra shot one and Sarge did, too. Henry took my place holding the hosses and I got to shoot one. Ezra and Sarge had their guns reloaded and Ezra wanted to shoot some more. Noah told him to wait for a young cow that didn't have no calf with her. Ezra said it didn't make him no never mind, as long as she's fat enough. He shot a cow with a calf right beside her. Both Sarge and Noah warned Ezra never to do that again.

"We had to work fast to get the meat loaded. We had enough to load the mules with all we dared put on them and then loaded Sarge and Ezra's horses, too, and started back to camp. Along the way we came real close to some buffler. The wind was right, I reckon. Ezra said he'd like to kill an old bull to feed the wolves, so Noah gave him a yes nod. Sarge and Ezra crawled a ways, toward the herd, and Noah, he followed.

"They stopped about twenty-five paces away from where Henry and me was. They was at the brow of a hill and Henry and me couldn't see the buffler very well. There was a big bull in rifle range and Ezra got off a shot. I could see him moving and Ezra reloaded his gun real fast, but by that time the old buffler staggered and fell down.

"The only thing left in range was a cow and a calf. By now I was close enough to hear Sarge warn Ezra not to shoot. Noah said we had all the meat we need and Indians don't like us to waste their buffler. Ezra said he didn't give a damn what Indians thought, so he cocked his rifle and started to aim. Sarge jerked up on Ezra's rifle. It fired a shot high into the air. Sarge jerked the gun away and stepped back a few steps. Ezra swore and grabbed his knife from his belt. Sarge could've used the butt of that big gun on Ezra but he didn't. He just tossed it to Noah. That's when Ezra rushed Sarge with a knife. Sarge stepped to one side and kicked the knife from his hand. He was off balance and by the time he straightened up, Ezra hit him hard. That was the last time he ever hit Sarge. Sarge went to work on him with both fists. When it looked like Ezra was goin' to stay down, Sarge said he was goin' to charge him with attempted murder. I sure learned something today—no man oughta ever pick a fight with Sarge! That's all I have to say."

Henry and Noah's testimonies were very much the same. Jed asked Ezra if he had anything to say, but he shook his head.

"Well, men that's it," said Jed. "Do you have enough information to make a fair decision?"

"Sure do," called Caleb.

Jed asked for a show of hands from those who thought Ezra was guilty. It looked like most of the hands were in the air, so he asked how many thought he was innocent. No hands went up.

Chet said, "Our constitution doesn't say what sentence should be given. What have other trains done in a situation like this?"

"Some have tied the man to a wagon wheel and used a whip on his back," said Jed. "I don't like that at all. That kind of punishment just fills the man with hate. Some have banned the man from the train. But if he has a family, like Ezra has, they'll be the ones to suffer and it isn't their fault. Sometimes they give a man another chance—but they take his gun away and watch him close. If the man doesn't settle down by the time the train reaches a fort, they leave him there and offer to see his family on to Oregon. Otherwise, the family will stay with him 'til another train comes along.

"It's hard to use the same justice on a wagon train you use in the states. One thing is for sure from the looks of Ezra, his face is going to remind him for a long time how reckless he was. You men have to decide what to do, that's not my job. Let's have some suggestions."

After a few seconds of quiet there was some murmuring among the crowd. Finally a man spoke up, "If we was back home, Ezra'd go to jail, but we ain't, so I suggest we give him another chance 'til we get to Fort Bridger. Maybe he won't try anything stupid again, because it looks like Sarge gave him a good education."

There was more murmuring in the crowd and finally Jed said, "Those in favor raise your hand."

So many hands were raised, Jed didn't bother to count them. He asked for a "no" vote and only a few raised their hands.

Jed said, "Ezra, you've been found guilty of attempted murder. Your sentence is that you act right from now on or be left at Fort Bridger. Understand?" Ezra's battered face bobbed up and down.

Jed spoke again. "The trial's over. Let's get back to work." It was important to check the dried meat carefully before it was packed away. If a piece cut too thick was found, it was thrown into a pot for cooking. In a short time, one piece of moist meat could spoil a whole batch. The meat drying continued until late evening. Jed felt happy about the amount of dried meat they had on hand—it would serve them well when they got to an area of poor hunting.

When Jed came to Ben and Molly's fire on his rounds that

evening, Ben was holding a cup of coffee and asked Jed if he'd like one.

"Sure," said Jed, "it's been a long day." Molly poured a cup for Jed and he thanked her for it, looking for a long moment into her eyes.

Ben took a sip and remarked, "You did a fine job at the trial. I liked the way you let the group decide the sentence."

"I just gave them a choice," answered Jed.

"There was really only one way to go," said Ben. "We've got a long trip ahead and I'm sure we don't need any more trouble if we can help it. You know Jed, I saw Gil stop Ezra from taking a shot at that Indian chief awhile back. That could have caused your death, but there's sure not much revenge in you today."

"My job is to get as many of you to Oregon as possible and I aim to do that," answered Jed.

"You're doing a good job of it so far," said Molly.

Jed handed his empty cup to Molly, smiled and said, "Thanks and goodnight."

Jed wanted to see how Sarge felt about Ezra's sentence so he stopped by his fire. Sarge wasn't in a very happy mood.

"It wasn't what you call a military sentence," said Sarge, "but I guess it's all right. We have to think of his family. I doubt if he'll ever try anything like that again. I know Noah will never take him hunting again." Sarge showed his hands to Jed and smiled faintly. "I'd rather have sore knuckles like this than have Ezra's face."

Jed grinned. He felt better about the situation now.

When the train approached the crossing of the North Platte, Jed was waiting by the ferries that were operated by some young Mormons. Although there was really no thought of fording the river—now a fast-moving mountain stream—Jed hinted that they'd build a ferry of their own if the charge was too high. A fair price was negotiated and the ferrying started.

The ferry the Mormons used consisted of two large cottonwood dugout canoes with a platform connecting them.

It was quite stable. Two by two, the wagons were eased onto the platform. The ferry owners guided their laden craft into the deep water and the current took it from there.

The Mormons had been ferrying travelers across for more than a year and had become quite skilled at it. However, immersed in the business of loading and unloading the ferry, they didn't notice a black cloud speeding toward them from the northwest—not until a blinding flash of lightning struck nearby. Instantly a gale sprang up and caught the ferry thirty feet from the south bank. It filled Pat and Maude's wagon cover like a sail and toppled it into the roiling North Platte. Sarge jumped aside and grabbed a wheel of the other wagon, which tipped but settled back down again.

Maude, on the ferry, shrieked, and Pat inside the wagon, bellowed in concert. The emigrants watched horrified as the wagon floundered in the water.

Jed, on the south bank on Blaze, raced downstream. He pulled his lariat from the saddle, judged the wind as best he could, and threw the loop toward the half-floating wagon. The first toss missed. The second caught the front wheel.

Blaze was guided to a nearby tree, and Jed jumped from the saddle and looped the rope around it. Gradually the wagon moved toward the riverbank, as the others rushed to help pull it back on land. Pat shakily climbed out.

"Guess the Lord was with us," Chet said, surveying the sodden contents.

"He sure was," agreed Jed. "I've seen 'em go under and never come up. Don't think they lost anything but cornmeal and flour. We can make it up."

That evening Jed called the whole wagon train together to tell them what was ahead. "Before we left Independence I told you we'd have to go through hell to get to Oregon," he said. "So far it hasn't been too bad, but now we're in for a rough time. For the next few days, we'll only have one good water source and that's at Willow Springs. We'll have to fill everything that holds water here, because from here to the springs the only water we'll find is poisonous. A lot of animals have died from drinking it. It'll take every available man and boy not driving the wagons to keep the loose stock away. There'll be very little grass on most of that stretch. It'll take a lot of working together to keep from losing our stock."

When Jed headed back to his bedroll, he noticed that Ben was away from his fire. He couldn't resist talking to Molly for a few minutes. Jimmy was nowhere in sight. Jed felt a little uneasy about what he was going to say but he was determined to do it.

He stammered for a few minutes about the weather and the trail ahead and then finally said, "Molly, if we were back in Illinois and you were living in a house, I'd ask you for permission to come calling. How can I do that here? I guess what I'm trying to say, would it be all right with you if I stop by and visit from time to time?"

Molly handed Jed a cup of coffee and she took the one she had poured for herself. She sat on a stool and motioned to Jed to sit on the other one. She smiled and spoke slowly.

"I guess the calling on a wagon train has to be done in public, doesn't it? Things happen fast out here. Sure, if you want to drop by and talk, I'd be pleased to see you."

Jed felt a surge of warmth. She'd be pleased, would she? He grinned. When Jed had finished his coffee, he saw Ben approaching and said goodnight. He still felt a little strained around Ben.

When he got to his bedroll, he felt so good he couldn't sleep. He gave a sigh of pleasure and a prayer of gratitude.

13

Jed awakened at the sound of a woman's scream. He jerked on his boots and grabbed his gun belt. He buckled it on while running in the direction of the sound.

He saw George, who was on guard duty, about eight wagons ahead of him, and he hurried toward him as his eyes became more accustomed to the faint light. A lantern was coming from the other direction and Jed heard several men shouting as he scrambled over the wagon tongue to get outside the circle.

George called to him, "Fight!" and that was easy to see in the light from the lantern. Two young men were going after each other with their fists. Jed could tell they were not experienced fighters because they were not defending themselves—just swinging wildly.

Several more men carrying lanterns showed up. The light was bright enough now so Jed could see a girl with a blanket draped around her about five paces away.

"Eva, what are you doing here?" questioned a man with a lantern. He moved quickly to her and roughly grabbed her arm, leading the tearful girl away.

Jed noticed a boy step over a wagon tongue and stand beside him. Jed leaned close to his ear. "Best not to say anything now. Just watch." There was enough light from the lantern so Jed

could see the rage in the young man's face. Jed knew the reason—
he was the boy Jed had seen on the blanket with Eva.

"She's mine and you leave her alone!" Jed heard one of the
brawlers say.

"You can't steal her from me," growled the other, and they
continued to slug each other. Then, both fell to the ground.
The one on top battered the boy below him with both fists.
When he started choking the loser, Jed quickly grabbed the
boy by his upper arms and lifted him to a standing position. He
held the struggling boy tightly.

Jed heard the other boy coughing, so he hollered, "Turn
him on his side so he doesn't choke on his own blood."

Two men moved in and rolled him over. After a minute or
so they raised him to his feet. He could barely stand. He was
bleeding from his nose and mouth and a deep cut over one eye.
The men holding him up said they'd take him to his Ma. Jed
turned the winner over to his brother. He'd stopped struggling,
but was panting and gasping for breath. Jed saw his face—it
was a sorry sight.

After the others had left, George and Jed talked a spell. "I
saw it start," said George. "When one boy and Eva were coming
toward the circle, t'other boy met them with swinging fists
and they got at it right away. The girl screamed and you know
the rest. I saw her out there the last time I was on guard duty,
but I don't know which boy was with her."

"I'd seen her out there, too," answered Jed. "It was a different
boy then—not one of them."

"Well, I'll be," said George. "She sure caused a lot of trouble,
and she might be in trouble, too."

Before they left the next morning, they filled every empty
container with water from the North Platte. They gave the
livestock a last chance to drink and before pushing on into the
high desert, Chet led them in a prayer for courage.

Then Zeb said, "Wait a minute—I don't know as much Bible
as Chet and Della do, but I remember the story about Hagar

going into the desert. The Lord brought her through, didn't
He?"

"Yes," answered Della. "She prayed for water and received
it for her son Ishmael. We will, too."

"God said to Hagar, 'Fear not,'" added Chet. "We also will
not be afraid."

It was difficult to understand that the water they passed
was bad, but they believed what Jed had told them. Keeping
the oxen from the alkali pools required heavy lashing. When
the thirsty animals smelled water, they'd bellow and run toward
it. The tired men used whips and clubs to keep them in line.
The horses used to herd the loose stock were suffering, too,
from the heat and lack of water.

The white-encrusted puddles were surrounded with decaying
ox carcasses bloated beyond recognition. Turkey vultures circled
lazily overhead. The stench was overwhelming. Jed tried to
guide the wagons to the windward side, but there was no escaping
the smell of death. It was everywhere.

Women and girls began driving ox teams to free the men to
keep the thirst-crazed animals from certain death. Jed could
hear the fretful wail of the baby, Jedidiah, and Nellie's crying,
but most of the children were as silent and determined as their
parents, conserving their energy for the trek, gritting their teeth
and moving forward.

After hours of torment, the lead wagon crested a knoll and
saw Jed atop Blaze pointing to a green oasis in the sea of beige. A
cheer went up when they saw it—Willow Springs and fresh
water. Once they were gathered around the spring and refilling
their water casks, Jed sought out Molly.

"Are you all right?" he asked, leaning down from Blaze.

She smiled up at him with cracked lips and whispered, "All
right."

"It'll get worse," he said. She nodded.

The sun beat down on them as they began the laborious
pull up Prospect Hill. It was the hardest pull they could remember
and some oxen balked at every step. Sun bonnets and caps gave

only the barest shade and the sun's glare stung their eyes.

The country was desolate now, with only small patches of sparse gray grass here and there. Jed had guessed correctly— Greasewood Creek was dry, and it was still a long way to the Sweetwater. On they plodded, past the alkali pools, toward their hope of a green land.

The night camps were a strain on both traveler and animals. The hungry and thirsty animals were unruly and hard to manage in their suffering. Sleep came slowly in the heat and was broken by the bawling of oxen. Among the emigrants, tempers flared and bitter words were spoken or swallowed along with the bitter alkali dust.

When the ordeal finally ended at the Sweetwater River, the thirsty animals and emigrants drank their fill of fresh mountain water. The oxen by then were drawn and exhausted.

When the smell of the Sweetwater first drifted to them, majestic Independence Rock came into view—the great, black turtle-like granite mound that was already a famed landmark. The grass was lush on the banks of the river west of the rock. Jed said they'd camp there for a few days, so the animals could begin to recover.

First they stopped at Independence Rock. The emigrants found they still had enough energy to climb to the top, which was not very difficult. They read the names that had been carved there in previous years—famous names, like Father Peter DeSmet, John C. Fremont, Tom Fitzpatrick, and Jim Beckwourth. New names were carved with the day's date—June 30, 1848.

Jimmy proudly showed Jed his name, which Ben had chiseled into the big rock.

"Can we go to the top?" Jimmy asked.

"Sure thing," said Jed.

Jimmy put one hand in Ben's and the other in Jed's, and they climbed to the crest, where several emigrants were standing, looking over the Sweetwater Valley. Noah edged up to Jed and pointed out the black specks in the distance. No words were spoken but Ben and Jed knew they'd have plenty of fresh buffalo meat for Sunday's meal.

Jed picked up Jimmy and, pointing to those specks, whispered in his ear, "Buffalo, Jimmy. Buffalo meat tomorrow, maybe even tonight." The child was thrilled at the sight.

"Gosh, Jed, can I go on the hunt?"

"Not this time, Jimmy. Maybe another time," he said kindly.

The wagons traveled a little over six miles farther and camped on the broad south bank of the Sweetwater River, next to the granite slash cut by the river and named Devil's Gate. When the animals were unhitched and turned out to graze on the lush grass, Noah took his party hunting.

Gil hailed Jed as he was heading toward Della's fire. "The families of the fightin' boys and the girl they were fightin' over are boilin' mad at each other. Everyone's ablamin' everyone else for what happened," he said grimly. "Eva's pa is a hot-headed feller and he blames the boys' families for not keepin' a rein on 'em. It's a mess. Whatcha think, Jed?"

"I suppose they're all to blame. I can give you my answer, but I'll ask you not to repeat it. Eva wanted to climb in bed with me one night. I sent her away. Does that answer your question?"

"Yep," said Gil. "I sure hope things settle down soon. It's bad for the train to have fightin'. Those boys have some powerful sore faces—they battered each other purty bad."

"I hope things don't get out of hand," said Jed, looking troubled. Gil shook his bushy head and walked slowly away.

The hunters returned before dark with a good supply of buffalo meat. Sunday the people would eat heartily.

That afternoon Henry fastened a forge from some rocks, mud, and the bellows and grate brought from Independence. He built a roaring fire in a circle somewhat larger than the wheels, let the coals settle down and heated the tires. He and Noah reset the tires on several wagons. The dry mountain air had shrunk the wood wheels so fast it was hard for Midwesterners to believe.

The steel tires on many wagons were very loose. The supply

wagon had wood shims which emigrants rammed between the loose tires and the wood of the wheels. If the wheels soaked overnight in the river, they'd be tight in the morning. Since they'd be fording the Sweetwater several times and other rivers west of South Pass, Sarge thought they might get by without setting those tires until they arrived at Fort Bridger, but some were still too loose. The smiths cut small sections from the tires, welded the ends together, quickly jammed them on the felloes and threw the wheels into the Sweetwater. Sizzling, steamy clouds exploded from the quenched iron.

Sarge and Jed had finished checking the wagon wheels by mid-afternoon. Sarge continued to supervise the work while Jed walked out of the circle to investigate an abandoned wagon not too far away. He noticed a man—it was Ezra!—sawing at the wagon tongue.

"Ezra, wait!" Jed called.

The startled Ezra stopped sawing and straightened up to scowl at the approaching trail guide.

"This wagon is junk—they left it behind," he said belligerently. "What's wrong with using it for firewood?"

Jed fought back his anger. "Ezra," he said evenly, "the train in front of us is having trouble. They've lost some oxen and this wagon's wheel collapsed. They took what they needed— the felloes, the iron tire, the reach, canvas cover, and hoops are gone. Now, the tongue is usable, too, and somebody behind us might need one, or the axle or box. If you just start sawing away, nobody'll be able to use anything."

"So what!" snapped Ezra. "What do I care about some other train?"

Jed felt his patience nearly evaporate. "Don't you remember what the Good Book says about doing unto others?"

"Aw, it was written a long time ago. It don't mean nothin' now. I gotta take care of myself, period."

Jed turned to see Gil, James, and Will arrive carrying a patched-up tongue.

"James had a accident the other day and we had to patch up

his wagon tongue," said Gil and they put their burden on the ground. "I saw this good one and figured we might make a trade. Is it spoke for?"

"Not at all—go right ahead," said Jed.

While James and Will carefully examined the saw marks on the tongue, Gil looked quizzically at Ezra, who returned an angry stare and walked away without a word.

"I kin see what almost happened here," said James, smiling at Jed. "I'm obliged to you for watching that polecat."

"Land a goshen," said Gil, shaking his head. "Ain't that man ever goin' to learn nothin'?"

Back at the campsite, Henry quit his work before five o'clock on Sunday and went to the river with Noah and Jed to wash. On the way to the river, Henry mentioned that he had heard Molly was not married to Ben after all. He added, "Dat's eine nice fraulein."

"Yep," answered Jed quickly, "and she gave me permission to call on her."

"Ach!" exclaimed Henry.

Jed couldn't tell how Henry felt about that. Maybe he was interested in Molly, too.

"It's a good thing you're getting cleaned up tonight," said Noah, "or you'd have to stay downwind of her."

"Is it really that bad?" asked Jed.

"Yep, it's that bad," said Noah, "and I don't think I'm any better with buffalo grease and blood on my clothes. Henry's lucky—he has enough smoke from the forge in his clothes to cover up any other smell!"

Earlier in the day, a few families had heated water to bathe in. The two pieces of canvas from the supply wagon were put to good use. Stakes were driven in the ground and the corners of the canvas were suspended from the stakes. The open end of the enclosure was about two feet from the outside wheel of a wagon. A blanket would be draped over the opening for complete privacy. Women made good use of the canvas wash house all afternoon. When it became muddy around the tubs, the whole thing was moved to a dry area.

After supper, Jed, full of roast buffalo, was lying in the grass talking with Gil, when he heard the sound of a fiddle. Gil stood up in all his six-foot-four height and said, "Let's go to the worship service that's afixin' to start!"

Jed found himself walking along with Gil, without even wanting an excuse not to go. They caught up with the rest of Gil's clan just before they arrived at the gathering. The fiddler Phineas began some familiar hymns. Jed didn't know the first one, so he just listened. The next song was one of his pa's favorites—"Amazing Grace"—and he knew it well, so he joined in.

To Jed's surprise, Caleb went to the front of the group, opened his worn Bible and read several passages from the Old and New Testament. Then Chet talked about ten minutes on Psalm 138—"I will praise thee with my whole heart"—and then led the group in prayer.

Jed knew the next hymn, "Ye Servants of God," and he sang out lustily, recalling with warmth the whitewashed one-room church of his youth. During the service Jed kept glancing at Molly as she stood next to Ben, holding Jimmy's hand. How lovely she looks, he thought.

After the service, small groups of people gathered to talk until Della called out, "There's pie and coffee at our wagon. Come by and say how-do!"

The crowd moved in that direction. Jed caught up with Molly.

"Would you like to take a walk to Devil's Gate?" he asked.

"Yes, I'd like that," said Molly. "Ben can stay with Jimmy." They slipped over the tongue and underneath the chain gate of Ben's wagon and started in the direction of the towering rocks. When they were a short distance away, they saw that some of their people had gone around and climbed to the top of the near rock. The climbers looked down on the Sweetwater, four hundred feet below, as it rushed through the opening in the rocks.

"I've never done that," said Jed, "but I bet it's quite a sight."

"It's beautiful right here," said Molly.

They sat on a boulder and watched the clear water flow between the majestic rocks that towered toward the sky.

"I wonder who named this Devil's Gate," said Molly.

"I don't know," answered Jed. "Some mountain man, I reckon. It's had that name as long as I've been coming here, but I know a lot of white people came by before I did."

"It's a beautiful place to camp," said Molly. "So green and pleasant by the water after such a desolate land we passed through."

"I hate that stretch from the crossing of the North Platte to Independence Rock," commented Jed. "I'm thinking of staying in Oregon this time and not worrying with a train again. Maybe I'll get me a farm."

Molly looked up at him. "Sounds like a good idea to me, Jed," she said.

"I ought to tell you, Molly—we've got some bad stretches of road ahead. It'll be real dry again along the Snake River and there's very little grass there. The animals have recovered some since getting here, but they'll not gain all of their flesh back. They'll suffer a lot. We'll have fairly good grass and water until we get there. We're a few days ahead of most people's goal, though—getting to Independence Rock by the Fourth of July."

"I think the people are rested and ready to travel again."

"I hope so," said Jed.

"I was glad to see you at the service this evening, Jed." Molly said. "You sing very well!"

"Thank you," Jed responded. "I used to sing a lot when I was a kid. When I started trapping beaver, my partner told me that singing at the wrong time could lead to an early grave. I got out of the habit and I guess I forgot how much I enjoyed it."

The sun was only half visible in the west. Jed rose to his feet and offered a hand to Molly, who reached out and took it. As soon as she was standing, Jed released her hand and they marveled at the beautiful sunset. They walked slowly back to camp.

Jed stepped over the wagon tongue and again offered his hand to Molly. She didn't need the help, but it gave him another excuse to touch her. Jed said goodnight and, after checking the herd, crawled into his bed. He looked up into the clear sky and thought what a happy man he'd be if he could marry Molly.

14

When the train rolled in the morning, the travelers spotted another of the great landmarks of the Oregon Trail. Split Rock—actually a split mountain—loomed on the western horizon. A giant cleft in the peak descended hundreds of feet.

The emigrants had to cross the shallow Sweetwater several more times before they left it. The water was good—cold and clear. Jed had told them that the route along the Sweetwater was easier than the deep sand route to the south, and it looked as if he was right. A day of pulling in the soft sand would be hard on the oxen and they'd lose weight. Those who walked alongside would be exhausted.

So Sarge chose to follow the river. They crossed it three times in about a mile, as the trail threaded its way through a high-walled gorge. Fording it as often as they did kept the wagon wheels wet enough to keep the tires tight.

A few miles west of the fifth crossing, the wagon train stopped at a bog along the trail known as Ice Slough. Most of the travelers knew it would be there, having heard about it miles earlier, but still it amazed them and lifted their spirits. They laughed as they dug into the bog and found a sheet of pure ice.

Josh especially was fascinated. "How can ice grow like that?"

167

he asked everyone within earshot.

"You had to dig through two feet of peat to get to the ice," Jed explained. "Water from the winter snows percolates through the peat, it freezes, and the peat keeps it as cold as our ice houses back home do."

Now that they were in high country, the nights were cold, even after a hot day. As soon as the sun went down it was time to get out jackets and blankets. Some days now, it was necessary to wear a coat, especially in the mornings. The July wind blew all day long and it brought an unwelcome chill. Mornings often began with a crust of ice on the water buckets.

Soon after leaving Devil's Gate, Noah had killed two large elk, which were still providing enough meat for everyone. The hunting party had shot a few buffalo, as well.

"That might be our last fresh buffalo meat. We'll be lucky if we get a few along the Bear River," Jed said.

One morning as the wagons were traveling across a nearly level plain, Jed halted the four leading columns. He told them to convey the word back—they were now on the divide at South Pass. A cheer rose up. This was another major milestone. The emigrants could see snow-capped mountain peaks on the north but they were on a broad saddle. It didn't seem possible they were on the divide—they could have been back in Kansas Territory.

Jed told them that in just a few miles they'd be at Pacific Springs, where the water would be running to the Pacific Ocean. The East was behind them forever—now even the streams would be moving west. When they reached the springs, they camped for the night.

"Ma! Ma!" Jimmy's shriek carried over the sound of the creaking wagons.

Molly ran to her startled boy, crying, "Jimmy! Are you all right?"

Jed looked to see the crying boy prone on the turf next to the reed-surrounded pond. In reaching for him, Molly almost lost her footing. Alarmed at first, Jed quickly realized what had happened and a smile crossed his face. He dismounted and walked casually toward the pair, now both on the ground.

"I don't think this is so funny," Molly said, exasperated. "What is it, an earthquake?"

"No, Molly," said Jed. "I don't know what it is, either—all I know is every time anyone walks to this little pond, the ground shakes. When you stop walking, it stops shaking."

"Then we're safe?" she asked.

"Sure, you are. Nobody's broken through yet that I know about. Go ahead and go to the pond. I think you'll find this the best water you've had on the Oregon Trail."

Other young people had discovered the phenomenon and were amusing themselves by walking, running, and jumping on the shaky ground.

"That oughta wear 'em out pretty quick," chuckled Sarge.

In the chill of the evening, Sarge and Gil met at Chet's campfire and listened as Jed described the Sublette Cutoff they'd encounter the next day. Sarge asked Jed which route he thought was best.

"The long way—it's got good water and grass. The cutoff has a stretch of about forty miles without any water. If we take that route we'd have to travel it all one night."

Sarge shook his head, and Chet frowned.

"And we'd have to force our animals—who will be almost crazy with thirst by then—to go the last fifteen or twenty miles," continued Jed. "Then, once they get a whiff of the Green River, it's almost impossible to hold them back, and that hill leading down to the water is one of the steepest you'll see."

"If we let the folks talk it over, they'll probably be split over which way to go," mused Sarge. "I say we go the road you pick out. That's what we hired you for." The others agreed.

Jed nodded. "We won't say anything about the cutoff, and if people complain that we're not using it, just send them to me."

He stared into the fire for a moment. "Say, I heard there was an accident this morning. A wheel ran over a six-year-old boy's foot—group "E," I think. Have you heard how he is, Gil?"

"It could be worse, I guess. The wheel just got the toes. He's lucky it was in soft ground. Still, there might be some toes broke and he'll lose all his toenails on that foot. That boy'll be riding in the wagon for quite a spell!"

"It's better for something like that to happen here than along the South Platte. It's funny, but infection doesn't set in very often in this high country," Jed said. "Five years ago Doc Whitman took a steel arrowhead out of Jim Bridger's back that had been in there for three years!"

"Three *years*?" echoed Gill.

Jed nodded. "Yep. When Whitman told Jim he was lucky he didn't die, Jim had an answer: 'Meat don't spile in the mountains.'"

Jed chuckled with the others and continued soberly, "Maybe the other kids will be more careful now after this."

The others silently remembered the stories they'd heard and the graves they'd passed.

The next day the train passed the Parting of the Ways, where those heading for California would turn off. It was split in the road, and Jed guided the train to the left with no comment. If anyone noticed, they said nothing about it.

That night they camped on the Little Sandy. There must have been a rain in the mountains because the creek was running bank full, and Jed usually found the stream nearly dry.

The next day was a short drive and they camped along the Big Sandy, only eight miles from its smaller cousin. As soon as the wagons had completed their circle, Jed was again drawn to Molly's wagon. But just as he said hello, he heard a scream. About thirty yards beyond the wagons he saw a crumpled form in the sage. It was Emma, and a few yards from her, the sinuous form of a rattlesnake.

Jed raced to the scene, drew a bead on the serpent with his pistol and fired once. The head parted neatly from the body and sailed another ten yards away, while the rest of the snake gyrated violently, then twitched and lay still.

Emma's apron was empty, but several buffalo chips lay nearby. Jed stooped to the still form as Gil and Chet rushed up to join him.

"I think she just fainted, Gil," Jed called out. "I'm not sure she got bit."

Gil crouched beside his wife just as she stirred. "My leg!" she moaned. "It bit me right there—" She lifted her heavy cotton skirt and Gil pulled down her stocking. Two red marks about an inch and a half apart stared at them.

"Here's a knife, Jed," said Gil. "Kin ye do it? I'm feelin' too shaky."

"No tellin' where that knife's been, Gil. I think I can do it without a knife," replied Jed. He leaned down and drew on the puncture wounds, sucking the venom and spitting it out at once.

"Worst tastin' stuff in the world," he grumbled. "That should do it, Emma. Does it still hurt?"

"Not like it used to," she replied huffily. "Think I kin git up now. Cain't say I appreciate all you menfolk staring at my ankle like that."

"Wonder why that snake didn't announce hisself," said Gil.

Just then Jimmy brought them the body of the snake and the question was answered. There were no rattles.

"How come, Jed?" asked Jimmy.

"I've seen 'em like this before," he replied thoughtfully. "Snakes aren't fast enough to get out of the way when buffalo stampede. Mostly they get squashed and die, but some of 'em just get their rattlers pulled off and go on living. That must have been what happened to this feller."

"Well, I shore 'preciate what you done," said Gil, "even if Emma don't. I got no appetite for raisin' them chilluns by mysef."

Emma coughed. "Reckon I 'preciate it too, Jed. You're quick."

Jed smiled and bowed. "Thank you, Emma. Guess that's the nicest thing you've ever said to me!"

Gil helped the grumbling Emma back to their wagon and Chet watched them go, shaking his head. "Never have seen two different people that got hitched," he said. "He's as kind as you get and she—well, she's not."

Jed laughed. "There's just no figuring some things."

On the day the train was to arrive at Green River, Jed rode on ahead through the bitter, alkaline desert. He wanted to find out if the river could be forded, or if a ferry was available. Some years it had been necessary to chink wagon boxes and make a ferry by using two boxes as boats. This was a very time-consuming operation. Jed was happy to see two young Mormon men with a dugout canoe ferry ready for business.

"Sure, we can do it," the older one said. "Yesterday we took a whole train across."

But when Jed heard the price they quoted, he shook his head and rode along the bank until he found a place where an earlier train had started to slope the bank down to make a ford. He knew Chet would never agree to such a high charge, so he instructed the men to start making a ford.

Jed led his little brown mare down the steep bank and mounted up, continuing into the Green River. It seemed shallow enough to ford.

When the wagons approached the Green River, they halted. The ferrymen watched as about forty men with spades and shovels swarmed over the steep bank. They moved a great deal of dirt in a few minutes. Soon the ferrymen approached and offered to cut the price by a dollar a wagon if they'd use the ferry. None of the workers so much as looked up. When he lowered the price another dollar, the dirt still moved but Sarge asked the men, "What do you say to that offer?"

"Not much," said big Pat as he kept on spading dirt.

"Ain't no use atalkin," said the bushy headed Gil, "let's finish the job and we kin save some money. I reckon the next twenty trains'll be as happy as cats with saucers of cream when they find a ford they kin use."

The last remark quieted the two young men. They approached Jed.

"What price you think will make them interested?" one asked.

"They're a pretty stubborn bunch. When they get their mind made up, nothing seems to change them much. I doubt if a ferrying charge of a dollar a wagon would even stop the digging."

When the excited young ferrymen made the dollar offer loud enough for all to hear, the earthmoving suddenly came to a halt. All the men kept straight faces as they walked back to their wagons. But when the wagons were safely ferried over, a few whoops of laughter were heard, and as Jed walked around the circle while the animals were unhitched that night, he received many thanks, smiles, and pats on the shoulder.

Chet smiled broadly at the supper table and remarked, "I consider myself a good Yankee trader, but the way you worked that deal was something!"

"It almost worked too good. For a while I thought the men were going to keep on digging, no matter how cheap the toll was," answered Jed, laughing.

That evening camp was made close to the Green River. Those in "A" group gathered to talk. They were impressed with the sight of the snow-covered peaks of the Wind River Range to the north.

"What's ahead, Jed?" asked Caleb.

"There'll be a lot of steep bank creek crossings from the Green to Fort Bridger," he said. "Then some more mountains'll be coming up."

Josh asked, "Jed, did you ever trap in the Wind River Mountains?"

"Yep," said Jed. "I trapped there and a few other places."

"Tell us about it."

"I guess I could," answered Jed. "Anybody want to listen?"

Jed was answered with a chorus, "Let's hear it."

"It was in the fall of '38, when my partner Bill and me found a place to trap. Bill was an expert at finding good places by then, but it was getting harder every year to find new territory. We did find some fair trapping and had about two-thirds of what we wanted.

"Bill and I holed up for the winter with four other trappers.

We had a good shelter, but there was lots of Indian sign that year. We kept a guard out all the time, even in bad weather. That was something we didn't do other years. When early spring came, we split up and went off in pairs to get more beaver pelts. It was tough going but we got some. We didn't have any horses left, so when it came time to meet the other four trappers, we packed our spring-caught pelts to the meeting place we'd agreed on.

"None of the others were there yet, so we cached our furs and went back after our other pelts. We left a signal to our friends that we'd been there. We found our fall-cached furs all right, but we saw so much Indian sign along the way, we moved cautiously. When we were packing down from the mountain stream, we came upon fresh tracks of an Indian going down the mountain in a hurry. Bill was sure we'd been spotted and it was a lone brave going after more help. I didn't question him, so we hurried to a spot Bill found on our way up.

"It was about dark when we got into a pile of rocks that gave us some protection. Under a big tree was an empty bear den that only a man like Bill could find. He crawled in and stashed a canteen of water and a pouch of dried meat. He laid some beaver pelts on the floor and the rest of his pack on the rocky ground where we were going to spend the night. We climbed a tree about thirty paces away and hid my furs in the branches. We didn't make a fire but ate dried meat and tried to get some rest. Only one of us slept at a time and then not too good.

"Just before daybreak, Bill was sure we had company but we couldn't see anything. I was leaning behind a rock, to keep out of sight, while Bill kept watch. It was still too dark to see very much when a rain of arrows clattered on the rocks. They had been arched high so they didn't have a lot of force, but one hit me—it was a sharp, steel arrow that split my rib."

Molly gasped. "What did you do?" cried Josh.

"I jerked it out and carried it into the den, along with my rifle. If I'd left the arrow behind with my blood on it, we might not of escaped. Bill crawled in behind me and filled the opening with rock. It had just started snowing and by the time our guests got to the rocks, it was snowing very hard. I think I liked that snowfall the best of any I'd ever been in.

"It was hard to breathe with the split rib, so I lay still and took very shallow breaths. At least I wasn't bleeding much."

"Why, you poor boy!" Della said.

"Go on!" commanded Josh, his eyes shining with excitement.

"At first daylight, Bill could see the heavy snow through a crack in the rocks. He could hear the Indians around the rocks, but he understood only a few words. They were going to look for us, that was for sure. The snow kept falling, and Bill was worried that our breathing and body heat might melt a telltale hole in the snow. He covered that area ever so carefully with beaver pelts. There was enough of a opening on the other end of the den to let in fresh air and some brush there hid the hole. We stayed very quiet all that day and the next night, knowing that any noise—like a rifle barrel bumping the rock—would mean certain death.

"The next morning a few Indians were still there, so we waited until about noon, when Bill slowly moved the rocks away and crawled out. He returned after awhile, sure that the Indians had left. I dragged myself out of the den—Lord, that rib hurt!—and Bill went to work on me. He tore one of our two remaining blankets into four-inch wide strips and wrapped me up tight.

"We found lots of tracks where the Indians had looked for us. They must've figured that we couldn't have gotten away, but they evidently gave up trying to find us. They found our pack of furs in the tree and those in the rocks, so all we had left was what we had in the den. Bill was sure we couldn't go down into the lower valley the way we usually went, so we took a much harder route. The deep snow made the traveling hard, especially for me, 'cause I couldn't breathe deep. We didn't dare light a fire that night, so we ate the last of our dried meat. From there on, we had to snare anything that was edible.

"We finally made it to the first rendezvous point. Two of the trappers were at the site waiting for us, but the other two weren't. We waited several nervous days, but they didn't show up. We were just getting ready to leave when one of them made it in. His partner had been killed, and he barely escaped with his life. He'd lost his rifle and pelts. He'd snared a rabbit and ate it raw on the way. We had to fill him up on what food we had and wait around another day for him to get strong enough to walk on with us.

"Bill and I had less than half the pelts we should've had and the other two had small packs, too. We made it to the second rendezvous site and found the other trappers didn't do well either. Some mighty experienced mountain men never made it back that year. The price for our pelts was very poor then, so I was through being a trapper forever.

"There was only one more rendezvous in that area after that—in 1840. The big fur business was about over. Small scale trapping will go on for a while, I reckon, but the big business that went on for so long is over."

Jed looked around the circle. Everyone was staring back at him wide-eyed in silence.

Finally Molly said, "Jed Jones, it's miracle you're even here! I'll never take you for granted again."

The wagons followed the Green River south the next day and then the Blacks Fork of the Green all the way to Fort Bridger. They had to cross it several times, but the water was shallow and clear, and there was good grazing along the banks. There were several dry creeks to cross as well, and the steep banks made them hard to negotiate.

On the third day after leaving the Green River, they came upon the wagon train that had left Fort Laramie two days ahead of them. A few wagons had gone too long with loose tires. Two wheels had completely collapsed, breaking some spokes, and many other wheels had loose tires. The people were then cannibalizing one wagon and making shims for the other wheels.

Jed's train stopped so Henry and Noah could look over the wheels and give them advice. They didn't have a blacksmith with them, but Jed assured them they'd find one at Fort Bridger. In the meantime, they could soak the wheels overnight in the stream. Then the tires would be tight enough to make it to the fort.

When the train arrived at Fort Bridger, Jed found that Jim, as usual, wasn't there, but the fort was open for business. A few men traded for some of the fat oxen that were available there. The well-watered valley where the fort was located offered excellent grass for all of the animals, so the train spent two nights nearby.

Jed bought some clothes, paying more for them than he wanted to. He felt he needed to change his ragged appearance now that he was visiting Molly. He also paid a high price for soap, but there wasn't much trading done at the fort among the emigrants. Sarge wanted to replace a couple of lame horses. When he found good horses at the fort, he decided to buy two more for the train. With the addition of the other wagons and the larger herd, more horses were needed for herding.

Before the second night was upon them, the other train pulled up to camp nearby. The blacksmith at the fort, who had set a few tires for Jed's train, worked far into the night setting tires for the other wagons. Some welcome visiting went on among the emigrants that evening. When they compared their backgrounds, several found that they had been near neighbors back home.

In the morning when Jed gave the order to roll, the fort blacksmith was still hard at work. He said he'd probably be busy setting tires for a couple days before the wagons in the other train would be in good repair. Jed led his group along Muddy Creek and on to the divide between the Green and Bear Rivers.

Jed had a good feeling that his train was ready for the trials ahead. The shoes on all the animals were in good shape because of the work of Henry and Noah. The cattle, horses and mules were all well-fed and rested from their stay at the fort.

Now Jed's biggest concern was Aaron's health. Gil told him Aaron seemed to be getter weaker daily. The long stretch of breathing dust had been very difficult on him.

After a few days of poor grazing, the train arrived at the Bear River Valley, where they had both grass and water. Noah and his hunters were getting enough antelope, grouse, and rabbits to furnish the train with meat at least every other day.

The emigrants were now in the land of the Shoshone, and they saw small bands of them occasionally. On two visits, they traded with them the few goods they still had. There was no trouble except the time that it took to complete the bartering.

Gil stopped by Molly's wagon one evening, looking for Jed. "I'm worried about Aaron," said Gil. "He insists on drivin' his oxen, even though Annie or one of my kids has had to hep him yoke 'em for the last week. He isn't strong enough to lift the yoke alone. The last time he did guard duty, over my fussin', I had to hep him mount the hoss. I told him these boys kin drive his oxen but he says he'll drive 'em as long as he kin."

"I've been watching him," agreed Jed, "and I don't see how he can go on much longer."

The air became cool very quickly that night, so Jed said goodnight and turned in early. His bedroll, like Noah's, served well in all kinds of weather. It was a heavy canvas strip nearly four feet wide and fourteen feet long. On top of the canvas was a three-foot-wide chunk of buffalo robe with the hair side up. One thin and one heavy blanket completed his bed. In rain or snow, he could pull the rolled up canvas over him.

His boots and extra blankets were stored below his feet. The chunk of buffalo robe made his bedroll a little heavy, but it was both comfortable and warm. He'd still get wet in a heavy rain but the two thicknesses of canvas kept off a lot of water.

The next day along the Bear River route was quiet. Jed rode leisurely ahead of the train, scouting a good campsite. He was leading the column as it arrived at the site. The circle was about half completed when he heard a loud "Whoa!" The shout went up and down the line and all the wagons stopped.

Jed galloped to Gil's group of wagons and saw Gil's tall frame bent over a man on the ground. Jed jumped off his horse and ran to them. It was Aaron. He had fallen in front of the wagon and both wheels had run over his neck. His head had been almost severed. Men came running to help, but there was nothing anyone could do.

Gil stood up and when his voice was under control, he said, "I talked with Aaron at the afternoon stop. He was sittin' on the hub of the front wheel spittin' blood. When he could talk a bit, he told me he wasn't gonna last long. His wish was that we not lose any time buryin' him. He asked me to do it at night, if necessary, and keep goin' to Oregon. He didn't have to ask me to see his family through to Oregon, he knew we'd do that."

Gil's voice cracked, so Jed continued, "We should honor his request. Let's circle the wagons and dig the grave. In the morning we'll pay our respects before we drive on."

It was a sad group of people who did the chore of burying that night. Gil's family had been close to Aaron's for years, so they did all they could to help his widow. Gil told Annie there'd always be a driver for her oxen. His boys would take care of the oxen, carry the water, and gather the fuel.

The next morning members of the train again gathered around the grave. Chet read Scripture, and Gil was given a chance to say a few words about his friend. He looked to the clear blue sky for a few seconds as if asking for Divine guidance.

"From the time Aaron was a boy, he was always one you could depend on to do what was right. He was a good husband, father, neighbor, and friend. Although he was never strong from the time we left Independence, he always did his job. He did his last night herdin' job when he was so weak I had to hep him on his hoss. He drove his team till the last, often holdin' onto the closest ox's yoke with one hand and a staff with the other. We pay our respect to his life this mornin'.

"I think the best thing we kin do to honor his life is to work together, to do the best job we kin and do our share of the hard work there is before us. He gave ever ounce of strength he had to get this far. That's all I gotta say."

Chet gave a short prayer and the people slowly returned to their wagons. When the train moved on, they could see the Sublette Cutoff join their trail near Sublette Creek. The train went northwest and crossed Smith's Fork of the Bear River. It flowed from the east and the water was good. Jed told those at the evening encampment that this had been the main area of the trapping industry.

When the train drew near to Soda Springs, Jed had a good campsite picked out and they found evergreen trees to use for fuel. Soda Springs was actually a cluster of phosphate cones, many spouting water. Steamboat Spring and Beer Spring were the most famous.

The travelers were overjoyed to find the bubbly water and filled their casks, then scrubbed up. After he was presentable, Jed got out the clothes he'd bought at Fort Bridger. They were plain work clothes but they were clean.

That evening felt special to Jed. He asked Molly to take a walk with him. So many people were gathered around the huffing, puffing, Steamboat Spring that the other side of the circle was almost deserted. The herd was quite far off, where the grass was plentiful and they hadn't yet been brought in close for the night watch.

The couple was alone for the first time since their walk to Devil's Gate. They walked to a clump of evergreen trees and sat on a fallen tree, talking about the beauty of the place.

Then Jed said, "You know I plan to stay in Oregon when we get there this fall. I've helped a lot of people get to Oregon— I figure I should enjoy some of that good farmland too, before it's all filled up. If I wait too long, it might be too late to find choice land."

Molly didn't say anything, but she smiled. Jed reached for her hand and she turned to look at him. He continued in a husky voice, "I've enjoyed our visits the last few weeks. It makes me realize my wanderings have made me miss a lot of things that people in the states take for granted." He paused and searched Molly's pretty face.

Molly said, "I've enjoyed our visits too. Now that it's over, I'm glad Ben and I quit living that lie. We were shielding ourselves from the world. It was all right for awhile, but we carried it on too long."

Jed stood up, gently pulled Molly's hand and she stood to face him. Jed's voice was just above a whisper, "May I kiss you, Molly?"

She didn't make a sound but she moved to him and he bent to kiss her gently. After a moment they pulled apart and looked into each other's eyes. Then her lips came to his again. His arms went around her and he brought her close to him.

She spoke softly. "I want to laugh at myself, Jed. When we started this trip, I was afraid of you."

"Afraid? I thought you were mad at me!"

"Oh, I was mad when you wouldn't let Jimmy take his dog. And you seemed so tough—forcing Pat to do his job and giving Bill a haircut in the middle of the night. But I also saw you risk your life to save a child and stop the train for a day waiting for a baby to be born. I know you care enough to push us when necessary and give us rest when we need it. I heard of your caring for Ezra's family—and he could have gotten you killed! You've done extra guard duty and all sorts of things to make life better for those of us on the train. So here I am in the arms of the man I once feared and I'm enjoying it!"

Jed's eyes turned to the herd moving in their direction, and he turned back to Molly. "I gotta get back," he said reluctantly. They kissed quickly and hand-in-hand they returned to the circle.

The wagon rolled west the next morning, past Sheep Rock, and turned north to leave the Bear River, passing through desolate country. Jed told them they should reach Fort Hall in four days, so they pressed on. There would be good grass around Fort Hall.

They were then in Snake Indian country. The Oregon-bound

visitors didn't do much business at Fort Hall, because it was owned by Hudson's Bay Company, and Americans still had a smoldering hatred of anything British.

"No, sir!" said Sarge, when John Lewis asked if he could look it over. "Your grandpap would roll in his grave. He fought them redcoats, remember."

The train followed the Snake River southwest for more than two days and then the trail gradually turned west, past the mouth of the Raft River. That valley carried California-bound travelers away from the Oregon Trail—Jed's train continued to the west.

When "A" group gathered to talk that night, Gil said he was reminded of a story. His youngest son was telling his grandfather about the sermon the preacher gave that day about Noah's Ark.

"Grampaw, were you on Noah's Ark?"

His grandpa smiled and said, "No."

"Then how did you keep from drownin'?"

Gil got a lot of laughs from the group with that one, and he couldn't resist telling another one.

"My old neighbor back in Kentucky liked to tell this story. They had a granddaughter who came to live with them one summer. The nine-year-old watched her granny bake bread a few times, but hadn't paid as much attention as she should of. When her grandparents left her alone one afternoon, the little girl thought she'd surprise her granny. She stirred up a batch of bread. But it didn't look right to her. Of course, she forgot to let it rise. She knowd her grampaw didn't like to see food wasted, so she thought she better get rid of the stuff. She got a spade an dug a shaller hole back of the house in the garden. She dumped the dough in the hole and covered it with a little bit of dirt. She got the pans all washed up and was sure that was the end of it.

"When her granny and grampaw got home, they saw a small mound in the garden and they thought it moved some. The grampa loaded his shotgun and walked close to the mound. When he saw the dirt moving more, he blasted the mound thinkin' he'd kill a gopher. There was dough scattered all over the place. I guess the old man was riled a little then, but by the time he got to tellin' me about it, he was laughin' so much he could hardly get it all told. He said he was covered with dirt and bread dough from head-to-toe."

Gil's stories were good medicine for the weary travelers.

The next day the train left the Raft River Valley and circled at Marsh Creek. The desert was fairly level without many grades to climb. The hot days and the lack of grass and water strained humans and animals alike. The animals were suffering from lack of water and losing weight fast. The dry desert air chapped lips. Buffalo tallow helped ease the soreness, but it collected the blowing dirt and eventually became rancid. Bonnets kept the sun off women's faces, but the hot dry winds took a toll. Only the desire to get to Oregon kept the tired people trudging forward day after day.

Jed felt it would have been foolish to waste the energy of the horses by trying to hunt in this area, so Noah led the train. Jed walked alongside the tired travelers all day. He started at the front of one column and visited briefly with each wagon group as he gradually walked to the rear of that string of wagons. Most people weren't in the mood for conversation, but he tried to cheer them up as he walked along with them. He knew from other years that riding a horse alongside added to their misery.

Sometimes the promise of plentiful water in the future brought a weak smile to their painful lips. Others just nodded slightly and endured their suffering in silence. Della's mouth was moving. "Lead me beside the still water, Lord," she whispered. "Let my cup run over."

When Jed finished the first column, he moved to the rear of the next group and worked his way forward. When he caught up with Gil's clan he walked beside his eldest son James, who looked glum. His bride wasn't in sight.

"Martha's sick again this morning and she's lying in the wagon. The last couple weeks have been mighty hard for her. She walks most afternoons, but the mornin's she feels poorly.

I know you cain't look back, but if we had it to do over again we shoulda waited 'til we got to Oregon to get married. I'm worried we could lose the baby, so I tell her she kin ride most of the time if she don't feel like walkin'."

"That's right," said Jed. "You don't have much weight in your wagon and you have good oxen, so tell her I said that riding is the right thing to do if she don't feel up to walking."

Jed was glad he didn't tell James of some of the similar situations he'd seen in prior years and the sad outcome.

The black walls of the Snake River in this area were very high and rose perpendicular to the ground. All the water in that river couldn't help them, because they couldn't get to it. Farther on, the weary travelers turned northwest and followed Rock Creek until they finally found a good place to ford it.

The train was so close to the spectacular Shoshone Falls and Twin Falls on the Snake River, they could hear the roar of the water, but most of the travelers were so exhausted they didn't want to waste energy to see them. When the train moved west of Twin Falls, it had to turn south to follow the bend of a creek with steep, rocky sides. Later they found that the south bank of the Snake was not as steep, so they could make better use of the big river. For a while they enjoyed traveling close to the water. They had a chance to trade the Indians fishhooks for fresh salmon, which was baked around an open fire that night. Most people ate their fill.

"Boy, that's the best fish I ever et," said Josh.

"Once you've had salmon cooked this away you'll never forget it," Jed answered.

When the Snake River made a loop to the north and came back the southwest, the wagons left the valley and cut across to the northwest. As they approached the Three Island Crossing, they descended a long steep hill to get near the river. Noah and Jed had scouted ahead and forded the river to check its depth. If it had been a foot deeper, they might have had to stay on the south side and take the torturous route over the barren hills.

Other trains had made their wagon boxes into boats to ferry across, but there was danger in that, too.

Jed had planned for this crossing, and many of the wagons were carrying large blocks that could be placed between the bolsters of the wagon gear and the boxes. This would raise the wagon boxes as much as twelve inches. The boxes were lashed tightly to the running gear and the loads in the wagons were made level to keep the boxes upright.

At first, about six wagons crossed a slough to the first and largest island at the lower end. The water wasn't very deep there. Four yoke of oxen were then hitched to the lead wagon. A fifty-foot chain was taken from the supply wagon and fastened to the chain of the lead yoke. Two yoke of oxen were placed at the end of the long chain and the wagon was ready to cross.

The family owning that wagon climbed in, and Jed gave the signal to start. Noah and Jed drove the two leading yokes of oxen far out in front from their horses and two more riders controlled the oxen close to the wagons. When the long chain to the lead oxen tightened, Jed dropped his upraised hand and the oxen all began to pull.

The second crossing, the widest, would be the hardest. It wouldn't touch the third island, now barely out of the water. Noah and Jed headed the lead oxen far upstream. The current was strong, but they kept the oxen facing it at an angle. The force of the current against the running gear of the wagons wouldn't be as likely to upset it if it flowed back at an angle. If they crossed at right angles to the current, there was more danger of the back of the wagon sliding downstream. If that happened, the wagon could jackknife from the animals and overturn. It was very important to keep the oxen aligned with the wagon.

The well-trained oxen responded satisfactorily to the shouts of the horsemen or the crack of a whip near their heads. The elevated wagon boxes stayed just above the rushing waters, and the people inside understood the need for high-wheeled wagons. Six yoke of oxen were necessary to fight the strong current. When the lead pair gained the bank and scrambled up, their pulling chain slackened a bit, but once they walked on solid ground they pulled all of the weight of the wagon.

When the first wagon was up on the level area, there was another wagon and twelve more oxen ready to go. The oxen making the first trip could rest a few minutes and the second wagon was taken over with a fresh set of eight to twelve oxen. Then the rested oxen recrossed the river and pulled the third wagon over on the north bank. When each set of twelve oxen had made three trips, the first six wagons were on the north bank. The blocks from the first wagons were taken back to the big island to be used by the other wagons. The tired animals were turned out to graze.

The riders mounted fresh horses and the fording continued. The bottom of the river was very solid but a few times a small ox was swept off its feet for a second or two. The water missed most of the wagon boxes by several inches, but occasionally touched the bottom of one. While the other riders changed off, Noah and Jed worked alongside the lead oxen for each crossing.

After twenty wagons had crossed, it was evident it would be impossible to get all of the wagons across before dark. Sarge decided that the remaining wagons would camp on the south side of the river that night. That created a problem because the barren area on the south bank didn't have enough grass for the stock. The oxen from the last wagons and the loose stock were driven across to the good grass on the north bank.

John Lewis rode one of their well-trained oxen to lead the herd because he had once ridden him while swimming a river in Missouri. The ox would go anywhere John Lewis asked him to. A half-dozen horses and riders kept the herd from drifting downstream. Careful attention of the riders was needed to keep the weaker animals from being swept away in the strong current.

When the last wagon of the day had crossed, the tired horses that had made so many trips across the river were turned loose to graze.

After the wagons were circled on the north bank, Jed and Noah rode into the ring and dismounted, limping. Their legs from the knees down were cold and stiff. They had worn moccasins to save their boots.

"Jed, I bet your feet are the cleanest they've been since we were here last year," said Noah.

He laughed along with the others. "More'n I can say for you, you varmit."

Molly brought them each a cup of hot coffee and their thanks brought a smile to her face.

Sarge asked what system other wagon trains used to get across.

"Some of them chain a lot of wagons together," replied Jed, "and they go across that way. It works, too, but there can be a big problem if a wagon overturns. It's hard to stop the train fast enough to help the people in the overturned wagon and they can pull others down. It's easier to get help to the one wagon than a whole train."

"Sure went smooth," said Sarge appreciatively. "Any more like that, Jed?"

"One, but it won't be as hard."

The next morning the oxen from the wagons of the south bank were sorted into a herd. With a group of horse riders surrounding them, John Lewis led them across, riding his big gentle ox. The river had risen a few inches during the night, so all the wagon supplies were carefully checked. Jed warned each family to make sure their flour and anything else that shouldn't get wet was placed at least a foot above the wagon floor. Even with the endgates caulked, water could seep into the boxes. The deeper water made the crossing more difficult than the day before.

This time, a hundred-foot rope was tied to the lead yoke and the other end fastened to the yoke of John Lewis' big oxen. John Lewis rode one beast leading the wagons through the dangerous channel. Although the rope slackened when they were in the deepest part, it tightened before the wagon entered the channel. John's powerful oxen were then in shallow water where they had solid footing. They kept the rope tight while the other animals were struggling to keep their feet in the strong current.

When the dangerous crossing of the wagons was completed and all of the wagons were on solid ground, Sarge said to Chet, "Once again Jed's knowledge of this trail has paid off. That was better done than any army crossing I've seen."

"I can say amen to that," answered Chet.

When the wagons finally moved away from the river, the people had a feeling of accomplishment: they had crossed the treacherous Snake River safely. Jed hadn't the heart to remind them they would have to do it again. The train headed in a northwesterly direction, winding around hills to avoid climbing them. This was dry country with little grass. Fine dirt blew into the wagons and soon everything was covered with the flour-like dust. Those walking beside the wagons couldn't escape it. Their clothes and hair were covered with it.

"Pickin' up a little weight!" said Gil. "My beard's gettin' so heavy I can hardly hold my head up."

The old complaints of parched, sore throats and cracking lips were back, coughing was heard all night long. The grass was coarse and dry but the livestock ate it—there was nothing else. The train struggled on through the dry, hot, dusty days.

They passed some hot springs, crossed Rattlesnake Creek, and finally John Lewis sang out, "Trees! That's trees ahead!" They had arrived at the Boise River. Stretched out below them were thousands of cottonwoods on both banks, extending to the horizon from east to west.

15

The Boise Valley had good grass and plenty of wood. The train stayed on the south side of the river until Jed found a good fording place. After the crossing, it was a day's travel in a northwesterly direction to Fort Boise.

It was near dusk when the shadowy fort came into view. The fort itself was dark—there were no outside windows. Jed knew the old Frenchman who operated the trading post would be nearby. When the fur trade died, the French trappers had nowhere to go but on the payroll of the Hudson's Bay Company.

Now they were close to their old friend and enemy, the Snake River. Again preparations were made to ford it, just west of the fort. The bottom of the river was solid but the water was an inch or two shallower than at the first crossing. There were two islands at this crossing also.

The travelers crossed easily and then headed north by northwest. They struggled over Keeney Pass and on to the Malheur River. Jed knew that "Malheur" meant "bad luck" in French—it certainly had been that for the wagon train that turned west there, away from the main trail, in an attempt to find a shortcut through the dreaded Blue Mountains. Jed escorted his train by a hot springs nearby, then kept them moving north.

There was nothing to fuel the noon fires except sagebrush.

The fires flashed quickly and then cooled before the coffee was warm. Later in the day the travelers came across coarse grass and willows in the river valley, a relief from the sagebrush desert.

Jed promised that the trail, which angled almost due north, would be rough the next day and it was. The country was broken, but soon they emerged on a level plain, sunburned, with eyes watering and throats rasping from the alkali dust. The humidity dropped, the temperature rose, and the animals bellowed and brayed for water.

That evening the train crested a knoll and there below them was the Snake River. This would be their last view of it, at Farewell Bend. The grass wasn't good in this section and the livestock suffered. The starving animals, in search of food, tried to get away. The herding force had to be doubled. Just before dark a dozen men and boys went on foot to corral the hungry herd in the circle. It would have been impossible to keep them from scattering in the dark of night. The usual night herders would be busy trying to keep the oxen from squeezing between the wagon tongues and the chain fence.

Jed checked the horses and mules that had pulled the two wagons from Independence. The mule owner had added two more sturdy mules at Fort Bridger, so he now had a total of eight. They had been getting along fairly well, but the last few days had ganted them up a lot. The old bachelor with his eight horses had traded the four thinnest ones at Fort Bridger for four well-fleshed ones. He was getting by, but he told Jed it hurt him to see them get so hungry. He had hoarded one bag of oats on the long journey and that evening he fed his horses the last of it.

Noah and a few others pushed on early the next day to the Snake, where they were able to bag enough rabbits and other small game to provide some fresh meat for the train. The hot, dusty trail was hard on both humans and animals, but at least the people had enough food. That evening there wasn't much talking or joking around the campfire for the weary travelers.

Sleep was difficult because of the constant bawling of the hungry cattle.

The next evening, after another long plodding march, the folks of "A" group silently began forming a half-circle around Chet and Della's fire. Their faces were drawn and haggard, their hair matted and their clothes caked with dust.

Chet looked at the dispirited group and said, "Maybe we ought to remind ourselves of why we're going to Oregon. I'll tell you why Della and me are going and then maybe the rest of you'll do the same."

He paused a minute and then began, "When I heard about the free land in Oregon, I was interested right away. My Yankee father always said that when opportunity walks in the door, you ought to stand up to greet it. We heard many good things about Oregon. We wanted to go while there'd still be choice land available. Della, you want to add anything?"

"Oh, the mild climate and how easy it is to grow fruit and vegetables. I thought it'd be worth the hardship of getting there to enjoy the beautiful valley," she said. "Illinois winters are too hard on a body."

"Caleb, you're next. Why're you going to Oregon?" asked Chet.

"The free land, of course. One of my brothers went out there two years ago and wrote back about how much he liked the valley," he answered.

"What about you, Sarah?" asked Chet. She turned to look at her husband, who was holding Nellie on his lap, and with her usual blank expression answered in a monotone, "Whither thou goest, I will go."

After a few seconds of silence, Chet turned to their son Josh. "Would you do it again if you got the chance, son?"

"Yep," was his answer. "It's been hard work, but I've seen a lot of country, and there's more to see yet. It's been a great adventure. I've enjoyed hunting with Noah and I've made some real good friends, too." He looked at John Lewis as he spoke.

Ben was the next to speak. "Most of my reasons have been

given but I could add something. I thought Oregon would be a good place to make a fresh start. What do you say, Molly?"

"I'm going to add another reason. We lived in Illinois, where there isn't slavery except on the passing riverboats. We have relatives who live in slave states and we've heard some terrible stories about it. But I've heard some abolitionists talk and they scare me—they talk about rioting and taking over the government by force. I hear there's none of that in Oregon."

"I agree," said Chet forcefully, "and I can't see how people can call themselves Christians and buy and sell human beings. You're next, Sarge."

"I've been in the army most of my life and I've been away from home too much. I want to put all of that behind me and be a full-time farmer in Oregon. John Lewis has done a man's work since he was thirteen years old. He and his ma have done most of the farm work without my help."

He looked at Molly.

"You're right about slavery—it makes me sick. A small percentage of the population owns most of the slaves, but they're very rich and powerful. Slave owners are politically very strong. I'm afraid we'll see the southern states withdraw from the union so we have two small countries or we'll have a civil war. If we split into two nations, we could easily be overpowered by a European country. If we go to a civil war, only God knows what will happen. I don't want to see John Lewis going off to war to fight his cousins. One thing's for sure, we must keep Oregon a free territory. Perhaps someday it'll be a state."

Once Sarge was silent, Jed could see the effect his words had on the group. Mary shook her head when asked to speak and John Lewis did the same. The somber crowd's eyes were all on Gil, who had joined the A group that evening.

"Well, I got a story for you tonight but it won't make you laugh. I guess I might say that with a clan of ten kids and a daughter-in-law we'll get a good-sized chunk of Oregon when we get settled. We've talked about goin' to Oregon for years but what happened last summer cinched our decision.

"I got word from my sister that my ma was real poorly. My ma had been livin' with my sister since Pa died. It was a fur piece to my sister's place, so I hurried there alone. I was lucky to get in a good day of visitin' with her before she slipped away. At the funeral, I saw a boyhood friend of mine I ain't seen for years. He wanted me to visit him, so I told him after I visited my brothers and sister a day or two, I'd come.

"When that day came, a big two-seated carriage pulled into my sister's yard pulled by two beautiful chestnuts. It was the fanciest rig I ever seen. The high steppin' team was driven by a light-colored slave. My friend Jim and me rode in the back seat. Emma and me named our first born son after Jim because we was such good friends when we was boys. Jim moved away when we was fifteen because his father had come into the land Jim now owned. We had a good visit reliving our boyhood days on our journey of three or four miles to his plantation.

"I was amazed at the size of his mansion when we got there. It was a huge house with white columns in the front and giant trees in the yard. Jim ordered the slave to drop us off at the house and the only words I heard him say was, 'Yes, Massa.'

"We crossed the porch and Jim showed me into the parlor. With all its fine furniture, it was bigger than the whole downstairs of our house. I was glad I had on my one-and-only suit and even then I felt out of place. We did some more talkin' of the past and I was really enjoyin' myself. A little later some of the older children came in the parlor, including two boys the same age as my two oldest. His wife and the resta the children came in and I got to meet all nine of 'em. They was all dressed so well it made me feel purty shabby. We had a good get-to-know-you visit, and it wasn't long before the youngest was sittin' on my lap. His wife Becky was a real nice lady, did her best to make me feel at home.

"When it was time for the evenin' meal, we went into the huge dinin' room. Jim sat at one end and Becky at t'other end of the long table. Some of you might find this hard to believe, but I didn't talk much while we was eatin.'" A few of his listeners smiled.

"The reason for me being quiet was all the fancy silver on the table and bein' served by three slave girls. Only one of 'em was really black and one of 'em was so light colored I couldn't believe my eyes. I could see the cook—who was very black—through the doorway and when we left the table, I could see the carriage driver eatin' at a table in the kitchen. We had a nice supper, including pie with a lot of whipped cream on it.

"We went back to the parlor and I told a few stories which had 'em laughin' and Jim entertained with a couple more. I told 'em of our plannin' to go to Oregon, and they couldn't understand that at all.

"I got the idea they felt they were livin' in a heaven on earth right there and wouldn't move for nothin'. When the others had retired, Jim showed me to the spacious guest room.

"I'd eaten too much supper and couldn't sleep, so after awhile I got up and went down one of the stairs to get outside. There musta been at least three stairways. The one I took brought me out to the side of the house. I walked around the area for awhile, but I thought I best not get too far away. They was about a quarter moon that night and I could see the overseer's house behind the big house and the slave cabins too. I could also see the big barns and t'other buildings that made up the plantation. After walkin' for awhile, I sat down in a comfortable seat under the trees."

Gil stopped talking for a few seconds and looked around at the women, who were watching him intently. "It's hard, but I just gotta say this. It was downright shameful how Jim and his overseers and big boys treated the slave girls." Gill stroked his bushy beard with both his hands and looked at the ground. "They was half-white slaves born ever' year on that plantation. It shore made my blood run hot. I gotta admit Jim talked kinda plain the next day because we'd been good friends when we growed up together. We had such a terrible fallin' out you wouldn't think it possible but we did.

"I was still madder'n hell when I got home so we all decided for sure to git goin' to Oregon where there ain't no slavery. I best not say nothin' else cause I get riled just thinkin' about it. I think slavery poisons a man's mind, and I agree with Sarge—a war's acoming, someday."

The light of the fire shone on the furrowed brow of the big man when he stood up. The usual smiling, joking Gil was frowning when he said goodnight and walked away. The rest of the group sat silent for a minute or two and started to leave.

"Wait," called Chet. "I don't like us going off like this. I wanted to raise our spirits and now everybody feels worse than they did before. I know what Della and me like to do when we feel this way—say the 91st Psalm, especially this part—" He began in a strong voice,

"I will say of the Lord, 'He is my refuge and my fortress, my God; in him will I trust." Della joined him,

"Surely he shall deliver thee from the snare of the fowler, and from the noisome pestilence.

"He shall cover thee with his feathers, and under his wings thou shall trust; his truth shall be thy shield and buckler."

Molly and Mary added their voices. "Thou shall not be afraid for the terror by night; nor for the arrow that flieth by day,

"Nor for the pestilence that walketh in the darkness; nor the destruction that wasteth at noonday." Jed felt the old, familiar words come to his lips.

"A thousand shall fall at thy side, and ten thousand at thy right hand, but it shall not come nigh thee.

"Only with thine eyes shalt thou behold and see the reward of the wicked.

"Because thou hast made the Lord, which is my refuge, even the most high, thy habitation; there shall no evil befall thee, neither shall any plague come nigh thy dwelling."

There was a moment of silence, and then Chet said, "Amen."

The next day the road again led north and called for a hard pull. The gaunt animals suffered as they strained at their traces. The desolate terrain looked scorched and the trail became even more rugged. They entered the narrow, rock-strewn gorge of the Burnt River.

Someone called out, "Hey, Jed! Is the road ahead anymore like hell than this?"

"Hang on, Joe," he said. "We're almost through the worst of it. There'll be grass ahead."

The train followed the trail out onto a dusty, alkali flat, and when the lead wagon struggled around a hill, Jed called a halt.

"What is it, Jed?"

"Look!"

Many of the emigrants came forward to see where Jed pointed. A long decline led into a sylvan valley of grass and toward more hills in the distance. Over those hills they could see the outliers of the Blue Mountains.

The emigrants stood in awe while the animals waited, unattended. There had been a great change in the ox teams since leaving Missouri, when the fat, half-trained brutes had to be watched every second. Now they stood silent, thin enough to show their ribs, and glad to get a chance to rest. They'd stand still for a long time with nothing moving but a twitching tail.

The travelers returned to their wagons and prepared for the long downhill route before them. This was a gentle hill, sideling in places, and Jed urged the men to keep a sharp eye on the tilting wagons. In the valley they found good water. They camped and the tired animals found good grass.

The train had traveled all day on the previous Sunday in the dry area, so the wagons didn't move the next day. After the chores were finished in the morning, most of the people rested without even cleaning up. Many of the men who usually shaved regularly had a week or two of whiskers on their faces. All their clothes were so dirty they would've been embarrassed back in the states, but now they didn't care. Most of the women were napping in the morning sunshine. The children, who usually played on the days the train didn't move, were sound asleep.

In the warm afternoon, the camp showed more signs of life. Women washed clothes and some of the men shaved. The people had a chance to bathe. By the time of the evening meal, everyone looked more presentable.

Jed finished the toy he'd been making for Jimmy. It was a wooden figure of man supported by four strings attached to a piece of wood. Called a dancing jack, it delighted the lad after he learned to work it. Jed's heart was warmed a half-hour later when he noticed Jimmy showing Nellie how to make the man dance, saying proudly, "Jed made this for me!"

When Chet and Noah had finished their coffee, Jed said, "I think now's the time to distribute the trade goods the company bought in Independence."

Before Chet could answer, Noah remarked, "I wonder if some of those who complained about the company buying too much stuff there will gripe when they've got something to trade for the dried salmon the Nez Perce have. I know most folks don't have any trade goods left."

Chet smiled as he put his cup down and walked to get Sarge. Jed took only a few minutes to get the tall Gil to the supply wagon, where Chet and Sarge had the trade needles and fishhooks placed on the tailgate. The count of the big salmon hooks proved they had enough, so each wagon could have several. They divided the hooks, needles, and thread into five different piles on the tailgate and then the men headed to the wagons to pass them out. The emigrants were told that there'd be at least one more chance to trade before they arrived at the Willamette.

"We'll trade with the Nez Perce Indians before we get out of the Blue Mountains," said Jed. "And maybe the Cayuse after that." "The Cayuse?" asked Sarge. "Aren't they the ones who murdered the Whitmans?

"Yes," answered Jed sadly. "I still don't understand it. They had helped the Cayuse for years."

It was almost dark when the dishes were finished. Some of the travelers gathered around the fire Noah had built and Jed told them the story of the Whitman Mission.

"They established a mission in that valley more than ten years ago. They had a nice spot to raise crops and gardens and they taught the Cayuse to farm. They also taught some of them English.

"The Whitmans were the kind of people who'd help anyone—Indian or white. He was a doctor, you know, as well as a missionary. And Narcissa, she was beautiful, inside and out. She loved to sing and she loved children. When Oregon-bound travelers ran low on food, they could always go to the Whitman's to get supplies.

"From what I understand, a number of white people came down with the measles last year and then the Cayuse got it from them. Many Cayuse died, but not many whites did. For some reason Indians die like flies from common diseases like measles.

"The Cayuse—some of them were about to become Christians by then—were sure Dr. Whitman was poisoning their children because they weren't good enough Christians. In a fit of rage they burst into the Whitman home and murdered Marcus and Narcissa. The Whitmans had taken in several children—their own daughter had drowned several years earlier—and some of those kids at the mission were killed, too. Almost sixty of the children were taken hostage."

"Mercy!" cried Della. Molly covered her eyes.

"The Whitmans were remarkable people," continued Jed. "They were the first to bring wheels this far west—that was 1836. Their first wagon broke down, so they made a two-wheeled cart from it and continued on. Narcissa and Eliza Spalding—another missionary wife—were the first white women to cross South Pass and Oregon Trail this far. Marcus went back east in the winter of '43 and brought back a large group of people that spring. He sure wanted Americans to settle the West.

"That was my first trip to Oregon. We all made it—875 people in all. I got to know Marcus, and I can't say enough good about him. He was probably the greatest man I've ever known. And he was killed by the people he had helped the most. I can't understand it," Jed finished huskily, "maybe you can."

"No, I can't, either," said Chet. "Of course we know the Lord works in mysterious ways. Maybe we shouldn't even try to understand it."

The next day the train crossed the Powder River and climbed the hills overlooking a most unusual valley—the Grande Ronde. As they descended into the nearly flat, nearly round saucer in the middle of the Blue Mountains, Jed told them it was about twenty miles across. Mountains surrounded it in every direction.

The emigrants camped by the rushing Grande Ronde River, which was lined with towering lodgepole pines and firs. Jed assured them they'd have plenty of firewood for the next week.

When the moon rose over the wagon train that night, there was very little activity. The night herders silently watched the animals, nearly a mile from the circle, where they found better grazing. Most of the tired people were asleep in their tents or under the stars in their bedrolls. A few were sitting by a dying fire with the last coffee of the day in their hands.

The following day was a work day to prepare for the rest of the journey. Shortly after daybreak, a band of Nez Perce Indians rode up to the circle. Jed greeted them and led them into the circle to trade. The emigrants were surprised at the color of their horses. Most of them had never seen horses like that. Some of the ponies were white and covered with small black spots, and others only a few spots on their rumps.

The trading was enthusiastic on both sides, if brief. The Oregon-bound people ended up with a lot of dried salmon, and the Indians went away with fishhooks and needles. Jed had said that the Nez Perce were good people to deal with.

Gil remarked to Jed as the Indians rode out of the circle, "I've saw dogs that color, but never horses."

"They're called Appaloosa," said Jed, "but don't ask me how to spell it."

The wheels of some of the wagons that had been bought in Independence were in bad shape. The tires had been set in Fort Laramie, but now were coming loose again. The wheels had been made of green lumber, and the hot dry air had shrunk the wood so much it'd be dangerous to continue into the mountains. The loose tires could fly off. Major repairs were needed.

Once again Henry put a forge together, using the metal grates and some metal sheets along with rocks and mud. The end of the bellows was stuck into the opening in the rocks under the grate and the forge was ready to fire up. This well-planned operation required several men to help.

Some cut firewood. Others removed the wheels from the wagons and placed them flat on four or five rocks. When the iron tires were removed, Henry used his round measuring wheel about six inches across to roll around the wood rim to measure its circumference. Then he measured the inside of the metal rim and determined how much smaller the rim should be. He made marks on the inside of the rim with a chisel and then placed the tire in the fire on the forge.

The blacksmith coke they had carried all the way from Independence proved to be very valuable now. While this was heating, the anvil from Henry's wagon was placed on a large, flat rock and the hardy—a heavy chisel with the sharp side facing up— was placed in the square hole of the anvil.

When the tire was heated to about white hot temperature, that spot on the tire was placed on the hardy. With a strong swing of a hammer, Henry cut the rim apart. The ends of the rim were placed in the forge again and heated to the right color to weld. Henry put flux powder on the hot ends of the rim and two men held the rim with heavy mitts as the ends overlapped to the chisel mark.

Henry used his hammer to weld the ends of the hot metal together. It was very important to have the heat just right to get a lasting weld. When he was satisfied it was welded right, he had them hold the widened area (that had twice the metal of the rest of the rim) on the hardy. With the careful use of the hammer the protruding hot metal was cut off. The rim was placed on the anvil for shaping the part of the welded section. The rim was left to cool for a few minutes. When the welded part had cooled down, the entire rim was placed on the fire.

The fires had been burning for a long time so there were a lot of coals to heat the iron until it was red hot. The wood rim of the wheel was swabbed with a wet sack when the rim was hot enough. Two men with long tongs placed the hot rim on the wheel and a couple of men with hammers drove it in place. Smoke rose from the wood rim, and as soon as the rim was on, the wheel was thrown in the river. For a few seconds steam clouded their vision. When the wheel was cool, the rim was tight enough to make the rest of the journey without any problems.

Henry checked the first wheel to make sure he hadn't cut too much out of the rim. If that happened, the wheel would be dished too much and it wouldn't stand the jolting trail that awaited them. One forge could do enough work to keep several fires going to heat the rims.

At daylight Noah left to hunt deer, but he was back before noon, empty-handed. He took over the forge work so Henry could eat dinner and get some rest. The other men took turns eating and the repair work kept going steadily. A few wagons needed other repairs, and all the wheels were greased. This job had occurred every five to seven days since the wagons left Missouri. Buffalo tallow had been added to the grease buckets when they were in buffalo country. This insured enough grease for the wheels all the way to Oregon.

That evening the people of the five "A" wagons talked awhile around the big fire. There was plenty of wood available so it wasn't necessary to skimp. They recalled the sagebrush they'd been using for fuel.

"Sure smelled good," said Mary.

"Yes, but I didn't like all that smoke in my eyes," said Molly.

The next day was Sunday, and the wagons didn't move at all. The animals needed to rest before the strenuous climb ahead.

Children picked huckleberries, which the women made into delicious pies. It was a time to catch up on rest and bathing. Jed asked Noah to trim his beard and mustache. As Noah got out the scissors, he asked, "Is this some kind of a special day? You're so fussy about your looks! You've got your new duds on, too."

"I'll have to wear them from now on—or wear my buckskins. My other clothes are nearly worn out," Jed said glumly.

After supper Jed walked slowly around the circle until he heard the fiddle announcing the worship service. He joined the crowd moving toward Chet's tent. During the hymn sing, he sang when he could remember the words, the rest of the time he just listened.

Afterward, Jed walked back to the wagons with Molly, Jimmy, and Ben. When they reached their campsite, Jed pulled out a small wooden horse from his shirt and gave it to Jimmy. He had carved it out of a chunk of pine earlier in the day.

"Oh, Jed! This is really fine! Thank you!"

When it was nearly dark, Molly and Jed left for a walk. Once outside the circle, Jed took Molly's hand and they headed for a grove of trees. Then he pulled Molly into his arms and kissed her gently. She responded warmly then laid her head against his chest. Jed rested his chin on the top of her head. He could feel the softness of her hair, which hung to her waist. They stood for a while in silence. Jed hoped this closeness would never end.

He raised his head slightly and spoke. "Molly, this has been a good day. I think most people are rested up now. They seem to be in a lot better mood than they were a week ago."

"Yes," answered Molly. "We were all exhausted. A week ago we didn't even care how dirty we were. Even Della, who is so clean with everything, looked the worst I've ever seen her. I know that I looked terrible, too, but no one else looked much better. It's nice to be clean again. You look so handsome with your beard and mustache trimmed!"

"Why, thank you," said Jed. "You look beautiful tonight,

Molly. Your hair is like silk."

She moved willingly to Jed's slight tug on her hands and they kissed again. Jed's next words came out with an effort. "Molly, there's something I have to tell you. You lost your husband. . . well, there was someone I lost, too. A woman, her name was Caroline—" Jed felt a lump in his throat and stopped.

Molly's face showed her concern. Tears filled her eyes. "You don't have to tell me, Jed," she said gently. "Not if it hurts too much."

He cleared his throat. "I want to," he said. "We were married—on the trail—in 1843, the first year I went across. She was a widow, like you, and she had a little boy, like Jimmy."

Molly looked at him in wonder.

Jed nodded. "Yes, strange, isn't it?" He paused a minute, then continued. "His name was Nathan. We made plans for the future, like every married couple does, and I loved being a pa. We were real happy."

"And then?" Molly asked softly.

"And then the Columbia River," Jed said flatly. "They both drowned in the rapids, only two days away from our new home. I haven't talked about it to anyone else and I don't let myself think about it much."

Her arms drew him close to her. They stood in silence for several minutes. Then Jed said, "Molly, getting to know you has made me happier than I can say. Just being close to you these evenings and days is wonderful. Even though we've been so busy we hardly had time to talk, it was nice just to see you.

"My greatest desire now is to get us all to Oregon where I can build a good home for you and Jimmy. I want to stay and farm in Oregon. Molly, I love you. Will you marry me when we get to the Willamette Valley?"

"Oh, yes! Jed, I love you, too." She snuggled closer and Jed felt his whole being wanting her. He put his cheek against hers and they held each other for a long time without saying anything. Jed could feel Molly's tears of joy against his cheek. He realized to his surprise that some of those tears were his, too. He suggested they sit on a nearby log.

Jed put his arm around Molly and she spoke softly. "I'm glad you had Caroline, even if it was for such a short time. Now I know you understand how I feel. I loved Jimmy's father very much. He was a good man and everything was nearly perfect until he died so suddenly. For a long time I never thought I could ever love another man like I loved him.

"You've made me so happy. I love you so much, Jed, I'll do everything I can to be worthy of you."

Jed took both of her hands in his. "We've both missed out on so much real living these past five years—you've been hiding behind Ben and I've been hiding along the trails. After Caroline, I vowed never to give my heart away again. But I have."

Molly kissed him, smiled and said, "Me, too. I think we have to risk it."

The happy couple talked quietly and then headed for Molly's tent where Jed held her close again and kissed her goodnight. He headed for his bedroll feeling the happiest he'd ever felt. On Monday morning the weather was clear when the rested animals started the long pull out of the Grande Ronde. The travelers were in good spirits as they made their almost ten-mile trek that day. They camped that evening where there was a little grass. Jed knew the next day would be very hard, so the animals should eat as much as possible. That evening he approached Noah.

"Noah, I promised to stand up with you when you get married. Would you do the same thing for me?"

"Would I!" exclaimed Noah, "you bet I will." He stuck out his hand to Jed and then gave his good friend a bear hug. "Molly is a fine woman. You're a lucky man, Jed. I'm happy for you both."

There was no snow yet in the Blue Mountains but the next day the going was very rough. There were times when they had to double-team the wagons to get them up the steep grades. The second trip up the hills left the thin oxen exhausted. A few minutes' rest was needed before they could continue.

The travelers were awed at the sight of the huge trees now surrounding them. After traveling so many miles without seeing a large tree, these were impressive indeed.

By evening it was quite cool, so everyone got out their jackets and coats. Jed put on his old beaver cap. Josh admired it.

"Did you trap it yourself?" he asked.

"Yep," said Jed. "And sewed it up myself, too. Maybe it's not as fancy as the top hats those dandies wear in New York City, but it's good enough for me."

When Jed was walking around the camp that evening, big Pat stepped away from his campfire to talk to him. "I never got around to thank you for getting me back to the train from Fort Laramie. I don't usually get that bad, but when I do I'm no good to anyone. I'm obliged to you for not leaving me at the fort."

"Don't mention it, Pat," said Jed. "You would of done the same for me."

"I hope so. Glad we got this extra stock, and that was your idea, too. We sure need them in these mountains. I was wrong to think we didn't need to guard them. Now I know they're the most important things we've got."

Jed nodded. "No need to dwell on the past. You've done a good job, Pat—you've always been there when heavy work needed to be done. Whether it was grave digging, moving rock off the trail, cutting wood or repairing wagons, we always count on you." The two men shook hands and Pat returned to his family.

The next day was much the same: Hard climbing on the steep grades and uneven ground. Several wagons broke axles and the train had to stop to fit the spares into place.

Some reaches broke and the wagon gears pulled apart letting the front end of the wagon box fall to the ground. That meant unloading the supplies and lifting the box up enough to back the front end with a new reach in place under the box.

Pat's great strength came in handy at times like that. So

many reaches had been replaced at one time or another, that it proved Jed right in having so many extras along. If they didn't have enough reaches or axles to get through the Blues or the Cascades, they at least had plenty of trees around to make new ones.

The wagons struggled up the mountain and when they reached the pass, Jed told them they'd be going downgrade. The travelers stood and looked down on the Umatilla Valley before they started down.

"Thank God we didn't run into snow," said Chet.

"So far," Jed said. "We still got the Cascades ahead."

The wagons proceeded cautiously down the trail to the Umatilla River and followed along its south bank. Jed, riding ahead, marked out the camp circle along the river and stepped down from his tall horse. He removed Blaze's bridle bit and let the hungry horse graze.

"You'll have tender grass when we get to the Willamette Valley, instead of this bunch grass," he told Blaze. "You sure have changed since I first rode you back in Independence—all for the better." Jed held the reins with his right hand and scratched behind the horse's ear with his left. He smiled, "Guess maybe I've changed for the better, too."

His thoughts kept him occupied while he waited for the train. I didn't have any goals then, he mused, but I sure do now. When Molly and me get married and start making a home in the valley with Jimmy and live next to the good people on this train, I'll become a solid citizen! Jed laughed out loud at his last thought and then felt a twinge of pain as he recalled the great plans he'd had five years earlier when they crossed the Blue Mountains. Caroline, Nathan, and his plans had all drowned at the same time. This time they would use the Barlow Road and the cursed river would not claim his family again.

He heard the wagon train approaching and then saw it moving slowly through a cloud of dust. Without looking at the first driver, he led them in the circle. Then he looked up and his broad smile faded at the sight of the grim faces he encountered.

More trouble, he thought as he wheeled Blaze in the direction of the "A" group.

Molly, Jimmy, and Ben were there—they were okay—and he could see the others, except Della and Mary. When Chet's oxen came to a stop, Chet ran to the back of his wagon and Jed could see Mary's head. He jumped from his horse as Chet helped Mary from the wagon then jumped in himself. Mary met Jed, and Molly joined them. Mary's usually strong voice sounded weak as she said, "Della is very, very sick. I just don't know what to do for her—"

"What happened?" demanded Jed, his heart hammering.

"She took sick at our afternoon stop so I've ridden with her since then. She spent most the time vomiting, or trying to, and she's very weak now."

Molly's sad eyes met Jed's for an instant, then turned to Mary. "What can we do to help?"

"We need to get the tent set up and move Della from the wagon as soon as possible. The wagon is so crowded and it's a real mess now. She needs some air."

Sarge appeared and helped Jed set up Chet and Della's large tent. Sarah brought clean blankets and a pillow. Then Mary, Molly, and Chet carried Della into the waiting tent. Jed got a glimpse of Della's deathly white face as she was placed inside. Ben hurried with the water and towels that Molly had ordered. Chet left the tent for a few minutes and found his oxen already unyoked. He stumbled for words while talking to his friends before returning to his desperately sick wife.

Sarge, Gil and Jed moved away from the tent to answer the many questions from those stopping by to inquire about Della's condition. Jed assured them that this was not cholera. They were out of cholera country.

While the rest of the camp went about their evening chores, Sarge, Jed, Gil, and Noah kept a vigil about twenty feet from the Della's tent. They didn't know what else to do. A half-hour later Molly emerged from the tent and from her expression they feared the worst. She collapsed in Jed's arms and was unable to speak for a few seconds. Finally the words came in a whisper. "She's unconscious—we can't reach her. She's just barely breathing."

Jed said slowly, "As long as she's still alive, there's hope. I've seen some mighty sick people recover—let's not give up hope."

Molly dried her eyes and turned toward the tent, while the four men looked at the ground. The sober-faced Gil spit a long stream of tobacco juice and said, "It must be something she et—but what? She can't tell us now."

Sarge moved a small rock around with his right boot and said, "We don't have a doctor to help us either."

"And Doc Whitman's gone," said Jed bitterly. "He would of come though, in a minute."

Chet emerged from the tent and moved to his now silent friends. His troubled face looked far older than his forty years. "Before she blacked out, Della said it was poison mushrooms or toadstools. She's always been so careful about picking the right ones at home, but she must have made a mistake in picking some in the Blue Mountains. She knows I don't like mushrooms, so she just ate a handful raw."

Chet's friends waited for his next words. They were slow in coming. "I . . . I feel so helpless. I can't do anything but pray."

Gil's long arm reached out to Chet's shoulder before he said, "Mebbe that's the best thing to do. There'll be a lot of prayin' done tonight, my friend. You kin count on that."

"Thanks, Gil." Without another word he returned to Della's side.

Jed rubbed his forehead and said, "Back in '43 we had some very sick kids in the Blues from eating bad berries. Doc Whitman told us then that if you eat poison mushrooms or get toadstools by mistake it's pretty serious."

"What's the outcome likely?" asked Noah hurriedly.

Jed frowned, looked at the ground and said softly, "Some wake up in a day or so, some never do."

There was only one fire going near the "A" group wagons that evening. Sarah amazed everyone by coming alive. She baked dozens of biscuits and fixed gravy with chunks of venison. Caleb invited them to eat at their table, a few at a time.

"Won't do Della no good if you skip a meal," he said.

Mary and Molly refused to leave Chet, so Caleb brought plates for all three of them. No one ate much. Not even Noah did justice to Sarah's efforts.

Sarah kept the fire going and the coffee pot on far into the night for those keeping vigil. Chet didn't leave his wife's side, and his lips kept moving in a heartfelt prayer. "Thy will be done, Lord," he repeated, tears streaming down his cheeks.

The group that had gathered near their tent began to sing softly,

"Oh, God, our help in agest past

"Our hope for years to come;

"Our shelter from the stormy blast

"And our eternal home."

Sleep didn't come quickly to most of the adults on the train and those keeping vigil didn't even try to sleep. Molly and Mary took turns staying with Chet at Della's side. It was past midnight before Noah and Jed finally moved their bedrolls close to the sick woman's tent.

Mary took Molly's place about an hour later. Jed and Molly walked slowly around the circle. They talked very little. Molly said, "Della taught me to give thanks for all things, no matter what, but it's hard to give thanks now."

Jed held her close for a few minutes, then they separated to get some rest. When Jed returned to his bedroll, Noah was still wide awake. In a voice that sounded forced, he said, "Della's been like a mother to me. She's as nice a person as I've ever known."

"I won't argue with you about that, my friend. She makes everyone feel good—like they're special."

When the camp began to stir at daybreak, Della was still alive but still in a coma. Sarge decided that the train wouldn't move until noon.

Gil said grimly, "We might be digging a grave by then."

The words were barely spoken before they heard Noah yell, "She's awake! She opened her eyes!"

He ran toward them shouting over and over, "She's awake! She's alive!" He only paused a few seconds in front of Jed before continuing around the circle with his happy message.

Jed's face lit up as he hollered, "Yahoo!"

"Hallelujah!" cried Gil as he slapped Jed on his shoulder.

"I'll say amen to that, Gil!" said Sarge jubilantly, throwing his hat in the air.

And the three friends stopped for a moment to give a silent prayer of thanksgiving. Sarge's right hand stroked his mustache and passed over two days' of dark stubble before he scratched his neck. "We still better wait a spell to see how she does."

The others agreed. Jed said, "I feel like I just dropped a hundred-pound weight from around my neck." His tired eyes mirrored the stress of the long night, but he smiled broadly at his two friends. "This could be a good time for folks to trade with the Cayuse Indians for fresh vegetables!"

Sarge laughed. "You never waste a minute, do you?"

When the wagons reached the best ford of the Umatilla later in the afternoon, Jed led them safely across. They did a little trading with a small band of Umatilla Indians, then continued on west and southwest. Afer two days of travel Della was still weak, but was able to sit up and drink a little gruel. She never tired of thanking people for their prayers and praising God for her recovery.

On the third day from the Umatilla, the emigrants had their first glimpse of the snow-capped Mount Hood. Jed told them that they'd be able to see the mountain most of the time on the rest of their journey.

"It's a lot farther away than it looks from here," Jed told them." I reckon it's 150 to 160 miles away as a crow flies."

"Well I'll be," mused Gil. "You must be joshing us, Jed. It

looks like three or four days travel to get right close to it."

"We'll be lucky if you can see the sun shining on the west side of the peak in less than two weeks."

"You never been wrong yet," said Gil. "Course maybe this is the first time." The tall man slapped Jed on the shoulder saying, "Let's get goin'! I want some of that there snow."

When the travelers returned to their wagons, Jed gave the signal and they moved west once more.

A day later the wagons crossed the John Day River, where they camped for the night. The clear stream was only ankle deep. Jed explained the route ahead at the campfire that evening. "We'll have a full day of travel tomorrow to get to Spanish Hollow. The next day you'll get to see the mighty Columbia River and some terrifying rapids. Then we'll leave it and go on the Barlow Road clear to Oregon City."

"Tell what this Barlow Road is, Jed," said Josh. "I heard of it."

"Sam Barlow started building the road in 1845. I've used it the last two years. It's a toll road and well worth the cost, compared to rafting down the Columbia. That costs money too, unless you build your own raft. It can also cost lives and property."

He caught Molly's eye and smiled. This time they'd all make it all the way home.

16

On a clear sunny morning the train rolled northwest for about eight miles before turning southwest to Spanish Hollow for the night's camp. At noon the next day the travelers received their first glimpse of the mighty Columbia River. They had heard many stories about the great river and now they could see it for themselves. From that height it appeared as a wide brown ribbon flowing peacefully to the west. There was no hint of the raging torrent it would become in just a few miles.

Gil turned from the river to look at Mount Hood. He grinned at Jed. "That mountain looks a heap bigger when we get closer to it, but it still looks a long way off. Maybe you's right after all, Jed."

"Mount Hood fools a lot of people," acknowledged Jed. "It's that way every year."

When they arrived at the mouth of the Deschutes River the next day, they found they'd have to ferry the wagons across. The river was too deep for fording. They felled some trees, cut off the branches, lashed the trunks together, and floated across. Immediately after reaching the west bank, they climbed a steep hill, further taxing the strength of the animals. Some of the milk cows that had gone dry because of the sparse grass were used to pull the wagons, giving the tired oxen a rest.

The banks of the Columbia River were impassable west of the mouth of Deschutes, so the train went southwest for a full day. Then the emigrants turned south, made a loop to the north and one to the south until they once again came close to the river.

Jed surprised the travelers with the announcement that when they made camp that evening, a few Cayuse Indians would be waiting to sell or trade them fish.

"I thought they were on the run after the Whitman Mission massacre," Ben said.

"Most of 'em are," said Jed. "But I imagine a few still want to trade with whites."

"How do they know we're here?"

"Indians know everything," said Jed.

"How can that be?" asked Josh.

"They know everything that goes on up and down the river," he explained. "Fort Vancouver will get the word about us in a few days. We're the first train of the season, you know."

The Cayuse indeed were waiting for the train with fish and potatoes. It was a treat to have potatoes again. In no time, Della had the fish fried, the potatoes cooked, and the biscuits baked. Dried apples were simmering in a saucepan over the fire. Noah and Chet had just sat down when Jed joined them. Della took the other stool and said the table grace with special gratitude for not having to eat bacon.

That night Jed asked the emigrants to take one last check of their supplies. Most of them thought they had enough to get to Oregon City. Some said they might run out of coffee, and their dried buffalo meat would soon be gone. Mary discovered that the bacon she'd packed in bran was still all right but the rest of the bacon was rancid.

As they relaxed later around the fire, Ben said to Jed, "Tell us about the old route to Oregon City, before the Barlow Road."

"All right," he replied. "We're now at the Dalles of the Columbia, and you'll see those awful rapids if you go near the water. This used to be the end of the line for the wagons. They were usually put on rafts made from pine logs, and there had to be portages along the falls and rapids. The animals were taken along the riverbanks.

"One thing about the river route to Fort Vancouver—there was always help waiting at the fort. Dr. John McLaughlin, the British factor who runs the fort, would send help to anyone who needed it, whether they were British or American. Those of us who supported the American Fur Company weren't supposed to like or trust him, but we sure heard a lot of good things about him.

"The sight of his snow white hair and his huge size might make a grizzly bear turn and run, but it was said no one ever left his place hungry. He staked a lot of Americans, too, in start-up supplies on credit."

"Ha!" said Sarge. "Bet the Brits loved that!" He laughed.

"Going the old way, when we arrived at the mouth of the Willamette, we went south to Oregon City and 'the promised land,' as some folks called it. I prefer the Barlow Road—it's much safer—but when we're struggling down some of those steep grades, you might cuss me for taking you this way."

The next morning the Columbia River and its beautiful scenery were left behind. They headed due south into the dry land. After the mid-morning stop they wound their way through large rolling hills in a southeasterly direction.

At noon Gil said to Jed, "According to the sun, you was takin' us back to Missouri this mornin', but now we're goin' southwest, so you must of changed your mind."

"If I'd taken you in a direct route, you would've been cussing me instead of joking me," replied Jed. He slapped his tall friend on the shoulder and, pulling his watch from his pocket, said, "We better get on the move. We'll be going south most of the day and a little south-by-southwest before we get to our campsite."

As Jed mounted his horse to start the train, Gil remarked,

"Guess I'll have to keep follerin' you whichever way you go. It's too late to turn back now!" He turned and took long strides back to his wagon. In a minute the wagons were rolling.

That evening, camp was made along a creek. As was his usual routine, Jed left the supper table to walk around the herd. To save his horse's strength, he let Blaze graze in the circle instead of riding him. He talked with each of the first two herders and then approached Sarge's son John Lewis.

The herding was easy there, so John Lewis dismounted and let his horse graze on the dry grass. Noah considered both John Lewis and his friend Josh expert hunters. They were also good drovers. Jed thought that either one would have made a good mountain man a few years ago. They were smart enough to have stayed alive when the going was rough. The old adage was that there were no stupid mountain men: They wouldn't survive very long.

"Some people say the soil looks good on these hills," said John Lewis. "They think you could grow grain here. It's pretty steep to farm, but I noticed the trails don't wash as deep as they do back in the states. Are the rains lighter here?"

"They don't get any rain to speak of here in the summer," answered Jed, "and they get just gentle rains in the winter and spring. The Cascades catch the heaviest moisture and only lighter rains get this far. There's good grass early, but it's all dry now. It's possible these hillsides could be farmed, but when you see the Willamette Valley you wouldn't want to try it here. This is Indian land anyway, so I don't know if it'll ever be farmed."

Jed turned back toward the circle and was surprised to find most of the folks from the "A" wagons plus Gil waiting for him. By the serious look on Gil's face, Jed knew there was something troubling him. Jed joined the circle of solemn people, and Sarge started talking.

"We've got something to discuss, so I suggest we sit down."

Some people had brought stools, but most of the men sat on the ground. Sarge turned to Jed. "You might not know what's going on. I'll start at the beginning. A little while ago Gil told

Chet and me that Eva's in trouble. It seems that she can't hide her morning sickness from her father any longer and he's ordering her out. She doesn't know who the father is—it could be one of three young men. Her father claims she's not his daughter anymore and says she's gotta leave his wagon—you know her mother died two years ago. Della's with Eva now.

"Eva's so desperate she was about to walk off into the night. Chet and Della want to take her in—they'll make a home for her when they get to the Willamette Valley. We thought everyone should know what's going on because we're all pretty close by now."

When Sarge paused, Sarah said, "I don't want the likes of her around Josh."

"Oh, Ma!" exclaimed Josh. "Don't worry about me. I know enough not to touch her."

Caleb asked, "Why do you want to take her in, Chet, when her own father is kicking her out? She ain't no good!"

"I think her father's wrong," answered Chet. "She's sinned, but she's a child of God as we all are. Jesus said to the woman at the well, 'Go and sin no more.' When another woman was about to be stoned, Jesus said, 'Let him among you who is without sin cast the first stone.' I don't think any of us is without sin—I'm sure not.

"Jesus also taught that if we expect our Father to forgive us, we must practice forgiveness ourselves. I believe He was right in saying that He hated the sin but loved the sinner. Can we do less than that? Eva is very troubled. Her father tied her up like an animal after the fight by the Platte. She needs love and care now, and I'm asking you to try to make her feel welcome in this group. It won't be too long till the end of our journey and then Della and I'll try to do our best for her."

Chet looked at each one sitting around the circle as he talked. Most of them met his eyes, but Sarah looked away.

"You can count on Ben and me to do our part," said Molly. "We can share our food."

Mary nodded. "As usual, Chet, you can preach a sermon

in a few words and after what you said, I don't think any of us who call ourselves Christians can refuse to help."

Chet said, "Thank you. I'll go get Della and Eva."

"I'll go with you, Chet," said Molly, and they left the circle.

When Molly returned, she came to Jed. They walked to the other side, where they could talk, and Molly said, "You didn't say anything tonight, but I'm guessing you approve of what Chet and Della are doing."

"Yes, I do," said Jed. "I just didn't have anything else to say. I've found that people can decide what to do without my interference. It was the right thing to do, but I wish I could have prevented what happened in the first place. I can help get the train over the mountains and I can find water, but I can't stop people from making mistakes. Perhaps I should have tried, but I didn't. When I first saw her with that fellow it might have already been too late."

"What could you have done?" asked Molly. "I know you wouldn't let Eva in bed with you—Ben told me about that. If you had gone to her father then, would he have believed you? Of course not! He would have blamed you."

"I know that, Molly, but it bothers me when people mess up their lives so bad. Two years ago something worse happened."

She looked at him, questioning, so he continued.

"One night a man came back to his wagon in the middle of his guard duty to get his chewing tobacco. Just as he got there, he saw his wife leave their tent with a man. He took a knife and followed them. When he found them, they were so busy they didn't see him coming. He crept up on them and cut the man's throat, spilling blood all over his wife.

"She screamed and that's what kept her from getting killed. We came on the run. It was a gory mess. We could see what had happened, so the man wasn't tried. The man who was killed was single, fortunately, but it was a very bad situation."

Molly shook her head. "Yes, it was."

"How's Eva doing?" Jed asked after a moment.

"Not too good, she was so dirty Della brought her in their

tent, lit the lantern, and started scrubbing. About all I did was heat that pan of water. Oh Jed, her back looks terrible! She has bad scars where her father beat her—this must have been going on for years. He probably gagged her when he used his whip after that fight by the Platte. If she hadn't been gagged, her screams would've roused the whole train. I don't know when I've felt so sorry for someone. One thing's for sure though, Chet and Della will do everything they can for her. They really live their faith, all the time."

"That's true. Chet's helped several families who are short on money. I'm sure glad they're on our train. I'm glad you are on this train too, Molly. I feel so lucky to have found you. It's easier to forget the sad things when I can think about the future with you and Jimmy."

Molly turned her face up to him and he bent down to kiss her.

When Jed went to his bedroll, he noticed Chet was sleeping outside of his tent. The next morning Eva was still in the tent. The potatoes they'd gotten from the Cayuse made breakfast special. Della served them hot from the frying pan. With lunch in his saddle bags, Jed moved on ahead for the day. He wondered about Eva, but had to concentrate on getting the train over the rugged Cascade Mountains.

That day the route was almost due south. The evening camp in a valley by a snow-fed mountain creek was only a couple miles west of their last night's camp, but the climb had been arduous.

Jed heard that Eva had ridden in Chet's wagon all morning, but she'd walked beside Della in the afternoon. There were only four stools at Della's table, so Jed filled his plate and sat on the ground. He liked being a little farther away from the new guest, whose eyes never left her plate.

Chet kept the conversation going about the road ahead and asked Jed several questions. After Eva finished eating, the sad-faced girl moved her stool nearer the fire and faced away from the table. But when Della started washing the dishes, Eva picked up the towel and started drying them.

Jed left to talk to Sarge and later ended up at Gil's fire. Gil asked how Eva was doing and Jed reported that she was getting along better. When Jed told him about the condition of her back, Gil's usually smiling face became grim and he said, "I knowd her pa uses a whip far too much on his oxen, but a feller who calls hisself a man and treats his own daughter like that is no man at all. I wouldn't mind usin' my own whip on his hide."

The next day the emigrants stayed in camp to make preparations for the climb ahead. The wagons were checked carefully and a few cracked reaches were replaced. No tires had to be set, but several wheels spent the day soaking in the creek to make sure they were tight. The animals' feet were checked. Sarge and Jed reminded the travelers to get their clothes and shoes in shape for the cold nights and cool days in the mountains. Shoe soles that were nearly worn out would go to pieces on the rough terrain. Much of their clothing had already been patched beyond recognition with parts of blankets and deer hide.

One woman held up a pair of her son's britches and laughed, "I patched them with buckskin a month ago and now look. The patches are the only thing that ain't worn out."

Jed knew from other trips how much women could do in one day mending clothes. Some mothers kept their young daughters busy with a needle. Many men were handy at repairing shoes, so several pairs of boots got new soles of buffalo hide. Jed's boots needed soles, too. He carefully cut some buckskin into narrow thongs and using a big needle and an awl—the kind the Indians liked to trade for—he sewed buffalo hide soles on. He decided he wouldn't mend his clothes anymore but would wear his buckskins the rest of the way.

Eva was still withdrawn and silent. The next evening Della asked Eva to patch some clothes while she prepared the evening meal. Molly brought her some of Jimmy's britches, too. Eva enjoyed the work and Della complimented her on the neat stitches. Gradually Eva began to warm up to Della and Molly and even began to play with Jimmy.

When he kissed Molly goodnight, Jed asked her if she'd still kiss him after he'd worn the same pair of buckskins clear across the mountains.

"I could hold my breath, kiss you, and run," she said, laughing, "or I could stay upwind and we could just hold hands—that is, if the wind is strong enough."

"In that case," Jed responded, "we better do a little more kissing now while I still smell all right." Molly laughingly accepted that offer.

The next morning the wagons pulled out of the valley and headed southwest. Later in the day the road turned almost west. They were in the foothills of the mighty Cascades now and that evening Jed told them they were close to the east gate of the Barlow Road. He had ridden on ahead and found men working on the road. They were awaiting the first wagon train.

That evening Chet and Jed figured what the total toll charge to take the road would be. Chet had to collect a little more money, but even Ezra didn't grumble much about the toll, although he wasn't very happy about it.

It was a clear morning when the wagons pushed on to the west. There was enough breeze to keep the dust away from those walking beside their wagons. After the tollkeepers counted the wagons, Chet paid the toll, accepting a receipt so someone wouldn't try to charge them on the other end.

The tollkeepers were buzzing with exciting news. Gold had been found in California, in some place called Sutter's Mill on a fork of the American River. The word was that folks were already leaving Oregon for the gold fields to get rich.

The news quickly spread from one end of the wagon train to the other. Jed let the wagons stand still for an extra fifteen minutes to let the talk of the gold continue before he waved them on. He guessed that when the news reached Fort Bridger or Fort Hall some wagons would turn down the Raft River and head for California. His train was too far west to do that. It was committed to Oregon.

Once in the mountains, the wagons followed a zig-zag course. There were some very hard pulls. At the noon stop, people were still talking about the gold strike in California. Some of the men wished they had turned south at the Raft River.

"I'd abeen rich!" said Caleb.

Noticing that Jed didn't seem excited, Ezra asked him if he already knew about the strike and had just not told them.

"How could I have known?" asked Jed angrily. "They didn't even discover it 'til I was somewhere east of Fort Bridger last winter!" Jed was irked that his integrity was questioned, but said nothing else.

The rest of the day the train continued in a westerly direction. At the evening campsite the talk of gold overshadowed all else. Jed left the discussion and headed for Gil.

"Still can't see the sun shining on the west side of Mount Hood, can you?" he asked.

"Think we ever will?" asked Gil.

"Oh, yes," answered Jed. "The next several days we'll be going almost directly toward it, but we won't get closer than six or seven miles from the cone."

"It don't look that far away now, but I reckon it's looked like that for about a week. Are you sure that mountain isn't sittin' on top of one of them—-uh, what do you call 'em— glaciers? Maybe it's sliding into the ocean and that's why we can't catch up with it!"

Jed laughed. "Don't think so. We'll be so busy the next few days you won't even notice that mountain. Besides, there'll be trees blocking our view most of the time."

"Man, what trees these be," said Gil. "Why didn't you just drag one of these along with you last fall and drop it off where all we had to burn was that measly little sagebrush? One of 'em would make a big enough fire for all the wagon trains through that desert for years. If we had one of them trees split in half, it'd make a good bridge across some of those creeks we had to cross."

"Why don't you saw one of them down and trim off those few branches, hitch a yoke of oxen to it, and drag it back to make a bridge. You could get rich charging a toll for it." They both laughed.

"Better 'n chasing after gold," Gil said. "Say, I reckon we'll be lucky if all our skinny critters can make it over 'em mountains."

"They'll do it," said Jed seriously. "A lot of worse looking animals than these have done it, but we'll have to take our time and change them off at noon."

Gil's said, "I'm sure glad you insisted on us takin' so many oxen. Lots of people who thought you was bein' foolish now think you're purty smart. Without extry animals we'd sure be stuck."

The next day was slow going. They didn't travel more than five miles, six at the most. Around the campfire that evening, Ben asked Jed about Sam Barlow.

"It was in 1845 that Barlow and his wagons got to the Dalles. When Sam found out how much it was going to cost to raft down the Columbia, he turned his wagons south and started this trail. He got somewhere between where we were camped last night and here, when they could go no farther. It was too late in the season and they were real tuckered out. They left their wagons here and packed on west to the settlements.

"They came back the next year and finished hacking out the trail so their wagons could get to Oregon City. They had to be a determined and ambitious bunch, that's for sure. Forty-six was my first year over this road and if you think it's bad now, you should of seen it then. They work on it every year."

"Let's talk about the gold strike," said Josh.

"Yeah!" agreed John Lewis. "Think we oughta go, Jed?"

"You going, Jed?" asked Josh.

Molly's eyes were on Jed when he answered. "No, I'm not going to look for gold. Molly and I are going to get married and stay in Oregon. Haven't you heard that?"

"Yep," said Josh, "but with all that gold just waiting to be taken, I thought you might of changed your mind."

Jed laughed a little before he answered. "You're young, Josh. I'm over thirty and I got the dream of a lifetime coming up in Oregon in a few days. I don't want to miss any of it. You young fellers can do your roaming if you want to, but I'm all through with that." The response from Molly's eyes was worth more than any gold mine to Jed.

"I've been thinking about what this gold'll mean to the states. By now, the ships will have the news in the East and up the rivers. I'll bet that next year the road we traveled will be jammed with folks headed to California—at least as far as Fort Hall. They won't all be solid people like you folks—farmers and their families. You people know how to take care of animals and know what they can do for you. Some people hungry for gold won't care about that. All they'll be thinking about is getting rich.

"That sounds like trouble to me. Big trouble. I'm glad I won't be leading a wagon train next year, that's for sure. And I wouldn't go to California for anything."

Josh and John Lewis looked crestfallen.

"I'll tell you what I'd do if I were a lot younger and wanted to make a lot of money," Jed continued. "I'd get some men who could get along together, load up a pack train with tools and food, and head right back to the North Platte River that we ferried across. Four or five men could build and operate a ferry for a few years and bring thousands of wagons across. There'll be a lot more business there than those young Mormons can handle. It'd be a lot less dangerous than fighting over gold. I could be wrong, Josh, but I doubt there'll ever be enough gold to make everyone rich—or happy. Men start getting greedy and then there's nothing but trouble."

The circle broke up. A little later Molly and Jed walked away from the wagons for privacy. Molly reached for Jed as soon as they were in the shadows. After kissing him soundly she said, "You made me very happy tonight when you said what you did. For a man to say that in front of others means a lot. I'll try very hard to keep the feelings we have between us. I hope it never ends, Jed."

"I only spoke the truth, Molly, nothing more." Jed changed the subject. "I've noticed Ben disappears most every evening for a while. It's not because of me being with you, is it?"

"No. I thought you knew everything that goes on in this wagon train! My brother's not the pushy type, in fact he's sort of shy, but he's been visiting Annie. He started cutting wood for her and carrying water and I guess she likes him because he keeps going to visit her. Gil's daughters have been a help to her and the children, too. She and Aaron knew for a long time that he was going to die, but they sure wanted to get to Oregon first. Before he died, he asked her to get married again. She's young and could have more children."

"Aaron was a good man—Gil sure thought a lot of him. I hope it works out with Ben and Annie," said Jed. "But I'm glad you didn't get married again right away after your husband died."

Jed pulled her close again and Molly whispered, "I'm glad too, Jed."

The next day, traveling was hard. Zeb struggled with his horses. They had made it through the Blue Mountains, but now they were in such pitiful condition they weren't able to make long hard pulls. It pained the old horseman to whip his emaciated horses to get them to use their last bit of strength.

When the teams had to double up on the steepest hills, his horses were helped to the top by four spare oxen. His animals were too exhausted to take their turn and help other wagons up the difficult slopes. Embarrassed, Zeb stood talking with the couple who used mules while the others battled their way uphill.

"I'm sure sorry I've been such a bother, and I'm mighty proud the way these folks have hepped me out. Sure wish I'd listened to Jed when he said 'no horses!' I never guessed it'd get this bad."

The next day the last of the tired travelers made it to the top of Barlow Pass. From there they could see the mighty Mount Hood. Its snow cone was stark white against the clear blue sky. The evergreen trees were deep green and the air was fresh and cool.

"It's purty enough up here to make you forgit your misery," said Gil. "Think I'll walk up and get me some snow."

"Bring some back for me!" called Jed. "Course you won't get back 'til tomorrow."

"How come?" asked Gil.

"The snow's a good four miles from here, and it's all uphill."

"Mebbe I won't go after all," said Gil. "Leastwise, not today."

After a rest at the pass, the emigrants moved to make camp nearby. Jed wanted everyone to be well rested for the next day's descent. The next morning, a crowd looked over at the trail as is plummeted between the towering trees.

Gil said, "We thought it was hard comin' up! It looks a whole lot worse goin' down. Hope we got enough rope."

"Look at those rope burns on the trees!" said Sarge. "Hey, Jed—is there room enough for us between those trees at the bottom?"

"Yep, we can make it, although there isn't much room to spare," answered Jed. "We'll rough lock the wheels, use ropes and drag trees. We don't dare make any mistakes on this hill."

It took hours to get all of the wagons down Laurel Hill safely, but they didn't have an accident. The wagons were lighter than when they went down the short steep banks of the Wakarusa River a few days after leaving Independence. The travelers were so used to working together now that they didn't waste time or energy as they edged down the mountain. They could sense what the wagons in front and behind needed and harmonized their movements accordingly. They were now a team, fuctioning as a unit.

It started to rain before the supper dishes were washed, and it rained all of that night and into the next day, Sunday. The exhausted travelers and their animals slept, waking only long enough to eat. Tents, blankets, and ground clothes were sodden, but the people slept anyway.

At the evening worship service, Chet prayed, giving voice to what was in the hearts of most of the travelers.

"Dear God, we gather to give thanks for our safe journey to our new land that we are about to enter. We thank Thee for seeing us through some very difficult times. You were there to comfort us in our loss of the Witherspoon girl and Aaron, the courageous young man who gave his last ounce of strength on this great venture. We pray you will give their families the strength to make new lives in this great valley.

We give thanks for all the people who worked so well together in crossing the rivers and mountains. We pray that our spirit of working together may continue through our lives as we go our separate ways. Thank You, God, for my wife's recovery and for the recovery of others who were sick.

Bless our leaders—Sarge for his devotion to his job, Gil for his friendliness and his care for the animals, Noah for his skill as a hunter, Henry for his blacksmith work, and Jed for his constant guidance—he led us to our own Promised Land. Amen."

When Chet asked if there were any announcements, Ben stood up.

"I don't like to speak in public," he said, "but I gotta say this—we oughta thank God for sending us a Christian man who lives the faith that he preaches."

"Amen!" said several voices and Chet blushed as Ben sat down.

Jed noticed that it was the largest crowd that he'd ever seen at a worship service. At the close of the service, Chet asked everyone to form a circle. They joined hands shyly and then Chet and Della led them into "Blessed Be The Tie That Binds."

Jed held Molly's hand with his right hand and Della's with his left. Tears ran freely down the cheeks of women and men alike. They all knew that this was their last worship service together.

When the last notes of the hymn had faded, John Lewis, Josh, Henry, and another young man descended on Jed. Just how should they go about setting up a ferry business?

"You'd better start back east pretty soon after we get to the settlements," said Jed. "It's possible the Blue Mountains will have snow while we're getting rain in the Cascades, but as long as you don't have wagons, you'll get through all right. Get a good riding horse in Oregon and a pack horse or mule each, plus a couple of extra horses or mules. You know the rest—food, tools, a good tent, and plenty of rope.

"You can travel more than twice as far in a day as the wagon train did—at least thirty miles a day. Of course, you might have to hole up a day or two now and then because of bad weather. You can get fresh horses at Fort Hall or Fort Bridger. If you have to layover for awhile because of the weather, just make sure you get over the Green River before the ice goes out. One way or another you know you must have your boat ready to go by the middle of June. Some of the gold seekers might be there even a little sooner—some of them will be packing too."

Later, Jed lay in his bedroll, but he couldn't sleep. He thought of more advice for Josh and John Lewis. He was glad Henry was going with them. Henry could repair or build almost anything and he was a good steady influence. Although they were young, John Lewis and Josh would handle themselves well.

Jed was glad there were only a few days left before getting to the settlements. Perhaps some of their success was luck, some of it was his experience and the good leaders he had to work with—Sarge, Chet, and Gil were the best he'd ever seen. There had been a spirit of harmony from the beginning.

The weather had been drier than usual, but being the first train of the season helped a lot. The livestock were thin, true, but the train had lost only two riding horses and eight oxen.

Yes, he thought, I have much to thank God for.

The morning was cool and damp with the dew dripping from the trees. The grass was saturated—anyone who ventured in the tall growth was wet to the waist. When the sun first peaked over the trees, the whole area smelled like it was brand new. Jed looked up the slope to the east. The trees glistened and the grass seemed to glow. It would be a good day. At breakfast Jed told the travelers that there'd be only one more night to camp on the trail.

There was a feeling of expectancy among the travelers as they pushed their way west. They knew they were nearly home. About an hour after the afternoon stop Jed and Noah spotted a wagon coming from the west. They could see two riders on horseback.

"Probably somebody wanting to sell us supplies," said Noah.

Soon they could see that one of the riders was a woman. Jed reached into his saddlebag, pulled out his spy glass, stretched it out, and handed it to Noah, whose mouth opened in disbelef.

"Yahoo!" Noah yelled, throwing his hat into the air and kicking his horse to a gallop. Jed slowly followed, delighting in the joyous reunion of Noah and his bride-to-be. The excited young man jumped from his horse as soon as it was reined to a stop and his arms caught Beth as she jumped from her steed.

The two fathers of the couple were riding in the supply wagon. Beth's younger brother was on the other horse. Jed directed the wagon to the center of where the campsite would be.

When the train was unhitched for the night, Jed helped them distribute the fresh vegetables and fruit from the wagon. That night dinner was a jolly affair, with people smacking their lips over the ripe tomatoes and fresh corn.

"Corn, Martha!" called James, holding up an ear. "Sweet as you ever saw along the Ohio!"

The grinning Noah introduced Beth to everyone on the train. The women noted her clean clothes, shining hair, and smooth face, and realized how disheveled they looked in comparison.

When the meal was over and the dishes washed, water was heated for bathing. Men stropped their razors and went to work. Scissors clicked away at snarls and straggling locks. Women washed their best dresses and hung them close to the fire to dry. Tomorrow they wanted to look as good as possible. Jed explained that most everyone in the settlements had gone through the same experience and would understand the sunburned faces and cracked lips, but they knew this would be one of the most important days of their lives.

Molly had just given Jimmy a bath. With his hair still wet, he came running to Jed, who was sitting on a packing crate near the supply wagon. "We're going to have eggs for breakfast!" he said. "Eggs!"

"Me, too, Jimmy," said Jed. There were enough eggs in the supply wagon, packed in oats, for everyone on the train.

"I can hardly remember what they taste like," said Jimmy.

"Oh, they're good. You'll like them. Say, I have something for you. Sit on my lap I'll show you how it works." When Jimmy clambered up, Jed unwrapped a piece of cloth.

"Oh, boy!" exclaimed Jimmy, "A whistle!"

Jed showed the boy how to hold it with his left hand and blow on it. Jimmy squirmed with excitement when the sound filled the air.

Jed instructed him. "Hold the whistle to your mouth and put two fingers over the holes on top." Jimmy's next blast was a different pitch. Soon he'd learned that he could get four different notes.

Jimmy jumped from Jed's lap with, "Thanks! Can I show Nellie my whistle, Mama?" he called to Molly.

Before he got an answer, Jed handed him another cloth-covered whistle. "Take this to Nellie and tell her I made one for her, too."

Jed laughed as the boy took off on the run. "I want Nellie's folks to know who's to blame if they don't like it," he said to Molly. "I thought everyone would be in such a good mood tonight they wouldn't mind the noise."

Molly laughed. "I know I'm the happiest I've been in a long time."

"I've been wonderin'," said Ben, who had just returned from Annie's wagon, "about how Noah's folks knew he was on this train. I know you told us about news going up and down the Columbia River on Indian canoes. Reckon the word got to the settlements that the first wagon train of the season was about to arrive that way? How would they know Noah was on it?"

A broad grin crossed Jed's face as he looked at Ben and Molly. He thought from the expressions on their faces they expected him to have some magic power. Again he smiled at the woman he loved and her good-natured brother. "Do you remember when we camped just a few miles east of the tollgate on the other side of the Cascades?" They nodded.

Jed continued, "I think I told you that I rode ahead to check things out. I guess I didn't tell you who else was there that night. Two men had arrived from the settlements about two days before with a load of supplies for the men working on the road. When they heard our train was coming, they wanted to get started back ahead of us. They knew we'd be too slow to follow. I sent them back with a note they agreed to deliver to Noah's pa.

"I paid them for their trouble, and I knew the empty wagon with four good horses would get to the Willamette River a lot quicker than we would. I wanted to surprise Noah, so I didn't tell anyone about it."

"How'd you know they'd deliver the note?" asked Ben. "They coulda just thrown it away and kept your money."

"I was sure they'd deliver it all right," answered Jed, "because I didn't seal it. I even read it to them. The note asked Noah's dad to pay them, too, and said I'd pay him back when we got there."

Ben laughed and said, "That'd keep 'em honest, that's for sure!"

Molly was quick to add, "That was a mighty kind thing to do, Jed. Noah is wild with joy and I know everybody's perked up since the wagonload of fresh food came."

Jimmy returned blowing his whistle. The whistle didn't

receive a rest until Molly took it away and led Jimmy to bed. The many bright campfires in the circle faded into a few coals glowing in the night air. Soon the only sound heard was that of crickets and locusts—sounds they hadn't heard since they left the states.

The camp came to life early the next morning. The emigrants moved quickly on this last day of their journey. They hurried through their breakfasts of fresh eggs, fresh bacon, and potatoes. Everything was packed up in record time. Almost six months of practice had taught them speed. The women spent more time than usual checking on their children's clothes and their own. Jed felt that most of them weren't happy with the end result.

He, however, thought the women looked wonderful. They had lived through so much hardship. During rainstorms they had slogged through the mud. They had escaped a prairie fire by crouching in the Platte River. They had fought an endless arid wind, flies, mosquitoes, alkali dust, terrible heat, and water that was barely drinkable. They had walked twenty miles some days and still cooked a good meal in the evening. Sometimes the dirt and dust was so thick they had to climb in a wagon to mix a batch of biscuits. They shared everything they had— food, water, medicines, blankets, and most of all, their love for each other and an amazing sense of humor. No, these women don't need new clothes to make them beautiful, Jed thought. They're already beautiful. May God bless them in their new homes in the valley.

The last morning of the long journey, all fifty-nine wagons rolled to the west. At noon, Jed led them into a circle. He moved into the center when the last wagon came to a stop.

The travelers listened to Jed's voice one last time. "We're now in the Willamette Valley of Oregon," he told them with pride. "Down yonder three miles are the falls of the Willamette. Our two-thousand-mile journey is over!"

A cheer rose all around the circle, drowning out anything else Jed might have tried to say. The roar of the crowd built as long-time trail companions turned to hug each other. Children jumped up and down. Mothers danced with their toddlers, tears streaming down their faces. Even the most reserved grinned and waved their bonnets.

Jed rode toward Molly's wagon, jumped from the saddle, and let Blaze go free. When Molly met him, he swept her off her feet and kissed her. Then he swooped up Jimmy.

"We're home!" he said. "We're home!"

17

It was decided that the train would camp at this spot a few miles from Oregon City until the next day. Eager as they were to begin building new homes, the company possessions would have to be sold and the financial settlement finished before the train could split up. Each family would have to decide where they would settle. At Oregon City they could learn which claims were available.

The first wagon train of the year was greeted warmly by Oregon City residents who flocked to the campsite. Relatives and friends greeted the travelers joyfully.

Jed delivered the letter to the Lee family from their daughter and family in Independence. He explained why they couldn't come yet, and the elder Lees agreed. Folks Jed had guided in previous years stopped by to shake hands with him. He proudly introduced Molly and said he was now going to settle down in Oregon.

In his usual business-like way, Chet made some "For Sale" signs on tablet paper to post around town that afternoon. The sale would begin at ten o'clock the next morning.

Shortly after noon, the first of the wagons rolled onto Abernethy Plain in Oregon City, known as the end of the Barlow Road and the Oregon Trail. Women and children stayed with the wagons, while the men walked to the business district. By the middle of the afternoon, the land office in Oregon City was crowded with hopeful emigrants. They exclaimed over the town's shops, the first they'd seen in almost six months.

The next morning, Gil acted as the auctioneer. He didn't lack for words when describing the items for sale and he entertained the crowd with his patter. The supplies in the company wagon were sold first. Jed bought one each of as many tools as he could. Then Gil pointed to the 150 feet of one-inch rope.

"Just lookit that there rope," he said. "It let the wagons down the bank of the Wakarusa, it hepped us down a steep hill in the Cascades, and it still ain't wore out. Buy that rope and stick it in your haymow now and you can tell your granchillun about it someday. That rope is part of the history of the Oregon Trail!"

Jed bought it. Henry, John Lewis, and Josh were bidding together, buying tools, all three pack saddles and the other saddles for their new venture.

When the supply wagon was on the block, Gil said, "Josh here is 'bout the only man that ever drove this wagon and he greased her up good every week. The grease bucket is empty but the wagon still has a lot of miles left in it."

Jed bought it, too. There were seven oxen to sell and the leanest went first. The settlers knew that a couple months on good grass would put a lot of weight on the thin animals. Jed bought the next yoke of oxen, and then Gil started on the sale of the best two.

"Look at them animals! They ain't no better yoke of oxen on this train. They look a little thin but they'll gain powerful fast. They're so gentle any kid kin drive 'em and strong enough to pull any load you want to hitch 'em to."

Ben, leading the oxen around the circle, picked up Jimmy and sat him on the nearest ox. The smiling boy proudly rode around the circle to the applause of the crowd. Jed took the animals.

The thinnest horses sold cheap, while the better looking

ones sold fairly well. The last horse up was Blaze. When Ben led him into the circle, he looked thin but healthy. The bidding kept going until Jed had a fairly good bid on him.

Gil continued, "What's a few dollars for a hoss like Blaze, the fastest one on the train? For the benefit of you people that weren't with us, I'll tell what happened. A train ahead of us along the Platte shot three Injun boys. The next day some braves of the same tribe mistook Jed and Blaze as bein' from the guilty train. Well Blaze was so fast, he outran the Injun ponies and we had plenty of time to circle up and get ready for 'em. That's the kinda hoss you got a chance to buy now. So what's a few—"

Gil stopped. Ben had turned Blaze loose, and he went straight to Jed, who scratched him behind the ears.

Gil watched for a few seconds and then said, "Jed's the man who was riding Blaze that day. Jed's the man who found us water when we didn't think there was any around. On account of Noah and Jed, we never ran outa food. Jed taught us how to travel light and smart. Oh, he had a lot of strict rules we complained about, but we got here, didn't we?"

The crowd cheered and Gil continued, "Jed's the real reason we made it here, and I think he oughta git Blaze for free. What d'you folks think of that?"

Applause was the answer. "Mark that hoss sold to Jedidiah Jones! The sale's over." Everyone continued to applaud—all were now on their feet.

Jed tried to thank them, but found his voice cracking, so he just waved and smiled.

Chet began to settle up the accounts, trading IOU's for cash. When the hurried noon meal was over, Molly pointed to Mount Hood. Jed put Jimmy up on his shoulders so he could see it better. He chirped, "It's so white, Mama!"

"Isn't that a thrilling sight, Jimmy!" Molly responded. "The mist has settled, and now it looks like it has an apron around its middle with its white peak pointing to heaven."

Others stopped to look at the remarkable scene.

"By gosh," said Gil. "I plum forgot to look before, but there's the sun, she's a-shining on the west side!"

The afternoon was spent in Oregon City getting supplies and deciding where to go the next day. Jed found a barbershop and came back to camp clean shaven. During the evening meal, Della remarked how handsome he looked without whiskers and Molly smiled her agreement.

After the meal, Gil's clan, Annie and Ben, Sarge, Mary, and the other from "A" group gathered near Chet and Della's fire.

Sarge said, "Don't like to think about splittin' up. In fact, I don't like it so much I wonder how you folks would like to settle in the same neighborhood."

"Yes!" everyone exclaimed at once. The next few hours were spent making plans. The excited group talked and laughed about getting settled on their new land. South and southwest, not far from the river, were several dozen unclaimed sections. A surveyor told Sarge that was the most fertile land in Oregon. All they had to do was build a cabin, break the ground, and live there a few years. Then it would be theirs, free and clear.

The strain of getting to the valley was all behind them. The fear of sickness, of Indians, of prairie fires and swift rivers was gone. They were near their new homes in this great fertile valley and at last they could relax. Their tired eyes and gaunt faces broke into smiles and hearty laughter echoed throughout the camp.

They decided that in the morning Jed's wagon would lead the other seven wagons south. When the travelers were ready to go to bed at last, the tall, bushy bearded Gil startled them by jumping to his feet and shouting, "Wait, folks! I got a question for you!"

All eyes were on Gil as he pointed at Jed. "Lookit that man, he's clean shaven and standin' there in his new store-bought clothes. He looks like a bank clerk! He don't look like no wagon train guide. You sure it'll be safe to foller him?"

With all eyes on the former mountain man, it was the usually serious Sarge who broke the silence with his guffaws. The others joined him as Jed's face turned red. Then he laughed too. Laughter followed them to their wagons and bedrolls.

When Jed took a last walk around the circle that night, he passed the Witherspoons, who had buried their little girl so far away, and looked in on little Jed, who'd been born months ago on the prairie. He nodded at Randy, waved to Will, and watched James help Martha into their tent. Perhaps Martha had changed the most—she had gone from a beautiful young bride to a haggard woman in a few months—Jed could hardly recall her sunny, youthful face. Yet he knew she would survive. Strength had replaced innocence.

Jed's tour ended at Molly's wagon. Her eyes shone as he approached her.

"Molly, I've been thinking about the house we're going to build," he said. "I want you to think about how you want it arranged."

"Oh?" she said, surprised. "I thought you'd just build it."

"I'm sort of selfish. If I can keep you happy, I'll be happy." He took her in his arms. No words were spoken and after a few minutes Jed realized his great desire for Molly was interfering with the plans he wanted to make. He forced himself away from her and hurried on with his words.

"We need to talk about what we're going to do when we get to our land. Ben and I think that Annie's wagon and our two should camp together. Ben can sleep in my tent till we get the houses built. It's going to be too wet to sleep outside from now on. We'll work together building the houses because Ben is a better carpenter than I am. As soon as we're done with one, you women and the children can move in, and we'll build the other one. I've talked to a couple of lads who'll help us. We can get a kitchen built in a hurry. We'll take a day off next week for Noah's wedding and then it's back to work again. I've got some money saved—enough to buy the lumber for a good house, the furniture, machinery and seed to plant for our first crop. It might be a year before we get the house finished, because I've got to plow and get the planting done. I can get some yards built for the livestock and start building a barn—"

"Jed!" put in Molly. "Slow down! You're talking so fast I can't keep up with you. Come here." She put her arms around him again and he stopped talking.

After a minute she said, "Aren't you forgetting something in your planning?"

"If you mean the wedding, no, I'm not. But that's your department. All you got to do is tell me when and where."

The fire died down and a few raindrops were falling. Jed rested his chin on Molly's head. After a moment he heard her say, "I'm so happy that I found you. I love you so much."

"I'm glad I found you, too, Molly. I love you more than anything in the world." The crackling of the small fire was the only sound heard and then Jed spoke almost in a whisper.

"Our venture to Oregon is over, but our venture *in* Oregon is just beginning."